SCIENCE VS SCIENCE

The Untold Story of Mysterious Science

GSD

SCIENCE VS SCIENCE

DISCLAIMER

This book is a work of fiction. All characters and events depicted herein are entirely imaginary, but some real locations are used as settings. Any resemblance to actual events, persons, or institutions is coincidental and unintentional. The depiction of these locations is fictional and not meant to reflect the real places. No offense is intended, and the book is written for entertainment purposes only.

TABLE OF CONTENTS

HAROLD AND THE GHOST

70 CENTURIES AGO – HIMALAYA

A humanoid creature, shrouded in a brown hooded cloak, is playing tag with a 7-year-old boy and a 15-year-old girl of olive-hued complexion in a clearing roughly fifty meters across at the forest's edge. Standing at an imposing 6 feet tall, its fearsome facial features, though unfamiliar to human eyes, radiate an otherworldly wisdom and kindness. The boy and girl wear expressions of godly innocence on their faces. The sweet songs of birds and the children's laughter are creating a lovely atmosphere. Nearby, a small hut stands, outside which Rashmi, a woman in her late thirties with a sorrow-etched face, is making bread on a clay stove, her gaze drifting toward the joyful scene.

Rashmi said, "A lot of mischief has happened today, let's eat bread!"

"Aagchhti Maat!" Arva, the boy, exclaimed eagerly.

"Mother is calling," the creature said in a low, thunderous tone, taking the wooden doll away from the girl.

"I'm not hungry," Prisha said, walking towards her mother with a red face.

Rashmi asked the creature, "Pranja, is their father still sitting in meditation?"

"Maybe he's still there!" Pranja replied.

"Please go and call him," Rashmi requested.

"No worries!" Pranja said, as he walked into the forest.

Chaitanya, 50 years old and Rashmi's husband, sat in meditation (Padmasana) under a tree, 100 metres from the hut. His body is flying two feet above the ground. Pranja approached through the bushes, hiding behind a tree, with a suspicious look in his eyes at Chaitanya. Cautiously, he emerged and inched closer to Chaitanya. There is a spiritual light on Chaitanya's face. His half-open eyes and upturned lids radiated an ocean-like peace. Pranja moved slowly, inspecting the scene with a mix of awe and curiosity by going near the ascetic. Sometimes, he peered behind the tree, under the ascetic, and other times, above the tree.

HALF AN HOUR LATER

"Pranja! What are you looking for?" Chaitanya spoke, opening his eyes with a very sweet and intoxicating voice.

Chaitanya's body began to descend slowly from a height of two feet back to the ground.

"How...?? How... how did you do that?" Pranja asked, speaking very excitedly like a child.

Chaitanya smiled and replied in a very calm tone, "It's not a big deal... but yes, it's not even in my own power."

"What do you mean, Master? I don't understand. You were flying in the air, and I don't even see any equipment... Please tell me how you did it?" Pranja said as he knelt on the ground, folding both his hands, and spoke in an eager and respectful tone.

Rashmi approached with a mild angry tone, saying, "Have you both made any plans to fast today? How long will I have to wait for you?"

"Did you know my master can fly without any equipment?" Pranja spoke with a childlike expression of great joy and wonder.

"How many times have I told you, if the Brahmans find out, they will kill us all," Rashmi said bitterly, expressing displeasure.

Chaitanya spoke very calmly, "Not all Brahmans are bad... Don't forget, my Guru was also a Brahman."

Rashmi said with a naïve face, expressing displeasure, "Whose own people disowned him. Tell me, why would his people spare his disciple? If you did not walk this way, we would not have to live in the forest today."

Pranja said, making an angry face, "Those Brahmans can't spoil anything while I am here. Master, teach me how I can fly. Then, see how I would take the Brahmans to a height higher than the mountain and throw them down one by one."

Chaitanya replied, "Even both clans are humans. Still, Brahmans do not like our Rakshasa clan at all. You are not even from this planet. If they see you, they would kill you on sight. Let them do whatever they want with me or my family, but you will never do anything to anyone. Don't go in front of them under any circumstances."

Pranja said, "If I get a little bit of power, then I will wipe out all the sinful Brahmans from the whole planet. Please, master! Make me your firm disciple."

"Ha ha ha!" Both Chaitanya and Rashmi laughed, looking at Pranja. Pranja smiled with a shy face.

PRESENT TIME - WORLD WAR II, 1945

Gunshots and bombs echo through the dense forest. Sikh soldiers and British troops from British India engage in fierce combat in a forest. Overhead, fighter planes roar through the sky, circling the battlefield like angels of death.

"Move forward! Not a single enemy should be spared!" Harold, a 50-year-old white commander sitting inside the front, spoke. The marks of war on his face are telling that he has spent half his life fighting in the army.

"Shaheed Singh...? The fauj has come for us..?" Zoraver Singh looked at a very strong and dangerous-looking Nihang Singh on a blue horse to the left of his front and spoke in surprise.

Zoraver Singh is a 25-year-old Sikh soldier standing over six feet tall, possessing a sturdy frame, a strong jawline, and piercing brown eyes that radiate courage and determination.

All his comrades were raining bullets on the enemy, causing the enemy to retreat.

"Zoraver...!! Zoraver...!!" A Sikh companion, advancing out of the front, shouted to Zoraver upon seeing him walking backwards from the front.

Zoraver did not hear anything. Before his eyes, a blue-clad Nihang Singh moved forward on his blue horse, beckoning him with a hand to follow.

"Come quickly, my lion! The troops are standing ready for you!" Nihang Singh called out.

Far from Zoraver, in an open field, an army of millions of Nihang Singhs could be seen, shaking the sky with their shouts of "Bole So Nihal, Sat Shri Akal," alongside the earth-shaking thunder of Nagara. In front of the entire army of Nihangs, there was a tent of luxurious cloth surrounded by a white light.

Seeing this scene, Zoraver's eyes turned red, and his nerves tensed with excitement.

"We don't recite Gurbani to see the Guru or his Singhs. We have to know the divine as per the Guru's words. Pay attention! Maya comes in any form during the last moments, and that can lead you astray," the words of a middle-aged man echoed in Zoraver's ears. As soon as the thought came, Zoraver's steps stopped abruptly.

"Zoraver! My Lion! Come on, let's save the world together!" Nihang Singh roared loudly.

On the other side, all the soldiers were moving forward, driving the enemy away. Commander Harold's eyes turned red with anger when he saw Zoraver.

"Zoraver....!! You coward...!! You can't run from the battlefield...!!" the commander shouted loudly, advancing towards the enemy.

Zoraver did not hear anything. He had entered another realm entirely.

"You're not what I'm thinking! No, you can't be that!" Zoraver's eyes, now red and drugged, spoke with a voice full of passion.

Thak..!! Zoraver drew his gun with lightning speed and fired at Nihang Singh. The bullet flew straight, hitting the left side of Nihang Singh's chest.

As soon as the bullet rang out, Nihang Singh became invisible, and suddenly, the melodious sounds of Bansuri, Sarangi, Ghungru, and Dholki began to ring in Zoraver's ears.

Zoraver is seeing a cosmic explosion unfold before him: light spread in all directions, transforming into a vision of himself as a white aura, then morphing into various forms, a stone , plants, insects, diverse animals and a wild man.

"Thak...!!" The commander fired at Zoraver.

The bullet came straight and hit Zoraver's neck from behind. Zoraver's face hit the ground, and all the scenes disappeared at once.

"Fucking slave..." the commander said, turning his back to Zoraver.

Now, all the enemies were retreating from the field, and the British soldiers were claiming their victory with loud and wild shouts.

"If this time someone kills you during the opening of the tenth gate, keep your senses strong and chase him until you know the whole truth," Zoraver recalled someone's words with his last breath.

"O Lord...!! How many more births will pass in the same way?" Zoraver's spirit emerged from his body, hands folded towards the sky in great sadness.

Some of Zoraver's companions looked at his body from a distance.

"Leave him for the animals!" The commander spoke, spitting as he did.

Zoraver looked at Harold, and a golden thread-like energy crawled around Harold's whole body like a snake.

Boom!! Suddenly, a bomb dropped by the plane exploded.

The bodies of most soldiers who had shouted victory in the encounter lay scattered around, alongside the wounded, including the commander, who groaned in pain on the ground.

"No, no, no...!!! You can't die yet. I won't let you escape without knowing the truth," Zoraver said, running towards the wounded commander in panic and anger.

FEW MONTHS LATER

The TV is broadcasting the ongoing celebration in London of the Second World War victory. Harold is sitting in his rest chair in a vast lobby, with a magnificent gold-plated cane resting between his thighs. Beside him, his wife, Helen, is sitting on a large couch. Helen is a sharp-featured Christian woman, of a quiet nature and one who speaks in a sweet tone.

"What do you think about Theo and Bella's marriage?" Helen asked.

"Bella and Theo? What does Theo think about it?" Harold spoke after thinking for a moment.

"I know my son; he really likes Bella. He would say yes even before I ask," Helen replied.

"You haven't even spoken to anyone yet and made up your mind to fix the marriage?" Harold said with a surprised smile and loving eyes.

"I need your permission first; the rest will see later," Helen said.

"If a girl like Bella, a good Christian girl who fears God, the daughter of a respected teacher, becomes our daughter-in-law, what else do we need? But children's consent is more important. You need to talk to both of them first," Harold said.

"That's what I expected from you. I was just talking to Bella's mother. Let's invite them for lunch tomorrow," Helen said suddenly with great joy.

"Tomorrow?" Harold spoke with surprise.

"Sorry, I blurted out in curiosity. You tell me, which day should we invite them?" Helen asked.

"I am going to the airbase tomorrow for some important work. It may take a while to come. You can invite them for dinner on this Sunday," Harold said.

Sitting cross-legged at the other end of the couch, Zoraver's soul looked up at Harold suspiciously.

EVENING TIME

"Father said yes, inviting your whole family for dinner," Theo spoke in very excitement. He is currently standing in his room with the telephone in his hand.

Theo is a more than 6-foot-tall gentleman with a very polite accent. His face exactly resembles his mother, Helen.

"Oh God, thank you so much, I can't believe it," Bella's sweet voice came from the other side.

Theo said, "I told you, father would have no objection to our marriage."

Bella said, "I think I'm dreaming. Finally, Jesus heard all my prayers. Tell me, what dress should I wear for dinner?"

Theo said, "You look like a flower in every dress."

"Wow man, you are also so afraid of your father!! I thought we are the only ones who scare from our father in the matter of love," Zoraver spoke with a smile, standing on the left side of Theo.

TWO DAYS LATER – NIGHT TIME

Zoraver was sitting on Harold's shoulders like a child, while Harold, using his cane and limping, made his way towards the front door of the house. He entered in quite a hurry, with a great deal of anxiety on his face. On one side,

Theo and his mother were sitting on the couch, but Harold didn't even glance at them and went straight into his room.

"This is madness, and it can't be done. They have no idea what could be at stake in the future," Harold himself spoke eloquently.

There is a secret room under Harold's bedroom that he entered through a burglar door and switched on the light bulb.

"Commander! Who are you?" Zoraver, standing behind Harold, spoke with great surprise after seeing the whole room.

The room was filled with an array of devices that appeared entirely non-human in origin. Amidst various mechanical equipment, jars contained an assortment of bizarre specimens, bones, nerves, eyes, and fragments of flesh. Harold approached the office table and chair positioned nearby, opened a drawer, and retrieved a file. He began sifting through its contents, which included numerous maps and photographs of the crashed UFO. Meanwhile, Zoraver climbed onto the table and sat on it next to Harold.

70 CENTURIES AGO

The sun is gradually hiding in the lap of the mountains with its golden rays. Pranja and the two children are sitting next to Chaitanya outside the hut.

Chaitanya said, "Mind and Maya are interrelated. Never think that Maya does not know what is in your mind. Whatever you are inside, Maya also creates the same environment for you outside. It confuses our whole life, and we never become aware of the reality of the universe."

Pranja asked, "What is Maya?"

Chaitanya said, "Every living creature and root object that makes us forget the God is Maya."

Pranja asked excitedly, "Can I fly without any equipment like you?"

Chaitanya said, "Don't even think about that power. There are a total of eighteen Siddhis, and all are different supernatural forms of Maya. Even if we have as many Siddhis as possible, we should not use these powers at all."

Prisha asked, "Father, if we cannot use any of the Siddhis, then why do they awaken with chanting the name of the God?"

Chaitanya said, "So that we stray from our path, forget the God and become an arrogant and worldly person."

Pranja asked speaking like a child, "If I chant the name of the God, will these forces try to mislead me, too?"

Chaitanya said, "Dear!! You are not human. If you want to worship, then you have to take birth as a human. And I can say that if you stay with us all your life, you would take the next birth as a human being."

Pranja asked, "Also you have been saying that we all have one soul, which means we all are equal. Then how can I be different?"

Chaitanya said, "You are a creature from another planet. Your body was not made for moksha. Only the human body can attain that level. When I first took you out of your crashed Vimana, I thought you were some demon companion of King Ravana. I thought you were an elusive creature of our clan. Then later I came to know from you that you are from another land. But don't worry. We will always consider you a part of our family. No one in this family will ever see you separately."

Prisha put her doll aside, hugged Pranja and said, "You are my dear friend and will always be."

Arva said while hugging Pranja, "You are my best friend."

Pranja smiled, looked lovingly at them, and took them in his arms. Chaitanya looking all three in a very compassionate way.

PRESENT TIME – HAROLD'S FARM HOUSE

Harold stands outside his house with his wife and Theo. All of them are looking at a car coming towards them from the dirt road towards the house between the fields in front.

"Hello, my friend, how are you?" A cheerful middle-aged man spoke while getting out of the car.

Harold said with a chuckle and hugged Bella's father, "I was fine like a horse even during the World War."

Bella and her mother, Margaret are seen in the back seat of the car. Both of them also came out and met Harald's family.

Bella looks like a doll with a shy pink face. She is well grown white girl. Her eyes have the expression of a spiritual nature.

"There are such types of spiritual people among the whites, too?" Zoraver said with a smile, expressing a little surprise.

Zoraver is standing on the top of the car and looking very respectfully towards Bella. He sees a spiritual light of white colour around her.

Bella and Theo sneak up on each other as they walk towards the house.

AFTER AN HOUR

Theo and Bella stood in the garden behind the house, while their parents were seated around a table in the open yard, enjoying their meal and engaging in lively conversation. Laughter and chatter drifted through the air. Zoraver perched on Harold's shoulders, gazing at Bella.

Bella asked, "What do you think, your father knows everything about us?"

Theo said with a smile, "Where is the time for a man to think about the common people like us who has been fighting battles for his whole life?"

Bella said, "It was quite a surprise! He said yes without any objection."

Theo said, "He is just a moody guy. I think mother just got him at the perfect time."

Bella said while moving her face to the left towards Zoraver, closing her eyes and smelling the air with great pleasure, "What a beautiful fragrance!"

Theo said while looking at flowers on his right side at a distance with a smile, "Yeah, you smell really good today."

Now Zoraver moved a little back from Bella.

Bella said while looking around in wonder, "No! It's not my smell. It smells like a flower, but I have never seen such a fragrance before."

"Hey! How are you love birds?" Harold spoke, walking towards them.

Now Bella blushed even more.

Theo said while stopping with a signal of facial expression, "Come on, Father! Now, Bella is going to be your daughter-in-law."

Zoraver, standing next to him, immediately climbed on and sat on Harold's shoulders.

Harold asked in a humorous tone, "Bella! So you really like my boy? You still have the time. Please tell me if someone forced you to say yes."

Bella is shying too much and isn't able to understand what to say. But both Theo and Harold are eager to hear the answer from her and smiling.

Bella replied, "Yes Mr Anderson... I agree with the decision of both families."

Harald said, "Oh, come on. Tell me which one of you had the plan to arrange this love marriage."

Bella lowered her face and pointed a finger at Theo with a naughty smile.

"Yes, mother?" Seeing the finger pointing towards him, Theo immediately called his mother and slipped away.

"Ha ha ha ha ha!" Harold and Bella started laughing as they saw Theo running away in panic.

Harold said, "Let's go to his mother and tease him."

Now Zoraver got off Harold's shoulders and began to follow both of them, going toward Helen. Bella is now looking around again, smelling the air in surprise.

70 CENTURIES AGO

Prisha said begging while looking at the Pranja flying in the air in front of her with surprise, "Please, I too want to fly."

Pranja is wearing advanced high-tech metal armour and flying 7 feet above the ground. He has blue skin with very thin layers of golden lines and a strong muscular body with golden hair.

Pranja said while looking at the girl with shrewd eyes, "Firstly, you need to promise that you won't tell anything about it to your father."

Prisha dropped her doll on the ground in excitement and replied, "Yes, yes! I promise. I won't tell my father anything."

Now Pranja takes her with him into the deep forest where his crashed flying saucer lies.

Prisha said to Pranja in a very calm voice as she moved towards the alien ship in front of her, "I can't go there."

Pranja said, "There is no need to be afraid. This is like a second home to me."

Prisha said, "No! Father said this is very strong and dangerous, Maya. Even King Ravana lost everything because of it. Sorry, I can't go inside with you."

Pranja said, "Ha ha ha! This is not King Ravana's ship! This is my personal ship."

Prisha said, "Whatever, I just can't! I can't go inside."

Pranja entered the plane while Prisha remained outside. After a few minutes, the plane lifted off, hovering just four feet above the ground. Prisha, both nervous and curious, watched intently as the ship ascended. Remarkably, it made no sound and did not blow dust. A few seconds later, the plane descended once more.

Prisha asked with great joy seeing Pranja coming out of the ship, "Did you fix it?"

Pranja replied, "Yes! I fixed it perfectly, and with it, I can also kill all the Brahmans who left your parents and brother to stumble in the forest. We can make your father the king of this whole continent."

Prisha said with sadness and an innocent expression, "But father does not hate Brahmans at all, and neither do they want any share of the state."

Pranja asked, "Do you really want your whole family to stay in the forest forever?"

Prisha replied, "No! I don't want to stay here. I miss my village friends a lot."

Pranja said with a sad face, "Don't you consider me your friend?"

Prisha said while hugging him, "No! You are my very dear friend."

Pranja asked, "Do you like stars?"

Prisha replied, "Yes. Very much. I always wonder what they are fixed with."

Pranja, pointing to the plane while walking inside, said, "Come inside! I will show you even beyond these stars."

Prisha is looking at the ship with a fearsome expression, but she looks exited as well.

PRESENT TIME – CHURCH

Today, Theo and Bella are about to embark on their journey as husband and wife. Standing before the priest in the beautifully adorned church, the bride and groom look adorable, radiating joy and anticipation. The atmosphere is filled with a sense of celebration, as nearly one hundred guests are seated, all eyes fixed on the charming couple as they prepare to exchange their vows.

The priest said after repeating the wedding vows to them, "Now you may kiss each other."

Bella and Theo kissed each other, and all the guests started cheering.

Zoraver is wandering in his old memory while standing in the middle of the last two rows of chairs and looking at Bella's face.

"Why do we need to fight for them? It's been only two months since our wedding. I don't want you to go anywhere." With folded hands, a very lovely, round-faced young woman said to Zoraver, who was sitting on the bed with her. She is expressing panic and displeasure with her words.

Zoraver said with a smile while explaining very lovingly, "It is not a matter of fighting for the British government. If their enemy defeats them and captures our land, then our condition will become worse than ever. I am not going to fight for them but for us."

Hearing Zoraver's words, his wife Shamshir Kaur did not say anything and started shedding tears with her innocent face bowed down.

"I don't know what Theo saw in this girl. I was bringing my sister's girl for him. My niece is a million more beautiful than her," a 50-year-old woman sitting on a chair on the right side close to Zoraver said to her husband.

Zoraver moved forward and hit her left thigh with a punch like a sword.

"Oh my God, I got a cramp!" The woman suddenly screamed.

Other women sitting next to them and other guests sitting along the row surrounded the woman to check if she was okay. The rest of the guests also started looking back.

"It's okay, it's okay, she is fine," the woman's husband spoke loudly in embarrassment, seeing the whole situation deteriorating.

Now the woman, overwhelmed with shame, sat down and tried to suppress her pain. Zoraver quietly walked over to Harold, who was standing with Helen, and sat on his shoulders.

NIGHT TIME – FARM HOUSE

Theo and Bella entered their room. Theo holds Bella in his arms. Both are laughing. Laying down Bella on the bed, Theo ran and locked the door. Bella smiles and snuggles up to see Theo, who is excited for the first night.

Theo said, moving towards Bella in a very romantic and naughty way, "You can't escape today! Been waiting for this chance for years."

Bella looks very happy, like she is living the best dream ever. Theo came, he laid her back on the bed and started kissing her.

Outside the door of the room, Zoraver is looking at the pair of dolls lying on the table on one side, ticking away in his thoughts.

While reading a letter written in ink on a piece of paper, Zoraver Singh's wife, Shamshir Kaur, sat on the door jamb, tears streaming down her face. In the yard of the house, Zoraver stood ready in his military uniform, his mother by his side.

"Mother, please take care of her," Zoraver said, looking at his wife sitting in the doorway with worried eyes.

"She is like my daughter, and you do not need to be worried about her," Zoraver's mother said.

"Finally, my lion is ready to roar in the war!" The voice of a middle age man came from behind, and Zoraver looked back with a very lovely face.

Deep in thought, Zoraver is surrounded by a huge circle of white light that extends all the way outside Harold's house. Outside this circle, many spirits are moving around in large numbers to come inside the house, but no spirit is able to enter inside this circle.

NEXT DAY

It's afternoon, and Harald is sitting in his secret office looking at the pictures of the ruins taken by the archaeology department in a file that presents historical evidence of interaction between aliens and human civilization. Some pages are also related to ancient scripts, and some pages have engraved interior maps of different ruins. Zoraver, sitting at the table, has been looking at the file very carefully.

Suddenly, Zoraver felt a strange tremor in his soul. He tried to move from his place, but an unseen force held him completely still. Then, as if gripped by some invisible power, Zoraver was suddenly dragged out of the room at an incredible speed. He passed through the walls of the house and merged into Bella's belly, who was sitting next to Helen and Theo on the couch in the lobby. Bella's face suddenly glowed with a divine light, and she felt a supernatural joy as she placed her hands on her stomach. A lovely fragrance of flowers seemed to emanate from her body, and her eyes closed in blissful contentment. Meanwhile, Theo and Helen, seated nearby, were engrossed in conversation about the beauty of one of the gifts given by their relatives.

"Trrrrrrrrn...!!! Trrrrrrrrrn...!!!"

Harold picked up the phone, put it to his ear, and said, "Yes?"

The officer said, "You won't believe what we got?"

Harold asked, "What do you mean?"

The officer replied, "Meet me at the airbase. Others are also arriving soon."

Harold put down the phone and exited his secret room in a hurry.

"Where are you going now...?" Helen asked Harold, who was hurrying through the lobby towards the main door.

Without looking at anyone, Herold replied, "Just got a call for an urgent meeting. I'll be back by the midnight."

THE WORLD ORDER

FIVE YEARS LATER – 1950

The capitals of Britain, France, Russia, Germany, America, India and China are being bombed by more than a hundred UFOs. Big buildings are crumbling in the blink of an eye. Thousands of people have died under the rubble and death is seen everywhere. Videos of the world's major political leaders and numerous industrialists, all of whom have been captured by humanoid aliens clad in advanced armour from head to toe, are being broadcast on news channels. Despite repeated attempts, the armies of every nation have been unable to inflict any damage on the aliens. Every time a missile or fighter jet approaches a UFO, it is swiftly destroyed, much like a moth consumed by the flame it dares to approach. There is no human presence on roads and public places in any area of every country. Everyone is hiding and praying for their safety. Hundreds of aliens are roaming with their heavy machinery and advanced weapons in multiple areas of major cities worldwide.

"Mother!! Will they kill us, too?" Godric, the four-year-old son sitting on her lap, placed his tiny hands on both cheeks of his mother, Bella, and said in awe.

Both Godric and Bella are sitting inside a bunker. Food and drinks and some beds in a 40×40 feet wide lobby are lying around.

Bella said, "No, son! No one can dare to hurt you. The God will destroy all these demons very soon."

Godric asked, "Are they from hell? Did Satan send them to kill the people?"

Bella replied, "Yes. This is Satan's army, and they will take all those people to the hell who killed millions of people in the first and second world wars."

Godric asked, "Does that mean they won't do anything to us?"

Bella replied, "No. They can't hurt those who love God."

Godric asked, "Does that mean they will only take the bad people from Earth with them?"

Bella said, "Yes! Only bad people."

Godric said, "Jayyy! I love Satan."

Bella said, "No! We only love God. Satan is a Devil."

Godric asked, "Why Can't Satan Be Loved?"

"Awwww! What a golden heart you have, my cutie," an angel siting against the wall said. She is five and a half feet tall, and her feathers and skin are like milk. Stunning eyes and her strong white aura are full of spiritual peace.

Godric smiled after seeing the angel admire his words.

Bella said, "I already told you. Satan disobeyed God, and that's why he was sent to hell. For those who don't obey God's command, God never shows them any favour."

Godric said, "But taking bad people to hell is good work."

Bella said, "It is very bad for Satan to provoke innocent people to do sins and then take them to hell."

Godric asked, "Do you mean Satan had caused world wars?"

Bella said, "Such a bad job can only be done by Satan."

Godric asked, "Is Satan doing all the bad things?"

Bella replied, "Yes! His job is to make people do bad things."

Godric said, "This means that all people are good and only Satan is responsible for the bad deeds."

Bella replied, "Yes! Satan is the only one who is responsible for all the sins."

Godric asked, "Why did God create Satan to do evil?"

Bella replied, "Ha ha ha! Oh my God, what can I do to stop you! How many questions are you gonna ask?"

Godric pleaded, "Mother! Please tell. Why did God create Satan?"

Bella replied, "God did not create him for evil deeds. Satan tried to be the equal to the God himself and was kicked out of the heaven. He is just a brat like you."

Godric asked, "Does everything happen by God's will?"

Bella replied, "Yes! Not even a leaf can move without His will."

Godric asked, "Does that mean God himself gave birth to a sinner and sent him to hell when he sinned? Then, what is the difference between God and Satan? Satan takes bad people to hell, and God also sends bad Satan to hell."

Bella said, "My dear boy! God did not cause Satan to do evil. Satan himself rebelled against the God, so he was cast out of the heaven. But Satan makes people do bad things by whispering in their ears and then throwing them into hell."

Godric said, "When everything happened by God's will, how would Satan's evil work be done by Satan?"

Bella replied with a smile while holding Godric tight in her arms, "I don't know the answer to this question, my child?"

Godric said, "I think God and Satan, are both father and son, are working together and playing a game with all of us."

"Ha ha ha ha ha!" Angel laughed.

Bella said, "Ha ha ha ha! Where do you get such rational thoughts from? Oh God! Please forgive my cute baby."

"Bella! Come outside! UAHW destroyed an Alien spaceship in France." Theo entered the room and spoke with great excitement and joy.

Bella asked, "Really?"

Godric celebrated, "Jayyyy!"

Bella quickly got up and followed Theo, holding Godric in her arms. They exited through the hatch of the bunker, which was built on the farm about 100 metres behind their house, and hurried towards the house. Helen was already in the lobby, sitting next to the radio and listening to the news. Bella and Theo joined her, sitting down to listen as well.

"We had lost hope, and no one understood anything about how to save our civilization, but the Army of Human World did what we could not imagine. Unfortunately, all the political leaders and industrialists who were abducted by aliens from many countries had to be sacrificed. Still, it became our compulsion to sacrifice a few people for the sake of millions of people around the globe. We hope that within the next twenty-four hours, we will destroy all the Aliens with their war ships." The voice of Army Chief Aldous was heard addressing the press conference on the radio.

"Sacrificing all the leaders for the sake of the whole of humanity seems to be completely right according to the situation, but don't you think that with the death of the presidents, prime ministers and industrialists of all the major powers, the order of the world will be disturbed," a journalist asked.

Aldous replied, "Don't worry about it at all. As soon as the Aliens are eliminated, UAHW's main task will be to prevent the spread of chaos in the world. Until the situation is settled, we will keep the entire world completely crime-free under UAHW."

"Does this mean UAHW will now control the entire world?" the second journalist asked.

Aldous replied, "Yes!! The world, which has been ruled by demons from another planet for the last two months, will again be ruled by humans over humans."

The third journalist asked, "Are you talking about the one government that will rule the whole world?"

An officer came to the army chief's ear and whispered something.

Army Chief said, "I just received another good news for you all. One more Alien war ship has been destroyed in Russia, too."

Everyone started clapping, expressing happiness.

A FEW DAYS LATER

Theo is driving the car, and Harold sits next to him in the passenger seat.

Theo asked, "Father! How were the fifteen out of a hundred UFOs suddenly destroyed after repeated failures."

Harold replied, "Alien's war ships were failing all our weapons with a special kind of very high music frequency. Our ears and all the devices are thousands of times weaker than that frequency, but our scientists found that scale and now, with the help of some eminent and renowned scientists of the world, we have made a more dangerous nuclear weapon. This weapon first notes the frequency of the alien's ship and then coordinates with that frequency, goes inside the UFO's safety zone, and gets blasted."

Theo said, "It was amazing. Do you think there may be more attacks by aliens in the future?"

Harald replied, "The way they retreated very quickly, it seems we are not safe yet. But without uniting the whole world now, the coming dangers cannot be avoided."

Theo said, "I agree with you dad, I consider myself very lucky. You and your entire team are great, and our family's name will now be etched in the pages of history."

Harald said, "There is no need to be so hasty. If we want to gain respect in history, we still need to struggle a lot. Tell me about your project. Have you received the delivery?"

Theo replied, "No! Tell him to make the delivery on time. If his work continues at this speed, then I will be seventy years old at the completion of this project, and you all will have gone to heaven."

Harold said, "Ha ha ha! I am not sure how long me and my fellas gonna live, but there will be no heaven waiting for us."

HEAD QUARTER UAHW UK

Inside the enormous hall, a long C-shaped table dominates the high stage, where the chief officers of UAHW and representatives from many countries are seated. Harold sits among them, his presence adding to the gravitas of the gathering. The front of the hall is crowded with journalists, prominent politicians, and social workers from around the globe, all eager to witness this pivotal moment. Outside, thousands of people have gathered around the headquarters, buzzing with anticipation. UAHW soldiers stand on full alert amidst the crowd, making them look like movie heroes to the admiring onlookers. Meanwhile, people of every country, race, and religion worldwide are tuned into the live broadcast of this conference on the radio.

"Good afternoon, everyone!! Today we announce the United Government of Human World, ushering in a new era in the presence of all the political and military representatives of the world," UAHW chief Aldous spoke with proud.

As soon as UGHW was announced, a wave of happiness spread everywhere. People started dancing and shouting in joy.

Aldous said, "Thousands of wars of man against man in the history of thousands of years, and then the First and Second World Wars are a symbol that humans cannot achieve anything by hating each other, and the first Alien War proved this to be true. It has been proven that if all human beings stand shoulder to shoulder with each other, then there is no break in our strength. All the hunger that has happened in the world till now, whosoever has borne the curse of poverty on his body, the women who have been raped and the children who have been deprived of their parents, the mutual division of our political people is responsible for all of that. Today! We promise that you would have never imagined the world you will see now. All forms of discrimination in the name of colour, race, caste and religion will be abolished. The process of drafting and implementing the constitution of UGHW will be completed within the next year. We will have a common government, a common culture, a common religion, a common language, a common bank, and a common currency. Maybe after hearing about common culture and religion, some people start thinking about what will happen to the hundreds of cultures and religions that already exist before. My people! There is no need to be afraid or panic; all your cultures and religions are safe, and no tampering with them will be done. In the new era that we are going to start today, every part of humanity will be renewed, and this earth is the birthplace of our ancestors, we eat the grain of this earth, we were born from the earth, We have drunk water, we have breathed from the earth and now the time has come that we should all unite and tell each and every civilization of the entire universe that we are the human beings and the earth is our mother."

Applause erupted from every corner, a wave of enthusiasm and relief sweeping over the gathering. Tears of happiness glistened in the eyes of many, reflecting the hope that now filled the air. A festive atmosphere enveloped the entire world, uniting people in a shared sense of joy and optimism. Everywhere, people could feel the warmth of a new sun rising in their lives.

ANGEL AND THE MASTERS

25 YEARS LATER – 1975

Harold said, "He had some dead human bodies inside the UFO. We checked all of them, and they were all radioactive. Then he also showed us some videos that gave us a big shock. The whole world seemed to be destroyed in minutes, death was raging everywhere, I could never have imagined that the end of the human race would be so bad, seeing all this our faith was strengthened for a great change, we started to meet continuously from that day. And within the coming five years, he united the whole world and saved the human race from the baseless leprosy of borders that was leading us to extinction."

Harold, now an elderly man, sat on a resting chair atop the roof of the large house perched on the hill. He has become very old and is currently talking to Godric with a heavy heart. Godric, a striking young Englishman standing over six feet tall with a broad build, sat beside Harold. His blue eyes, resembled those of his grandfather.

Godric said, "I can understand how much pressure it must have been on you, but now the world is prosperous, and all the credit goes to you and your team."

Harold said, "Even though we did a great job and got success in it, the souls of thousands of people on whose dead bodies we built the foundation of UGHW still haunt me. We have been lying to the whole world for twenty-five years."

Godric said, "A truth and a lie are not the words, it's your intention! If your intention is negative, then a true word becomes a lie! But if your attention is positive, then a word that looks like a lie is actually the truth. So whatever we say to the world, we shouldn't go after the words but must look at our intention! In order to save the entire humanity, one or many sacrifices have to be made, and you have done nothing wrong."

Harold replied, "It is very easy to say, but it is very difficult to bear the weight of it. If not today, someday the world will end. How long can our race exist? I sometimes feel like we played a dirty game with nature. We killed thousands of innocent people out of fear of annihilation from which the human race cannot survive forever."

Now Harold's eyes are wet.

Godric said, "Grandpa!! Once you told me to follow the social, religious and political order strictly but do not take anything seriously. And now, why are you taking the political and social order you followed seriously? Everything you did was the need of time."

"Hello, Mr Anderson!! Are you ready for the meeting?" Herold's secretary, Isla, asked.

The face of this five and a half feet tall white young lady is a perfect combination of innocence and Royal attitude.

Harold said, "Just wait downstairs, I will be there soon."

Isla replied, "Okay Sir! I will wait for you."

Harold asked in a very low and mischievous voice while seeing Isla heading back downstairs, "Did you ask her for the date or not?"

Godric responded, "Come on, grandpa, this is not the best time yet."

Harold said, "Even your mother likes Isla a lot, what is the problem if a girl who gets along well with all of us comes into your life?"

Godric making a childlike mouth replied, "I'm nervous."

Harold teased, "My grandson is scared of a girl?"

Godric responded, "It is harder for me to approach a girl than kill a man."

Harold said, getting up from the chair and speaking in disappointment, "If I were in your place, I would have killed few people by now for that goddess. Why are you such a loser?"

Godric said, "Marriage thing does not work for me."

Harold exclaimed as he walked down the roof without looking at Godric, "Looooser!"

EVENING – UGHW CENTER FOR SOCIAL AND SPIRITUAL RESEARCH

"Today, every common man is working six hours a day to raise his family! Thirty years ago, no one would have thought that our future would be easy like this," said Anne, a girl of Irish descent walking alongside Godric.

Both of them are wearing white lab coats.

Godric said, "It is very important for people to have more time for themselves and family. If the husband and wife do not have time for each other, then the family cannot be in perfect balance and as you know the family is the smallest but the most important unit of society, and a happy family is the only one that."

Anne interrupted, paraphrasing Godric's speech, "Can create a happy society."

Godric continued while entering the lab, "Stop eating my brain again and again for your presentation and focus on the work."

Anne replied, "Sorry, bro! I'm just a bit nervous."

Godric asked a Chinese-born scientist in the lab, "Is it all ready?"

Inside the lab, five elderly men representing different religions stood alongside the scientist. Each man was dressed in traditional attire that reflected his country and religion.

Scientist replied, "Yeah! All the signatures have been taken, so you can start your work without any worry. All the masters are yours now."

Godric said, "Thanks, Doctor!"

"You are doing a great job," said a 55-year-old Tibetan monk, Chodrak, standing among the elders.

Godric said, "I am not doing anything great. This is just my hobby, great are you who came forward to share your precious knowledge with the whole world. It was not an easy task for us to find you guys. Thousands of people offered to teach spiritual knowledge and share their spiritual experiences. But only five of you passed the test for the Great World Religion. Twenty-four years have passed since the creation of this organisation, and we have prepared a great book for GWR in sixteen years, but we have not found a single enlightened man to date so that the scriptures can be preached on a very large scale to the whole world. So from this year, we will give spiritual education to our subjects to make them worthy of attaining the Moksha, and we need your help a lot."

"Many births are required to attain Moksha. We cannot make any claim about that this institution will make someone attain that power with our education. I have spent my entire life gathering the knowledge. May my next birth be my first step towards moksha!" said Vedant, a 60-year-old Hindu saint.

Anne asked, "The knowledge that took you decades to acquire, if someone gets that knowledge in a day?"

Vedant spoke with surprise, "This can only be possible with a miracle."

Anne said, "We are going to show you the same miracle today. We will give that knowledge to a thousand subjects within a few days, as much knowledge you all have spent to gain all your life, each of our subjects will become equally knowledgeable of you five within minutes."

"Five spiritual men who have accumulated so much knowledge over a lifetime, putting it all into a man's mind? Sure, he will go mad," said Gurbaksh Singh, a 70-year-old Sikh.

Godric responded, "You don't have to worry about it at all. These one thousand subjects are not ordinary people, they were born inside the lab, and we are not going to gather your knowledge in the way you think. We need the consciousness of your knowledge, not the weight of millions of words."

"I also have a question," said a 65 years old Muslim fakir.

Godric said, "Yes Mr. Mansoor?"

Mansoor said, "I appreciate your sentiment, you who are establishing the kingdom of Allah in this world. I am completely with you in this work, but as you said, you are giving the spiritual education of all of us to each of your subjects, I don't think it will do you any good by doing this, we are all from different sects and religions, our destination is one but the paths to reach it are very different, no man can cross the ocean in two boats. How would it be possible with five?"

"Ha ha ha ha!" All the spiritual men laughed a little among themselves.

Godric said while walking towards a machine in the corner of the lab, "Let me explain our whole plan to you."

Anselm, a 55-year-old Christian priest, said to Mansoor, "Good question, I had the same dilemma."

Godric continued, "This machine has given us thousands of social workers and economists, just as we are going to use it today to store your spiritual consciousness in one place, the same way... twenty years ago, we stored the consciousness of some of the world's greatest social workers and transferred that into our subjects. At the same time, we started gathering the consciousness of economists, and that work continues even today. Uniting the whole world after the first alien war was not easy. We started using this machine to create a perfect economic structure for the entire world and for that we started a huge project by sending all our economists to different corners of the world and within ten years we were able to build a very big and strong system from the economics side, and the complete success was achieved. Besides, a common subject of sociology was also taught in every school and college by subjects proficient in sociology to create a common human society around the globe, even though all our social workers belong to different regions, religions, and races. But still, we have had complete success in implementing the Great Social Order, and want to see similar success in relation to The Great World Religion. Now, coming to your question, you must be thinking that just as we store the information in our minds by reading many books, we may store the spiritual information from our minds into the machine and then transfer that in the minds of our subjects. But it is not like that at all. Could any of you tell me please.. Do we start living our lives completely according to our religion after learning all the teachings mentioned in the scriptures?"

Anselm said, "No, it takes decades of practice."

Godric replied, "Exactly! That's why we will not take the information of words from your mind, and we will take your consciousness, which is the essence of the knowledge of your whole life."

Chodrak asked, "You mean you want to create Karma Yogis through our consciousness?"

Godric exclaimed, "I love this guy!! Yes sir! You are right. We are going to do exactly that!"

Mansoor said, "This is a very great breakthrough effort."

Anne said in a very attractive manner, "Let's change the era, guys!"

Following this, each individual was placed on the machine one by one. The machine featured three rings revolving at 360 degrees around the chair, each rotating in opposite directions. These rings not only received consciousness from the brain but also captured and stored it as energy from every part of the body, from the head to the feet and through every vein beneath the skin.

NEXT DAY

Godric is kissing Isla standing by a tree trunk fallen on the ground in a garden, and Godric's angel lying on the trunk behind Isla, looking at both of them with a shy tone and making a sour face.

"Could you leave us alone for a minute please?" Godric turned to the angel and spoke with a loving tone.

Isla said with a smile and a surprised expression, "Oh God! Is she sneaking around?"

Godric replied looking at the angel's face with a slight frown, "She always does that."

Angel spoke in a very sweet voice, "I am just a cute angel."

Godric said, "No! You are not cute!"

Isla exclaimed, "Nooo! Don't talk to her like that!"

Godric said with a slight look of displeasure at the angel, "If you could see her expressions, you would agree with me completely."

Angel said nothing further and silently hugged Isla from the left side, pressing her cheek against hers, claiming to be more special to Isla than Godric.

Isla said, "Listen! I have a surprise for you."

Godric guessed, "Let me guess! You told your father about us."

Isla replied, "No! Not yet, he still doesn't like your work. No matter how hard I try, directly or indirectly, he doesn't like to hear a single word about the concept of this Great World Religion."

Godric said, "It seems that now we have to tell the whole thing to my grandfather."

Isla replied, "No, not yet! They are very good friends. I don't want their friendship to sour."

Godric said, "Oh, come on. Same thing every time. My whole family likes you. We've known each other since childhood and love each other from the heart. If your father gets angry, that's not our fault."

As soon as the angel heard Godric, she stood between the two with a resentful face towards Godric.

Isla said, "Why don't you understand? I am a girl. Things don't work in a girl's life as you think. Just leave this topic and listen carefully! I got the video of the nuclear destruction."

Godric said, "I forbade you to do that, didn't I? What if anyone found out?"

Now, the angel standing in the middle flew and sat on the tree.

Isla said in a very lovely tone while putting her arms around Godric's neck, "I didn't steal it. Mr. Anderson gave it to me on his own."

Godric asked, "How can this be possible?"

Isla replied, "I just talked about the video, and he gave it to me like someone gives an old toy to a child. Also, this video was in your house, in his secret room."

Godric said in a mischievous accent, "Really? That old man is so bold. I don't think he's been with any lady since Grandma died."

"Hee hee hee," laughed the angel sitting on the tree.

Isla said with a smile, "Oh, come on! He always treats me like his own granddaughter."

Godric said, "Nah! I have zero percent trust in that man. I am afraid one day that old mule will propose to you for marriage."

Isla said with a sad tone while walking away, "Oh my god! You know Godric, I am done for today."

Godric said while ran after Isla, "Isla! That was just a joke."

Isla exclaimed, "Stop chasing me!"

Godric asked, "Can you show me the video? Please."

Isla stopped and glared back at Godric. Godric also stopped at a distance of five to seven feet from her.

Isla asked, "So you came after me to watch the video? Do you really care about any of my feelings?"

The angel came and stood between the two, her face etched with sadness as she watched them fighting.

A FEW DAYS LATER

Harold and Isla sat on chairs around a C-shaped table in a spacious white room, accompanied by six members of the research centre's management. Godric stood in front of them, next to a projector screen displaying photos of five spiritual masters. Anne stood in the corner, holding a remote control in her hands.

Godric said, "Five masters that we chose for our project, we have saved the consciousness of all these spiritual masters. So far, we have successfully transmitted consciousness to the minds of five subjects."

Various videos and photos related to each word that Godric is speaking are also being played on the projector screen.

"How much change did you see within the subjects after this whole process was completed?" asked a 55-year-old French chairman.

Godric replied, "The success we have achieved with regard to social science and economics, we have not found such results with regard to our spiritual subjects."

Hearing Godric's words, everyone's faces were filled with dismay and despair.

"So all your effort to find the masters was just a waste of time?" Surprisingly, a 50-year-old African woman said.

Godric replied, "No, no! You do not need to be sad, this is only a small problem. Our subjects have become spiritual beings, but they don't know which direction they should go. In the subject of sociology and economics, we transmitted consciousness to the subjects on the basis of memory and intelligence. However the subject of spirituality is very complex. If we talk about the subcontinent of Asia, there are more than a hundred ways of attaining Moksha in the religious scriptures there. Apart from this, all these methods are also connected to each other. We are preparing our subjects for the propagation of a common religion. Still, the difficulty is that if we give them spiritual knowledge based on memory, we cannot give them the same knowledge. Since the knowledge of all the subjects is different, they will never be part of one link, and in the future, they can create their separate cults instead of the same religion. We have found a solution to this problem, and instead of memory, we gave our subjects the actionable consciousness of spiritual masters, which is the essence of spiritual knowledge. But now the problem is that our subjects have become people who show good character and desire to gain divine knowledge, but they do not have even a drop of real knowledge. If we give knowledge based on memory, then all these will not be able to propagate under one roof. On the other hand, on the basis of consciousness, we can make them of very high character, aspiring to spiritual pursuits but cannot transmit spiritual knowledge to them."

"That means now we have to find a guru for them," said, a 55-year-old Arabian man with a thin body sitting in front.

Godric replied, "Yes! We need masters for our subjects. But there is no need to worry about it. We already have these five masters to teach them."

Chairman said, "They all are different from each other. Can they give the same type of knowledge?"

Godric replied, "They are all the same."

Chairman asked, "If they are the same, then what is the problem in transferring their memory into the minds of our subjects?"

Godric explained, "The problem is that these masters belong to different religions."

Harold, in a slightly irritated tone while controlling his anger, said, "Godric! Firstly, you should decide whether those five people are the same or different from each other."

Godric said, "Don't you worry. I'll explain in detail. When any person follows a religion for fifteen to twenty years with complete determination, they become a spiritual person. Religions are different paths, but they all become one when they reach spirituality. These five people have two types of personalities in them. One personality is that of a religious person who belongs to a specific religion, and the other is that of a spiritual person. Both their personalities are mixed in their memory like milk mixed with water. This is the main reason we have given our subjects their consciousness and not the memory. We have no technology that can separate spiritual memory from religious memory. However, these five spiritual men are completely expert in their work to teach someone who is willing to understand the matrix of nature."

A forty-year-old man of French descent, sitting to the left of the chairman, asked, "So now if we have to depend on them, how long will our subjects acquire spiritual knowledge from them?"

Godric replied, "One year would be plenty in my opinion. But for this, we will give knowledge to only our five subjects, and when they become fully expert, we will transmit their consciousness and memory to all the other subjects. Problem solved! Any other questions?"

Everyone consulted among themselves in very low voices. The expressions on their faces indicated that they liked Godric's advice.

EVENING TIME

Bella sat in the backyard of the house, sipping coffee. The angel perched on the table in front of her, watching with a serene expression as Godric walked towards Bella, his face radiating love.

Godric said with a hug from behind, "I got it, mother. They all agree with me now."

Bella, speaking in a slightly resentful tone but smiling without any physical movement, replied, "You are so mean! It's a billion-dollar project, and you just tricked them all for your own deed."

Godric, speaking in a mischievous tone while sitting on a nearby chair, said, "What they have waited two decades for, if they do it for one more year, what started to deteriorate?"

Bella smiled and said, "You can't be anyone's trustworthy in matters of spirituality."

Godric responded, "Mother! If you read the book of World Religion, you would see the spiritual research committee has done a great job. But alas, I never got to meet them. Now, to understand such a big and valuable book, what is the harm in taking the help of five masters?"

Bella replied, "I love my Bible enough. You can read whatever you want."

Hearing Bella's words, the angel's face suddenly became very happy. She flew off the table, sat on Bella's lap, hugged her, and tried to tease Godric with her tongue like a child.

Godric said, "It has the spiritual teachings of all religions, including the Bible."

Bella spoke in a mocking tone, "It has been more than twenty years since your religion came into existence, but how many people follow it? Until now, you could not even bring your scripture before the people."

Godric replied, "We have no enlightened person; otherwise, we would have at least forty percent of the people with us from all over the globe."

Bella, putting the cup on the table, said, "To establish every religion, God himself sends a messiah! Common humans can't do this work."

Godric remained silent, offering a loving smile to his mother. Meanwhile, Angel, captivated by Bella's words, kissed her face repeatedly with childlike affection.

NEXT DAY - THE GREAT WORLD RELIGION CENTER

The five masters sat in large chairs positioned beside a long, straight table. In front of them, high officials of UGHW, including Harold and Aldous, were seated on chairs around a C-shaped table situated on a lower platform. Between the two groups, a small table, measuring 2 by 2 feet and standing four feet high, lay a book titled The Great World Scripture.

"If anyone is the most valuable to us today, it is you five masters. We have a great scripture for the world, but no one can preach it to the people. As you know, the entire team who did the work of writing this book was attacked and killed by an anti-world religion terrorist group. After that, we did not understand how this world religion would be preached until four years later, Godric joined this organisation and offered us his service to find religious gurus from different regions of the world to take this project forward with the help of clones. We need the cooperation of all of you. I assure you that we will keep all your information and your families safe," said the army chief of the United Army of Human World in a very respectful way. He is 55 years old, six and a half feet tall, American man.

Chodrak said, "This is a great task, when we were selected, we all read and understood this scripture completely according to our own understanding. Soon, we will have a mutual understanding among all of us about each verse, and then, we will explain each page of this scripture to the students you have selected."

MIDNIGHT

A 30-year-old Indian man, bound in iron chains, is being sacrificed by priests on the altar of an ancient temple, surrounded by a crowd of onlookers. His legs and arms are tightly secured, and his agonised screams pierce the dead of night, creating a heart-wrenching and terrifying noise.

Godric is sleeping on his bed, trying to move here and there, but his body is completely numb and his face is covered with sweat.

A priest raised an arm high, where an advanced technological weapon was attached to his hand. The weapon featured six pointed fingers spinning at an extremely high speed. The priest plunged the weapon into the man's stomach, reducing his intestines to mincemeat.

Godric's eyes snapped open and heaved a deep sigh.

A YEAR AGO

Inside a bunker, Theo, Harold and Aldous are standing in front of a machine that looks like an 8×8 feet chamber designed with very advanced technology. Three other scientists are also standing with them. It is clear to see that all the parts of this machine are a combination of human and alien science.

Harold said, "I am very proud of you. This research of you and your colleagues will prove to be a boon to the entire humanity."

"Thanks Father!" Theo added, beaming with pride.

Aldous placed a hand on Harold's shoulder in an expression of concern. "Harold! Think again," he urged. "We have more people to do this work. If there is any kind of disturbance, we won't be able to save you."

Harold replied in a calm expression, "I have lived my life, my every breath is a bonus. After all, Michael was my soldier, no one can explain him our situation except me. If you go yourself, he will scatter your head like a melon before you even start to speak."

Aldous with a calm expression said, "I have no doubt about that. My son's attitude intelligence training was way ahead of our time."

"Can we start now?" an elderly scientist with a hunchbacked body spoke.

Theo said, "Father! You really need to be careful about your time window."

Harold replied, "Don't worry, son! I am a soldier and father of a great scientist. Let's get to work now."

SECOND WORLD WAR – 1945

Sounds of bombardment and gunshots are coming from all sides. Harold lies unconscious with his soldiers wounded.

At a distance of 100 metres from them, Harold came out from a wormhole. He is in the uniform of British army and has a gun in his hands. On his left wrist is an alien technology watch. Now he started moving forward slowly, looking around the forest.

"May God never make me see such a day again," said Harold to himself, sitting in the cover of the bushes while looking at the wounded body of his past lying on the ground.

No active soldiers are visible far and wide. Harold is constantly looking at his military unit, which is a victim of a warplane's bomb.

"Where are you, my beast?" Harold said, while looking through the binoculars at the soldiers lying on the ground.

Suddenly, a silence like a cemetery spread all around. It seemed as if time had stopped.

No, no, no!! It can't be. I seem to be stuck in the thoughts of my mind instead of going to the past," Harold said suddenly in panic.

PRESENT TIME – RESEARCH CENTER

Godric sat inside the expansive lab of World Religion, surrounded by five lab subjects of diverse backgrounds, all dressed in white. In front of them, five masters stood on a raised platform, with a projector screen positioned before them. The lab was cluttered with religious scriptures, ancient books, and various sacred idols and artefacts.

Mansoor, "Every religion talks about the God. He is one, but he has many forms as well. The first form is called Akaal, which is beyond the time. The second form is Mahakal, which is linked to the creation and rules over the cycle of the time. Some religions speak only about the Mahakal form of God and some worship many powers of nature as gods and goddesses who are many other forms within the Mahakal form. Some religions worship only The God, and some religions worship The God and his thousands of other forms as well. So, mainly, all the religions worship only the One, The creator, the Lord. Only the ways to connect him and the names of the creator are different. To make what I said easier, look carefully at these different images that illustrate the world's four main spiritual approaches in a very simple way," he spoke, pointing to the images running on the projector screen.

Vedant explained, "In this image, you are looking at Sanatan, which has existed for thousands of years within the subcontinent of Asia. In fact, it is not a religion but a form of spiritual life style. The research on this spiritual approach has been done by many spiritual gurus for thousands of years. This form of spirituality is now called Hinduism. In this religion, Akaal, then his Mahakala form, then positive and negative forms of Mahakala and then the sub-forms of positive and negative both are worshiped by naming different deities. Instead of dividing the whole creation of Akaal into wrong or right, it is called Leela of Akaal by Hindu saints. Leela means a game in which good or bad does not matter; only the order of Akaal matters. According to this religion, a person can worship any power of the Mahakala form of Akaal, by his or her own will or the power he or she has to worship. This religion believes in the hell and the heaven. To avoid hell, Hinduism teaches the lesson of humanity and teaches humans to do good deeds to attain heaven. But its main teaching encourages its followers not to limit themselves to heaven like the Abrahamic religions, but to strive for the attainment of Moksha, that is to say, merge into the One. Hindu scriptures do not point the existence of the hell as an opposing side of heaven. It is believed, these both sides, I mean hell and the heaven are mutually related to each other and the chaotic relation between both is considered as a necessary factor for the existence of creation. The power that runs the hell is also considered as a god and is fully respected. In this religion, while worshiping the God's various powers, it has been taught to gradually cut the cycle of the Mahakal's creation to merge into his highest form. I mean the Akaal. This religion believes in reincarnation and claims to teach the perfect way to liberate our soul from the never-ending cycle of heaven and hell based on the principle of karma. More than one hundred paths are mentioned in the Sanatana for the attainment of Moksha or Brahmgyan."

Gurbaksh explained, "This image represents the spiritual understanding of Sikhism, which came into existence five hundred years ago. Sikhism worships only the Akaal. In this religion, the existence of the Akaal, the Mahakal form of the Akaal, the positive and negative powers of the Mahakal form and further their sub-powers like gods and goddesses etcetera, have been fully recognised, but this religion apart from the Akaal, does not worship any of the powers that come under the influence of the creation or run the creation. Sikhism refuses to worship any gods and goddesses. This religion also believes in hell and heaven and instead of dividing it into good and bad, it considers it as an essential part of the Mahakala that governs the creation. This religion also has absolute belief in reincarnation. While the Sikh Gurus have instructed their followers to stay away from hell by teaching them the lesson of serving the humanity, at the same time, while worshipping the Akaal, they have instilled in their minds the desire to stay away from heaven as well, from the game of transmigration that is going on under Mahakal. It has been taught by Sikhism how to go out of the endless cycle of the creation forever and get absorbed in that wonderful wonder by fixing the attention within the one creator, Akaal. In simple words, this religion's main goal is teaching its disciples how they can attain Brahmgyan or Moksha."

Chodrak explained, "This image depicts the spiritual ideology of Buddhism. Buddhism does not mention any power that governs the creation. The creation itself is considered in charge of everything. In this religion, the followers have been taught to do meditation in order to know about their own existence. The followers of this religion give priority to the principle of non-violence in their social life. This religion also believes in the existence of hell and heaven and emphasises the attainment of Moksha or Brahmgyan by talking about the rebirth of the soul according to karma that is being stuck in transmigration for billions of years."

Anselm, "This image describes the spiritual approach of the Abrahamic religions. All these religions believe in one creator only. His abode is considered to be within the whole creation. Any kind of Idol worshipping is forbidden in all Abrahamic religions. The concept of Leela does not exist in any of these religions. Main focus of these religions is creating a strong and well ordered social structure along with worshiping only one God. These religions mainly encourage their follower to follow the commandments given in the scriptures so they can get their way to live in the heaven after the death. The concept of Moksha or Brahmgyan does not exist in these religions. That's it! If anyone has questions please ask," spoke explaining every aspect of the film in a great detail.

Mansoor asked, "Any questions?"

Subject 1 asked, "The Akaal, then Mahakal and then there are more forms; why are there so many forms of the creator?"

Anselm replied, "Various forms are necessary for the phenomenon of his Leela; without them, the Leela is not possible. But he is one in many. He cannot be seen in isolation based on the various types or powers of the creation. We are discussing His various forms only to give you a spiritual understanding of creation and the creator."

Subject 3 asked, "If God is one, then why are all religions different?"

Gurbaksh Singh replied, "If you look carefully, every religion is just a discipline. Every religion teaches you the truthful way of life. Every religion in the world teaches humanity in its basic form. The basic teachings of all religions are exactly the same. We see the differences in them only because of the cultural and regional differences. But if we take a look at the psychology of each religion, it is exactly the same. So basically, no religion is different, big or small."

Subject 4 asked, "Do the hell and heaven really exist?"

Gurbaksh Singh replied, "If we want to teach a kid to stay away from bad habits with the help of creating a fear of something in his mind, would that be our bad parenting?"

Subject 4 responded, "No! If the intention is positive, then creating a fear in the kid's mind is totally fine."

Gurbaksh Singh asked, "If we give a reward to our kid for his good habits, will he become a bad kid, or he will adopt more good habits?"

Subject said, "Obliviously, the kid will adopt more good habits for more rewards."

Gurbaksh Singh remarked, "So does the hell and the heaven! They do not exist the way religions talk about them in words. We need to understand the deep meanings behind these teachings. Actually, the heaven is the positive part of our life and it's within the emotions of compassion, love, pleasure, happiness, joy, sympathy, etcetera. On the other hand, the hell is considered to be within the emotions of hatred, pain, anxiety, anger and jealousy. Both hell and heaven are within and around us. These both states of our mind are part of the creation. But we need to get rid of the birth cycle that keeps us in tangle with hell and heaven through our earthly attachments and for that, we need to merge with the God, inside and outside of the Creation."

Subject 2 inquired, "Does it mean those who just focus on the heaven, can't break the cycle of the birth and the death?"

Chodrak asked, "Estimate, how many people can attain Moksha out of ten million people."

Subject 5 answered, "There can be thousands."

Chodrak laughed and said, "Ha ha ha ha! There are thousands only of those who want to follow the path of attaining Moksha. If we talk about how many get success in that, then only one person would get it after ten million."

Subject 1 said with great surprise, "I was thinking, it would be about ten thousand?"

Chodrak replied with a smile, "Ten thousand out of ten million are only those who truly feared God and chanted His name all the time."

Vedant said, "Now think for yourself: if only one person after ten million attains Moksha, then what would the rest of the people understand about the top-notch spiritualism? It's impossible to make everyone understand about the top level of spirituality. Therefore, if every religion succeeds in teaching the lesson of humanity to the whole world, that would be more than enough.

So the concept of hell and heaven is really great, and we experience both of these all the time. It's not fake, but yes, the way of presenting it is different from its true existence.

Subject 4 asked, "Can people of two different religions learn to worship the God in each other's way by sharing information with each other?"

Godric replied, "This is the foundation of the Great World Religion. The book of this religion has been prepared by collecting the teachings of all the religions in one place."

Mansoor said, "All religions can be differentiated due to the cultural differences of their regions, but spirituality is absolutely common. Spirituality cannot be seen on the basis of any location, language, religion, caste, colour or culture. All the enlightened ones in the world to date have never seen the religion, country or race of any guru while receiving spiritual education, nor have they ever had any relationship with anyone on the basis of religion, country or race before they started giving spiritual education to someone. Religions never stops us from exchanging education with each other. These are some political people who spread hatred by creating division among people in the name of religion."

Godric added, "We have gathered the teachings of all religions in one place and that one place is called The Great World Religion. The common social order of the New World Order has spread to almost every corner of the world in the last two decades. So, our religion will be very easily adopted by people from every corner of the world."

Subject 1 asked, "If someone already believes in a religion, why would he adopt The Great World Religion?"

Godric answered, "All the people in the world are following any religion only on the basis of the beliefs of their family. In the old social structure, people do not adopt religion themselves, rather, it is inherited. But now we have implemented a very strict law under the new social order according to which no parent can impose their religion on their child. We will promote World Religion in the whole world through our education system and we are preparing you for that great mission. But we are not going to force anyone to believe in the Great World Religion."

30 YEARS AGO – 1945

Harold, accompanied by his fellow officers, scientists, and businessmen, arrived at a room with a black glass wall at the front. They all took their seats around a large, round table.

Harold said, "I don't think we need to make any contact with the inhabitants of any other planet. They are far ahead of us in science. If they want to occupy us tomorrow, I don't think we would be able to last more than an hour."

"If we do not make any contact, then what's going to change? Did they just fly into the infinite universe and fall here accidentally? These aliens already would have known about us, everything," Oscar, a 50 years old British business man sitting in front of Harold, said.

"How do they get here all of a sudden? What do you think about that?!" Army Chief Aldous asked Oscar.

"We think they didn't just pop up today. Surely they have been here for a very long time. Analysis of the Pyramids of Egypt and some other civilisations shows that humans have never been away from people from other planets. The only difference is that these alien civilisations never lived like common people. In ancient times, people used to consider them as gods, or say, some of the ancient gods are aliens," said a businessman named Newton, sitting next to Oscar.

"Do you really think they're never going to intend to occupy our planet?" Harold asked. "They came here, made our people worship them for some time, and then disappeared? Now, after many centuries, they suddenly fell from the sky! Seriously? It can't be just an accident."

Oscar responded, "I think it's just an accident. If you have a better theory, we're listening. Tell me."

"Who knows if there is another alien civilisation that is an enemy of these aliens and wanted to kill them, and during a fight between them, their ships crashed? I find this whole episode very negative," Harold replied.

Now all the people sitting around started whispering to each other. Harold's words forced everyone to think.

Newton said, "Did you ever think that if we get hold of their science, we could rule the world?"

"If you can copy their science and rule the world, then think what they can do to the whole world. I agree with Harold. We need to think seriously about this whole incident," an army officer said.

Oscar argued, "We all know that our planet is not hidden from them. If they had to take control over it, they would have done it long ago. I think we should try to make friendly relations with them. However, since their civilisation is way ahead of us, I don't think our planet will be of any use to them."

"Chief! In my opinion, we should get as much information about alien technology as we can through reverse engineering of their spaceships. There is a chance that some other countries may have got all this alien junk too. Even if it is not found by them right now, who knows? Other nations might get their hands on this type of useful alien tech in the future!" said a 40-year-old scientist.

"Absolutely!! I agree with you," Newton exclaimed. "We should speed up the work on this project without losing any time. The enemy may be weak today, but who knows about tomorrow."

Aldous added, "I agree with all of you. You all have strong opinions. But we should not rush into this issue. I don't want us to enter the first inter-world war after the Second World War."

A 60-year-old scientist in a white coat entered the room and stood in front of everyone.

"Welcome, everyone. Today is a very extraordinary day for humankind, but also... We have some very bad news," the scientist standing in front spoke.

Aldous asked, "Tell me the bad news first."

"The Earth is going to be completely destroyed in the third decade of the twenty-first century," the scientist stated.

"Ha ha ha ha!" everyone started laughing.

Aldous asked with a smile, "May I know who gave you this so-called bad news?"

"Lights, please!" the scientist requested.

Suddenly, a light on the other side of the black glass wall in front turned on, and everyone stood up from their chairs with an expression of surprise.

PRESENT TIME

Outside the house, Godric and Isla stood with their backs against a car. Isla held a cup of coffee in her hand, while Godric watched a video on his tablet, depicting the destruction of the entire planet. Angel, perched on the roof of the car behind them, leaned forward, trying to get a closer look at the tablet.

"How many more times do you have to watch it?" Isla asked.

"Something is wrong with the video," Godric said, watching the video with suspicion.

"Something wrong?" Isla exclaimed. "The destruction of the whole world is not just something wrong! It's a hundred percent apocalypse."

"I knew that old man would have tricked you," Godric replied.

"What do you mean?" Isla questioned.

"This video is not real," Godric stated confidently.

"How can you be so sure?" Isla demanded.

"Just leave it. I will explain later. This is his old habit. He thinks no one can be smarter than him. But... I am relaxed now. It shows he has no plan to propose to you," Godric said, the last words spoken in a very mischievous tone with a smile.

Isla retorted, "Don't you dare start that again. You... Just change the topic. How is the work on World Religion going on? What are they teaching you these days?"

"God is one. He has an eternal form, which exists in thousands of forms, that is, hell, heaven, gods, angels, and men, as well as each particle of the whole creation," Godric explained.

"What!? I didn't understand even one percent of what you said," Isla said.

"Now, what can I say more simply?" Godric asked, turning off the tablet.

Isla sighed, "Don't you think all this is just too boring?"

After listening to Isla, Angel sat back on the roof of the car, her lips pursed in displeasure as she looked at Godric, waiting for an answer.

Godric replied, "This is the path of self-discovery. You are walking outward, and I am swimming inward."

"Again, the same boring words," Isla said with a sigh. "Please, talk about something like love."

"The real source of love is God. If we want to talk about love, it cannot be discussed without mentioning God," Godric explained.

"I am talking about our love!" Isla said, her voice slightly irritated. "Can we talk about our love for each other?"

"God is the cause of your love. In fact, people think love is an action of emotions between two bodies towards each other, but no one knows what love actually is. The real secret can be understood only after connecting with God. After that, we get to know... measuring the depth of love is beyond our mind and body," Godric replied.

Angel flew down from the car and sat on the ground, giving a tight hug to Godric's right leg.

"All right, tell me about this love thing in detail," Isla said, softening. "But only in very simple words."

"It means something very bitter. Can you bear the truth?" Godric asked, looking at her seriously.

"I am listening. Go on," Isla encouraged him.

"Do you want to hear an answer that you would like to hear, or do you want to hear the answer?" Godric asked.

"Tell me the... answer," Isla said with a smile.

"When God created the universe, His energy spread in all directions. Our souls are the most awakened part of that energy, and every soul is always agonising to be reunited with the source of its origin. That agonising manifests itself in all of us through the sense of sex. The attraction to the opposite sex in all humans and animals is actually the desire of the soul to meet with God," Godric explained.

By now, thousands of angels had gathered around Godric and Isla. All of them were listening to Godric very carefully.

"Animals also have the same soul as us?" Isla asked, genuinely intrigued. "I mean, exactly the same life force?"

"Yes!" Godric confirmed. "Whether the soul is in a stone, plant, an animal, or a human body, it is the same life force. Only according to the body, its consciousness is different, more or less. Always keep in mind that the soul is not a human being. It acts like a human because it is in a human body and depends on the senses that nature gifted to the human body."

"Okay... that's interesting!" Isla said, her interest piqued. "Now tell me what you were going to say about the soul and God."

"When we are attracted to any human being, it is actually the hunger of the soul to meet with God. All our souls are a part of God, or we can say the drips of an ocean that parted with Him billions of years ago and now crave to merge with Him all the time. So when our body has affection for another person, it means our soul has the illusion that God is close to it. We call that passion of the soul for God as lust or love. But actually, it is not a physical act but a spiritual act of contact between one soul and another through the physical bodies," Godric concluded, looking at Isla.

Isla trying to digest the complex explanation, and asked, "That means we both do not love each other, but our spirits brought us closer to each other thinking that the person in front of us is God?"

Godric nodded and replied, "Exactly right! And when two people have sex with each other, that moment is the closest link of one soul dissolving into another soul. Then, during sex, there comes a moment when the duality between man and woman ceases, and both of them forget gender differences and become one. At that moment, the soul feels the closeness of the other soul as if it is entering into its original source. But as soon as a man and a woman reach the extreme limit of sexual desire and achieve orgasm, during that moment of orgasmic joy, we get a very subtle glimpse of meeting with God in a very small part of a second. But at the same time, the energy of our body fades away, and the spirits remain untied. Then we have sex again and again so that we can go forward in that pleasure, but we cannot dive into that pleasure from the other's body. Therefore, the attraction of love between two people starts decreasing after a few months of relationship."

Isla asked, "Why? Why would the love fade away after having sex for a few months?"

Godric replied calmly, "Because the soul gets to know that the body is not connecting it to the eternal joy with which it wants to connect."

"Does that mean love doesn't exist?" Isla questioned, her voice tinged with disbelief.

"No!" Godric exclaimed, shaking his head. "It is only an illusion. This is the reason why a person can never keep another person connected to him or her at the spiritual level forever. But the soul becomes intoxicated with lust, and this is the reason why people go to the extremes of insanity for sex, and some actually become insane. This wandering of the soul for God has been going on for billions of years within every living being in the entire universe. Only a true Guru can eradicate this leprosy."

Isla rolled her eyes, sarcastically replying, "Wow! What a great way to justify cheating. Looks like you love it a lot. I think I should meet your masters personally."

Godric, sensing her sarcasm, said, "That's it? You start hesitating only after hearing half of the story? I already told you that! You cannot bear the truth."

"Go on! I am listening!" Isla insisted.

Godric continued, "Instead of wasting our sex energy to get joy from other people through the reproductive organs below our body, if we take this sex energy to the tenth door on the upper side of our body, then the peace and liberation that we can attain, the joy of sex is not even a fraction of that. Our soul can become one with God, not through Linga or Yoni, but only and only through Dasam Dwar, or we can say the tenth gate. In this way, we can end our wandering of billions of years and millions of births from the matrix of Mahakal."

Thousands of angels gathered around the porch listened intently to Godric's words, their expressions filled with rapt attention, as if each were a lover absorbed in the affection of their beloved.

Isla, who seemed less convinced, asked, "What is Dasam Dwar?"

"The mouth, eyes, nose, ears, and below the excrement, as well as the reproductive organs, are the total of nine gates of our body," Godric explained. "The tenth door is between our eyebrows, and this door is secret. Only with its opening the soul can merge with God."

Isla laughed, her scepticism evident. "Does this mean there are eleven gates in a woman's body? Ha ha ha!"

Now all the angels got irritated hearing Isla's childish talk and looked at each other's faces, shaking their heads as if saying that nothing could be taught to this idiot.

Godric sighed, his expression a mix of amusement. "Come on, do you really think about humour in the midst of such a great conversation? Right now, you can't even imagine how many angels are looking at us."

Isla replied, "What to me? I think they are also lustful like you who come here to listen to your lascivious words."

A collective "Boooooo!!" resonated through the air as the angels voiced their disapproval.

Godric said, "She can't hear you're boo! So relax and listen. Miss Isla... Yes! The women also have ten gates."

"Are they booing me now?" Isla asked with great surprise.

Godric replied, "Should I answer the question?"

Isla said, "Okay... go on!" while looking around with a sore face.

Godric continued, "Suppose a house has a big gate that remains open twenty-four hours and seven days a week, and there are two other small doors at the back of that gate, which are opened only when needed. Now tell me, do we call that big gate the main gate of the house, or shall we call the two doors on the inside the two main gates of the house?"

Isla asked, "Whose gate remains always open?"

Godric answered, "Ask to the owners of the house, what to me? Give me the answer, ma'am."

Isla retorted, "Tell to your soul! This hot body belongs to me only. Don't you dare to trick me with your heavy spiritual words to see other girls."

Godric exclaimed, "What? When did I say that?"

"You know better what I mean," Isla said while going back inside the house.

Godric surveyed the surrounding angels, who smiled at Isla's innocence and the profound depth of her love for him.

THE TIME BRANCH

FEW MONTHS LATER

All five masters and Godric are currently sitting in front of Harold in the backyard of their farmhouse.

"Godric! My sweet, sweet grandson," Harold began, "I tried so hard to make sure you are not part of any conspiracy. All the interviews of hundreds of people, their names, and addresses are there, but I could not find a single legit documentation about the way you found these five guys. It looks like you just picked them without going through a fair process. Tell me! What are you guys cooking?" Harold spoke in a stern army officer's tone.

Godric responded, "You've misunderstood," speaking as if the other person's point was completely unfounded.

Harold countered, "Thanks to God, your issue has not reached the head office of intelligence yet."

"But I did nothing wrong. I am doing my job very well," Godric protested.

"The way you found these five masters from all over the world, it seems as if you and your masters have a secret connection with the anti-world religion group that killed the team that prepared the scripture for the world religion. It looks like you do not want this religion to make any kind of progress," Harold said, making very strong eye contact with everyone.

"We are serving this religion wholeheartedly day and night. Those you are talking about are our enemies too. Grandpa! You have got a big misunderstanding," Godric insisted.

"If you are serving this religion, then why did you lie to us to keep these men in our research centre? You don't even have an idea how big an investigation UG has done on all the work of every department. Anne told me everything. You didn't want these people to transmit their consciousness and go back. She said you wanted to stop them here to get spiritual education for yourself, which does not make any sense to me. Some of the families of all the masters chosen by you are rebelling against the New World Order and have died by our army's bullets. It is clear that you and your friends are part of a big conspiracy," Harold accused.

"You are greatly misunderstood," Godric maintained.

"I will talk to you later," Harold said, turning his attention elsewhere. "Gurbaksh Singh! You never mentioned that any member of your family participated in World War II."

Gurbaksh Singh spoke very easily without feeling any surprise. "I already felt that I could not hide this from you."

"Who was that man?" Harold demanded. "Don't try to hide anything from me."

"He was my only son," Gurbaksh Singh admitted.

Harold pressed on, "Why didn't you ever talk about him yourself?"

Gurbaksh Singh replied, "What will I achieve by mentioning it? Was he a martyr of the Second World War that I should discuss him? He was mistakenly shot by his own commander, not by any enemy. There is nothing to discuss about him."

"Why would a commander kill his soldier? Do you have an explanation for this?" Harold questioned.

"Yes, of course!" Gurbaksh Singh answered. "My son was a spiritual type of person. When he was fighting the war, he was seeing Shaheed Singhs during the firing, and he left the front and followed the Shaheed Singhs. He thought that the army of Shaheed Singhs had come to help him, but he did not know that Maya was playing with him. When he was going after the Shaheed Singhs, his commander felt that he might be running away from the field."

Harold asked, "And what happened then?"

"The commander shot him from behind," Gurbaksh Singh explained.

Harold shook his head, saying, "I have also lived among Sikh soldiers in India, and they used to talk about the guard of Shaheed Singhs. But till today, I consider all this just a fantasy. But sorry, I still don't understand what you are saying. May I know who told you that he was seeing an invisible army?"

"One of his friends came back alive from the war," Gurbaksh Singh replied. "He was very injured, so he left the body only a month after coming to the village. Before he died, he mentioned to me that Zoraver was muttering to himself while sitting in front. He was looking outside the front on his left as if someone was calling him. He was repeatedly saying, 'Shaheed Singhs have arrived.' Then he got out of the front and walked backwards instead of moving forward. That soldier called out to Zoraver several times, but Zoraver did not look back at all. After this, the commander shot him."

Harold said, "He had no idea how dangerous it could be to leave the front like that?"

"It is not a normal incident for a Singh to see Shaheed Singhs during the war," Gurbaksh Singh explained. "But what he was seeing as Singhs were not Singhs. It was Maya in the form of the Singhs to fool him once again."

"How can you say with such confidence that they were not Singhs?" Harold asked.

"If they were real Shaheed Singhs, they would not have allowed your bullet to hit my son," Gurbaksh Singh replied.

Harold's expression changed, and he said, "It means you knew that your boy was killed by my bullet and you came close to Godric to avenge him. I know the blood of your race very well! You can go to any extent for revenge. Didn't I say that right? And some of yours have also died at the hands of the United Government's army. I have strong evidence for that too. Revenge is not a bad thing, but you all messed up with the wrong person."

Suddenly, UAHW soldiers who had been hidden 50 metres away sprang up, their guns aimed at the masters from all directions.

Gurbaksh Singh said, "Listen! My colleagues and I have no need to take any kind of revenge against you or your army. Also, I know very well that you fired that shot out of misunderstanding. Not only I, but Godric and the rest of my companions are well aware of this."

Harold asked, "Godric! Did you already know about this crazy story?"

Godric declared, "I am Zoraver! You killed me in my past life," holding both hands in the air.

Chodrak added, "Not only in the past life; you killed him four times before that too."

Harold exclaimed, "What the fuck are you guys talking about? And how can you be Zoraver?"

Godric replied, "Grandpa! I can explain all the truth to you, but before that, you need to understand that I have not slacked at all in the work of World Religion. We all have done that work with full determination. All my masters are good people. None of us is conspiring against you and the government."

Gurbaksh Singh said, "My son was killed by Maya. I do not blame you at all."

Harold retorted, "Stop bullshitting. What do you think I'm going to believe in your religious fairy tales? You have no idea about the truth of the universe. I know the level of science that people like you worship as divine power for thousands of years."

Gurbaksh Singh replied, "Just look to your left."

As Harold turned his head to the left, he was met with a vast assembly of millions of Shaheed Singhs. Ready for war, he began to tremble as the sky echoed with the shouts and chants of the Khalsa army.

"Soldiers! Put your guns down, you have no idea what we're dealing with right now," Harold said, raising his arms in surrender with a very frightened voice.

Godric asked, "Have you ever wondered how you survived the war? Do you remember anything between opening your eyes in the army hospital after the bomb blast?" He stood from his place and moved towards Harold, speaking with wide-open red eyes.

"I was unconscious, so how could I remember?" Harold spoke nervously with a trembling voice.

"Did anyone ever tell you who took you to the army camp?" Godric asked.

"What are you trying to say?" Harold responded.

RESEARCH CENTER

All the masters sat in the vast lab with Godric and Harold. Spiritual knowledge and consciousness were being transmitted to the clones through numerous machines positioned in front of them. The institute's scientists, deeply focused on their tasks, closely monitored the process. Anne, also present, found herself unable to meet Godric's intense gaze, as he looked visibly angry.

Harold said, "I am amazed at how much you fooled us all to solve your mysterious dreams. How mean are you, grandson?"

Godric replied, "I hit two targets with one arrow. All these subjects have become masters in spirituality and are now fully prepared to preach the world religion. Although I chose my masters for my own sake, I never turned away from my duty."

"You could have found more masters like us, but I cannot claim that you would have found better ones than us," Vedant, sitting to the left of Harold, spoke in a mischievous tone.

Harold said, "Don't know how you all the freaks got together."

Mansoor spoke in a strong accent, "We have fulfilled our promise. Now it is your duty to solve our problem."

Harold asked, "Are you requesting or scaring me?"

Chodrak said, "You have been scaring our disciple for many past lives. It's been centuries. You have no idea how much we all love you. Now it's time to open up properly."

Harold responded, "I have fixed the meeting, and we shall be pleased to help you all in your fairy tale mission."

A FEW DAYS LATER – A BUNKER

Godric, Theo, Harold, Aldous, all the masters, and three scientists were sitting around a round table.

Aldous said, "We need both sides to share all the details in this meeting that have led to our current suspicions. I have full confidence in my friend Harold, which is why I called this meeting today. Otherwise, we would have turned you all into a pile of rubbish by now. This is your last chance, so I will not tolerate any trickery at all." He spoke very casually to Godric and his team in a serious tone.

Anselm responded, "Don't worry, chief! We won't hide anything from you, but I am wondering why you are giving us such a chance for the sake of friendship. The army can't be so emotional before its duty?"

Godric said, "Don't you know? They are afraid of the army of Shaheed Singhs. These are army people and respect their equals only."

Harold interjected, "Oh, stop your bullshit! The existence of our entire world is in danger, your team accuses me of killing you five times, and you're still joking around?"

Godric apologised, "Sorry, Grandpa! I am silent now," as he put his finger on his lips.

Aldous continued, "The claims you made about Godric's five past lives do not fit our interest. But yes, one thing is definitely true about your claim: Harold reaching the army hospital in a supernatural way while critically injured. I want Theo to open up to everyone about this matter."

Theo said, "Thanks, Chief! My fellow scientists and I have been building a machine for the past two decades through which we can travel to any time zone in the past and the future. We succeeded in that project last year."

Godric exclaimed, "You made a time machine?" with great surprise.

Theo retorted, "Shut the fuck up and listen! You... don't you dare interrupt me again!"

Godric said, "Sorry, Dad! The stage is yours!" raising both hands and smiling.

Theo continued, "First of all, we have done a lot of research on the behaviour of time to get the exact work from this machine. During this research, we also discovered that the timeline we were living in twenty-five years ago has now branched into a new, weaker timeline. In result of that... our whole world could turn into ashes at any time."

Anselm asked, "If time has changed its course, how can it be dangerous for us?"

Aldous urged, "Theo, you need to tell them the whole thing!"

Theo agreed, "As you wish, Chief! Your question is quite correct: how can we become ashes due to a change in the course of time? Normally, time keeps changing, and a change in pace cannot be attributed as the reason for our extinction. But three decades ago today, an event occurred that separated us from our timeline. Our superiors were contacted by a being from another planet who presented evidence related to our future and claimed that after a few decades, our entire world would be turned into a pile of ashes due to nuclear war."

Gurbaksh Singh asked in great surprise, "Are there people from other planets in your contact?"

Theo replied, "Thanks, Godric! At least you did not leak all the information."

Vedant asked, "You knew about the aliens?"

Godric confirmed, "Oh yes! I knew."

All the masters looked at Godric with displeasure and suspicion.

"Come on, guys! I can't share the secrets of others with you. That's a sin!" Godric spoke like a wise man to all his companions.

Harold remarked, "That means my grandchild can't be trusted by anyone. Ha ha ha!"

"Dad! Can I finish, please?" Theo said with a hint of displeasure.

"Sorry, son! You can carry on!" Harold replied.

"Listen, you all! If any one of you interrupts me again, I will shoot you right in your forehead!" Theo said angrily, drawing his pistol.

All the people, including Godric, sat completely still with their fingers over their lips.

"Why are your hands up?" Theo asked the scientists.

The three nervous scientists put their hands down.

Theo continued, "The Aliens presented evidence and told us that our world would end soon and they offered us a solution to avoid our extinction. Thanks to that, we brought a new order to the whole world. The whole structure of our world today was prepared by those Aliens. As they told us, we continued to follow their instructions, and soon the government of the whole world came into power. We all thought we might have saved our world from ending, but when I discovered some hidden secrets related to the time while building the time machine, I concluded that if our world was about to end, it means only a few decades of vitality remained in our timeline. We have now gone beyond the original timeline and created a time branch, not a new timeline. All the energy of this branch is coming from the original timeline, and we all know that the energy of that timeline was about to end. This means that this time branch does not have a solid source of energy to keep moving forward. Just as the branches of a drying tree dry up along with its roots and trunk, we can make as many branches of time as we want from the main timeline by going back to it again and again. But when the original timeline ends, all its branches will fade away simultaneously."

After hearing Theo's words, everyone's faces fell into sorrow.

"Why were those Aliens so kind to us?" Chodrak asked.

"We'll talk about that another time," Harold replied.

"May we also meet those Aliens?" Vedant asked.

"Till this day, even Theo and Godric have not had that chance," Harold said with strictness.

"Don't worry, master. Meeting them is a far-fetched thing. We haven't even been told how they look or where their base is," Godric said.

"Can't you even trust your own family?" Mansoor asked Harold.

"Huh! Look at the face of this brat. Do you really think I would trust him?" Harold said to Mansoor, pointing at Godric's face.

"This face belongs to your family," Godric said.

"The world is about to end. Where are your brains? Focus on the matter and talk your bullshit later," Theo scolded.

"Shhhhhhhh!!!" Godric put his finger over his lips and motioned for everyone to disperse.

"Do you have any solution to the timeline issue?" Gurbaksh Singh asked.

"Yes!" Theo replied. "We have to go back to the main timeline and stop the disaster in its future. If we do this, the timeline will continue to move forward, and our time branch will also be completely green. We already have a precise plan for this work."

"May we know the plan?" Godric asked.

"Absolutely!" Theo said. "That is why we have invited you here. We will go to the past with the help of a time machine to meet a very special, reliable, and dying friend to give him the mission to reset the future of the main timeline."

Anselm asked, "What is the need to give this mission to someone else? I mean, when you yourself have a complete understanding of all this, is it okay to trust someone else?"

"Good question!" Theo responded. "It has a very easy answer. We are now connected to a separate time branch. Our future is different from the timeline. If we try to go to the future, then our future is where we stand today. Therefore, we need a person from the main timeline, and that too a person who is close to death. If such a person is saved from death and sent to the future, then the balance of the timeline will not be damaged in any way. He will still be dead for the main timeline, and there would be no harm in him going into the future and dying with the rest of the world if he could not complete his mission. We are using Michael, who died during World War II and... He was our army chief's son."

"Oh! Sorry to hear this, chief!" Gurbaksh Singh said.

"It must be hard for you to choose your own son for the death route again," Chodrak added.

"Huh! I have three more sons, and they are all very alive!" Aldous said with a chuckle.

"So when are you going to execute your plan to save the world?" Godric asked.

"We have already tried a few times," Theo explained, "but every time we attempt this mission, something happens for which we have no answer so far. But now, if that incident is seen in connection with your claim related to Zoraver Singh, then we can understand that what your grandfather saw was not an imaginary dream."

"What do you want to say? What dream?" Chodrak asked.

Theo said, "Father! It will be better if you tell about it yourself."

"When I went to the past through the time machine," Harold began, "the bloody scene of the war and the smell of the ammunition were exciting every nerve in me to pick up my gun and join the war. The corpses of my soldiers seemed to me like the crematorium of my sons. I barely controlled my inner warrior soldier and focused on my plan, starting to look for Michael's body. But after a while, I saw the unconscious bodies of myself and some of my soldiers starting to fly in the air. It seemed as if a supernatural power had taken over control of the entire atmosphere. All of a sudden, there was silence everywhere, and not even the leaves of the trees were moving. My feet were held by the earth in the same way as iron is held by a magnet. My whole body had become a statue. As soon as I saw all the bodies flying far away towards the direction of the army camp, my body returned to its normal state. Ever since I came back from the war, I have dreamed many times that my body is being carried in the air by some force towards the army camp. So I thought maybe there was a malfunction in the machine. Then I quickly came back to the present time branch."

"We tried many times," Theo said, "but every time the same incident occurred, which puzzled my father again and again in his mission. We all were thinking that maybe this machine is taking father to some dimension of his own dreams instead of taking him to the past."

"Look at the results of thinking too much!" Mansoor said.

"Ha ha ha ha ha," Godric and all of his masters started laughing.

Aldous said, "Why do you guys not take it seriously? This incident is the only reason you are alive. When Godric told Harold how he saved him in the war, Harold believed that because he had already seen it due to the time machine. That's why we are meeting you here. Otherwise, you all are subjects of treason with UG for your selfish work." He spoke in a rather stern tone.

Godric asked, "First! Why did you choose an old man for this job? Secondly, if something was freezing him again and again, he should have finished his mission after waiting for some time."

Aldous replied, "Michael can be handled by Harold only. He won't listen to anyone else. As for waiting a little longer, Harold was afraid that he would be trapped inside his dream forever. So, we stopped trying after five attempts."

Godric said, "That's not a dream. It was Zoraver who took you to the very safe army camp so that he could stay with you to find out who you are, who has been continuously killing him for many lives." He said this to Harold.

Harold responded, "I had no enmity with Zoraver. Even Gurbaksh Singh has admitted that he was killed by mistake."

Gurbaksh Singh said, "I agree that you did not commit the murder deliberately to settle a grudge from any previous birth, but that does not mean the murder was just a misunderstanding. The karma cycle is very strange. Neither the victim knows who is going to kill them, nor does the killer know when they are going to kill someone. Both of you have some kind of connection from previous births, so it is very important to find the reason why this incident happens continuously."

Anselm commented, "See! Even in this birth, Harold took Godric as his enemy. Karma is not shying away from playing its game at all, and instead of finding a solution, we all have prepared reasons for that miserable incident to happen again."

Harold said, "I promise! I will never cause any harm to my grandson. Now that the whole issue has been cleared for us, I think we should complete this mission together and save the whole world."

Godric asked, "Can we use the time machine to see my past lives?"

Theo replied, "No, no, no! I can't help you with the time machine."

Aldous said, "Relax, Theo! If they help us complete our mission first, then we will definitely let them use the time machine. Now tell me, who is ready to go on a mission with Harold?"

Godric and all his masters raised their right hands.

Theo said, "Godric! You can't go with them."

Mansoor agreed, "I agree. There is an atmosphere of war now, and who knows if he'll shoot our disciple again." He pointed to Harold.

Chodrak added, "I agree with you."

Theo clarified, "I didn't mean that. Godric is still young, and you all are old. Even if one half dies, we won't suffer any loss."

Vedant laughed and said, "Ha ha ha! I am pleased to see Dhritarashtra in white skin."

Theo asked, "What do you mean? Are you being racist?"

Harold said suddenly, "Theo! Please focus on the topic."

Aldous asked, "What is your concern about their mission and the time machine?"

Theo replied, "Our mission shall be successfully completed, which would happen because we have a proper plan. To use the time machine, it is very important to have complete accurate information about the time, place, and event. We have all that information for our mission, but how can it be possible to trace Godric's past lives with a time machine?"

Godric stood up from his chair and said stood in front of Theo and said with a serious smile, "Father! What do you think, how would I have found my five masters? Did I choose them by playing rock-paper-scissors?"

NEXT DAY

Godric sat on a couch in a cabin nestled in the heart of the forest, with Isla nestled in his left arm. Her head rested on his shoulder, and her face appeared very pale. At the table in front of them, the angel gazed at the pair with deep affection, her left elbow resting on her left knee and her chin cradled in her left palm.

Isla asked, "How can you so firmly believe that you were Zoraver in your past life?"

Godric explained, "There is a big difference between a normal dream and a glimpse of a previous birth. So I went to every place I saw in my dreams under the pretext of finding masters for world religion. When I met Gurbaksh Singh and shared a dream with him, he told me the rest of my dreams himself. Zoraver had also seen the same dreams as mine. I can't forget the shine in Gurbaksh Singh's eyes. It was a great experience meeting him."

Isla said, "You have no idea how much money you've wasted for your own sake. What was the need to hide all this from me?"

Godric replied, "First thing, I did not waste money; I saved a lot from being wasted. No one else could find such good masters for world religion. Second thing, I didn't want you to think of me as a psychopath. I didn't want any rift in our relationship."

Isla asked, "Do you think my love is that weak? I can die for you. Just don't hide things from me again. I've known you since childhood. As far as I know, you're the best." She said, giving him a tight hug.

Godric said, "Yeah, I admit that. I have no competition. I'm a bloody genius!"

Isla smiled, "Oh, come on, you arrogant person. I was surprised that you used the research centre's funding for your own purposes."

Godric said, "The funding? Huh! I used the entire research centre for myself. But if someone else were in my place, they would have used even more funding and still not found perfect masters."

Isla asked, "How can you claim that the masters you found are the perfect ones?"

Godric answered, "Angels always wander around me. What's a big deal for a person like me to find a spiritual master?"

Isla inquired, "How was Zoraver's family? Did you feel anything special?"

Godric replied, "No, nothing like that happened, but the family is very sweet. I met Zoraver's son and his four-year-old grandson as well."

Isla asked, "And his wife?"

Godric said, "Alas, poor girl could not bear the pain of separation caused by Zoraver's death, and she died only two years after his death."

Isla questioned, "If you were Zoraver, wouldn't you still love your wife from your past life?" She lifted her head from Godric's shoulder and sat up straight.

Godric said, "My crazy girlfriend! I don't remember anything from any of my previous births, nor do I feel any emotional connection with Gurbaksh Singh or his family. I just wanted to know my secret, and now I've come very close to knowing it well." He spoke lovingly, gesturing with both hands.

Isla asked, "Did you see any photo of her? Was she more beautiful than me?"

Godric said, "Oh God! Please bless some wisdom to my cute girlfriend."

Isla pressed, "Tell me! I want to know! Was she hot?"

Godric replied, "No! She was just an average-looking girl, but her face had a spiritual innocence. She was like someone who submitted her whole life to the Lord and breathed only to wait for the death that happens while you're alive."

Isla said suspiciously, "It means you liked her."

Godric said, "Well, I like my mother too. Just because I admire someone doesn't mean what you're trying to prove here. She could not bear the pain of her husband's death and died in grief. She could have married someone else, but she didn't. Shouldn't we praise her?"

Isla observed, "I can see a lot of love in your eyes for her. My sweetheart! Please let me know if I'm wrong." She spoke in a naughty accent.

Godric said, "Yes, this is love but not sexualised love. It's something beyond our bodily limits. When I heard about her grief and saw her photo, that lady was the reflection of God, a pure soul. I have a lot of respect for her and anyone else like her."

Isla said, "I also see God in you."

Godric replied, "And you are my goddess! I love you soooo much. But please don't bother me in this critical hour. The person who has been killing me every time I come close to enlightenment for the past five lives is my grandfather in this life. Even more strangely, he kills me every time by mistake or due to some misunderstanding. But I don't want to leave my body without being enlightened again this time."

Isla said, "Sorry, my love! I won't bother you anymore. Could you tell me what enlightenment is, please?"

Godric said, "Wow! First time someone questioned me in my interest."

Isla asked, "Come on... I'm not kidding. Please tell me what it is."

Godric said, "Now listen carefully. When God created the universe, His energy spread everywhere, and along with it, time was born. As time progressed, creation continued to expand and is still happening today. As I told you that day, our soul is a part of God and wants to reunite with its original source. That reunion is called Brahmgyan, Moksha, or enlightenment."

Thousands of angels had gathered both inside and outside the hut. Inside, they filled every available space, while outside, they sat on the ground and perched on nearby trees. Enraptured by Godric's talk about God, they appeared almost intoxicated by spiritual talk.

Isla asked, "How could it all be! I mean, what is the experience of the soul connecting with God?"

Godric replied, "It's just like a drop of water meeting the ocean."

Isla said, "When the drop and the ocean come together, the drop will disappear. Does that mean... you will die?" She spoke with a panicked expression on her face.

Godric answered, "The drop does not end after merging with the ocean but becomes the ocean itself."

The angel sitting in front immediately jumped up and hugged Godric very tightly in bliss.

Isla asked, "Does this mean we become God?"

Godric replied, "You have to worship the Akaal yourself to know the secret. I can only guide you as my masters did for me."

Isla said suddenly, very excitedly, "It means... I can also be enlightened?"

Godric affirmed, "Yes! Absolutely you can be. But this level can't be attained by the devotion of one birth alone. It takes many births to get there."

Isla said, "Nah! I can't do this. Who would wait for so many births? I can't even wait for our marriage."

Godric said, "Don't you see any difference between millions of births and five to seven births? This is the endless time cycle. You will not end by dying. For billions of years, every soul in the universe is going through an endless cycle of becoming stones, trees, insects, animals, and birds millions of times. Your soul is not the human being; it's your body that is human."

Isla asked, "Then what is the soul?"

Godric replied, "That is the main secret to know. We all have been changing bodies and types of births for billions of years and are stuck in the time cycle."

Isla said, "Means... I am also taking births again and again."

Godric responded, "You didn't fall from the sky! Of course, you are also changing bodies like everyone else. Our main purpose is to break this cycle and merge again with God."

Isla asked, "My life is going well. What is the problem with the human body?"

Godric said, "If you remembered your previous birth, you would understand in a few seconds what is the problem of the soul. Suppose someone were to take you away from me and lock you in a cell. You might be kept hungry, beaten, raped, and never see the warmth of our love or the light of the sun again. Wouldn't you crave for your old life in such a situation?"

Isla responded, "Why did you say that? It's horrible!" She spoke in great sadness.

The angel flew away from Godric and hugged Isla with full expression of love and care.

Godric said, "What our soul has seen in the past millions of years is nothing compared to these words of mine. Don't you want to be free from this matrix of nature?"

Isla said, "I don't know. I'm just worried about you a lot. Promise you won't leave me?"

Godric answered, "Oh my life. Why would I leave you?"

Isla asked, "When you find God, will you continue to love me the same as today?"

"Awwweeee." All the angels made a cute noise at once.

Godric replied, "You too are part of God. What do you think, God brought us together for no reason? Surely, we have a relationship from previous births. No ordinary soul can come close to a spiritual person like me. But first, think of those old people whom my father is preparing to send to the Second World War at this old age."

Isla said, "Nothing will happen to them!"

Godric replied, "No! This mission is very dangerous. Especially for an old man."

Isla said, "You just said that no ordinary soul can come close to you. Do you consider your masters to be ordinary men?"

Godric said, "Actually, my concern is... who would teach me divine knowledge if they died?"

Isla responded, "Oh Godric! Those old men are putting their lives at risk for you, and you are worried about yourself! How can you be so mean?" She spoke suddenly in great surprise.

Godric replied, "Ask the Lord. He wired me this way!"

"Ha ha ha ha ha ha ha!" All the angels laughed.

"You spoiled brat! Come here, let me teach you some love," Isla said pulling Godric towards herself.

As Godric and Isla shared their intimate moment, the angels felt a wave of shyness and glanced at each other awkwardly. Gradually, they began to drift out of the hut, their movements slow and tinged with a sense of embarrassment. Meanwhile, Godric's angel, sitting with her back to the pair, smiled gently at the scene.

MAIN TIMELINE – WORLD WAR II 1945

Harold and the Masters crouched behind the bushes, all dressed in British Army uniforms with modern guns slung over their shoulders. In front of them, the bodies of Harold and his three wounded soldiers are floating four feet above the ground, drifting slowly away from the scene. The trees around them stood motionless, their leaves frozen in place. Time seems to have stopped, and an eerie silence blankets the area. Everyone's feet were rooted to the ground, rendering them immobile.

Chodrak said, "Gurbaksh Singh! You were right, Zoraver was truly too powerful."

Vedant remarked, "I am amazed at how much he controlled his own strength despite having so much power."

Listening to them, Harold felt embarrassed, and the regret of his actions against Zoraver was evident on his face.

Gurbaksh Singh responded, "Miracles become destruction if we misuse them! And he was fully aware of this. That's why he never used any Siddhi."

Anselm added, "It takes a lot to raise a son like him. You are a great master."

Gurbaksh Singh said, "I was just doing my duty and came here for the same reason today. Harold! Where is the corpse of Zoraver's body?"

Harold pointed to the corpse of Zoraver, which was lying 50 metres away.

Gurbaksh Singh said, "Thank you!"

Harold instructed, "When time resumes, you both will pick up Michael's body and bring it to me," addressing Vedant and Chodrak.

After waiting for a few more minutes, when the time resumed, the once-still leaves began to rustle, and distant sounds of gunfire and explosions echoed through the air. Vedant and Chodrak moved towards Michael's body, while Gurbaksh Singh headed towards Zoraver's dead body.

In front of Chodrak and Vedant, Michael lies in a pool of blood, gravely injured and gasping for his last breaths. The left side of his face is injured, revealing torn flesh. His left arm is severely damaged, with the bone exposed three inches between the elbow and wrist, and his left thigh is also shattered like a melon.

Chodrak remarked, "He seems very heavy."

Chodrak and Vedant both are reaching closer to Michael's body very carefully.

Vedant replied, "He's not going to survive anyway. Just hold one of his legs, and I'll do the same. We both need to pull him towards Harold."

Chodrak said, "It looks like a cruel way of helping."

Vedant asked, "Do you have a better idea?"

Meanwhile, Gurbaksh Singh reached the lifeless body of his son, who had a visible bullet wound on his blood-stained neck. Gurbaksh gently straightened Zoraver's body and placed his head on his lap. The bullet had exited from the left side of Zoraver's neck, causing a large tear in his throat. His mouth and chin were smeared with blood from the right side.

"My Lion! I am proud that you followed the way to know the secret instead of killing your murderer at the last moment," Gurbaksh Singh said with a slight moisture in his red eyes while closing Zoraver's eyelids with his left hand.

PRESENT TIME BRANCH – BUNKER

There is a one-foot-wide wormhole inside the time machine. Outside, Theo, Aldous, and two scientists are standing in considerable anxiety.

"It must be done this time!" Theo said.

The wormhole suddenly became quite large, and blood-stained masters and Harold came out of it with Michael's body in their hands.

FEW MINUTES LATER

Breathing slightly, Michael's body lay on a table, and a four-foot-tall spider-shaped machine with many robotic hands scanning it.

"Seeing my own child dying in front of my eyes is really very hard," Aldous said.

"He is already dead in the past. You need to control your emotions," Theo replied.

"And this is the only thing that I am good at," Aldous said.

All the masters and Harold were sitting on chairs at some distance to one side.

"Harold! What are they doing now?" Anselm asked slowly.

Harold responded, "The machine needs time to learn about Michael's body. As we don't know how to operate it and also would not have enough time in the past, they need to do most of the process here on this body."

RESEARCH CENTER

Godric is observing a thousand subjects seated in Padmasana, meditating inside a vast lab. Energy data for all the clones is being displayed on numerous computer screens around the room. Isla and Anne are standing beside him, also watching the scene.

Anne said, "I know you are upset, but I had no choice."

Godric replied, "Nah! I am not upset. Your action just opened the door for me to know something that would not be possible for me and my masters to get through within a decade."

Anne asked, "What do you mean?"

Godric answered, "I can't tell you the whole thing, but your words did not harm me or any of my masters. They resulted in something positive."

Anne said, "I really feel so guilty."

Isla chimed in, "It's totally fine, Anne. You did nothing wrong."

Anne admitted, "I just feel embarrassed all the time."

Godric reassured her, "You have no need to say that. I can understand your situation."

Isla added, "Whatever happened, Godric is responsible for that. You were just hiding a lie for your friend. I would have done the same."

Anne asked, "Really? Are we still friends?"

Godric replied, "Yes! You are my friend!"

Anne said, "Thanks. I thought we wouldn't be the same again."

Godric assured her, "It never changed for me. Now concentrate on your work. Is there any change in their energy level?"

Anne responded, "Nah! It's still the same."

Isla asked, "Godric, do you think they have a soul?" She said this while looking at the subjects sitting in the rows.

Godric replied, "How are they breathing, then?"

Isla questioned, "But they didn't born like us."

Godric explained, "The whole universe is conscious. Nothing is sterile here. The soul is even in every single stone as well. How can a human body be without a soul?"

Isla concluded, "So they have a soul."

Godric replied, "Yes, they have a soul like you, me, and others," he said, a little annoyed, and spoke with a smile.

Isla asked, "How did they get the soul?"

Godric explained further, "The soul is not something that has to be picked up from one side and placed on the other. Every single atom of the universe has consciousness. When that consciousness finds a body, it shows its effect according to the sense ability of that body. The body of an animal is an animal, a human body is a human, but the soul is neither an animal nor a human."

Isla inquired, "Will they all be enlightened?" She said this while pointing her finger at the subjects.

Godric replied, "At least one should be. But others will get enough energy to preach to the people. Maybe some of them will get supernatural powers as well."

Isla asked, surprised, "Really? Supernatural powers? How?"

Godric explained, "Those powers are just part of the illusion of nature to stop you from being enlightened."

Isla said, incredulously, "How does that work? I can't believe that."

Godric retorted, "I have no need to make you believe. Just read Scripture, live accordingly, and in time, you will know the reality."

Isla replied, "That's rude! Tell me if you also do these things yourself?"

Godric said, "Suppose a newly married girl walking down the street is stopped by a stranger and asked how her nights are going with her husband. Would that be an appropriate question to ask?"

Isla teased, "Do you have sex with God?"

Godric exclaimed, "That's an analogy, you dumb!"

Anne laughed, "Ha ha ha ha!"

Isla joined in, "Ha ha ha ha ha!"

Laughing, Anne and Isla did a high five.

Anne said, "You guys just reminded me of our school days. She is still the best at gaslighting you!"

Godric twisted Isla's arm backwards and gave her two light strokes on the back, but at the same time, he was also smiling.

Isla exclaimed, laughing, "Ha ha ha ha! I will tell your mum. This is domestic violence. Anne! Please save this poor bird ha ha ha ha!" She said, speaking while hiding behind Anne after she got her arm released from Godric.

MAIN TIMELINE – WORLD WAR II

Harold and the Five Masters arrived close to the dying Michael and placed his previously dead body twenty foot away behind a tree. A four-foot-long, one-foot-wide, and three-inch-thick box-sized alien machine is hanging over Vedant's back. He took off the machine from his back and positioned it over Michael's breathing body.

"You four look around while we put the machine on him," Harold said to Gurbaksh Singh, Mansoor, Chodrak, and Anselm.

All these four people held their guns in their hands and stood at a short distance in different directions. Harold placed his hand on the machine's screen, and as it was scanned, mechanical arms emerged from the device and began to heal Michael. Two of the machine's arms administering blood through needles, while the remaining arms swiftly mending broken bones and restoring the skin to its normal state.

"This is not less than any miracle," Vedant said aloud, watching the machine work.

Harold nodded. "I said the same thing when I saw it working for the first time. After witnessing many such miracles, we made an agreement with that alien."

Vedant replied, "I can understand. If anyone were in your place, they would never shy away from shaking hands with such powerful beings."

The machine fixed all of Michael's broken bones in five minutes and sprinkled a special type of chemical on the deep wounds, making his whole body completely fresh, including the damaged face. Michael is breathing but remained unconscious. Gurbaksh Singh, Mansoor, Chodrak, and Anselm, who had been monitoring the area, approached Harold and stood beside him. The machine completed a final scan of Michael's body and bound his hands and legs with plastic wires. Harold and the Masters drew their guns, aiming at Michael. When the machine delivered a powerful electric shock, Michael's eyes flew open, and he began to thrash about uncontrollably. The machine quickly retracted its hands and transformed back into a box.

Harold laughed and spoke very proudly, "Ha ha ha ha! Welcome back, my beast!"

Michael is trying to hide behind the trunk of the tree next to him.

"Who are you?" Michael said, trying to get rid of his tied hands and legs, speaking very annoyingly.

"You can call us gods. Welcome back to the chaos. You are born again!" Anselm said with a chuckle.

Michael immediately bit through the latch and grabbed the nearby gun.

Thak...!! Gurbaksh Singh shot Michael in the shoulder. As soon as the shot was fired, Michael groaned in pain, and the gun fell from his hands.

Harold said, "Good shot, young man!"

"You are welcome!" Gurbaksh Singh replied.

"Let's fix him again," Vedant said while looking at the machine.

PRESENT TIME BRANCH - BUNKER

Theo, Aldous, Godric, and a scientist are sitting around the table next to the Time Machine.

Godric asked, "Will he understand everything in ten hours?"

"According to me, two hours will be enough," Aldous replied.

Theo said, "I hope everything goes smoothly. Now tell us what time and place we need to go to find out about your previous births."

"We already know about my past birth. So now we need to visit Afghanistan, Tibet, South India, and South Western Germany to know about the other four," Godric explained.

"What would be the exact time frame for each birthplace?" Theo asked.

"The South Indian temple I see in my dreams was built around 750 AD. That's the first place and the time frame to visit. I think my own people sacrificed me in front of that temple for some kind of ritual," Godric explained. "Then Tibet could be the best second place to visit around 1100 AD. My very own disciple killed me in that birth... And my third birth was during the witch-hunting period of South Western Germany... Sadly, I was killed by a witch. That's it."

"What about Afghanistan?" The Scientist inquired.

"I don't know much about the fourth birth. Even that could be elsewhere because I guess that's Afghanistan only on the basis of the clothing style of the people who I see in the dream from that birth. The time frame could be around the middle of the ninth century," Godric speculated.

Theo said, "Okay! At least we know about three time frames. What was the year for the first birth?"

"Around 750 AD," Godric confirmed.

"We will visit there first and will follow the sequence one by one," Theo stated.

The Scientist remarked, "Seeing everything that has happened in the past days, it seems as if we need to rewrite all the books of human science."

"No matter how much research you want to do and write new books, no one can understand the game of God," Godric said. "Father! I don't understand one thing. Instead of the change in our same timeline, how did this new time branch come into existence? I can't digest what you said that day."

Theo explained, "As far as my understanding works, the reason can only be that the alien who laid the foundation of the New World Order from our people are not from the same time frame that we live in. They came from the future. This could be the only reason. An outside intervention in the whole world's order separated us as a branch from our main timeline. Time is a very complex subject. We still need to do a lot of research to understand its nature. If only those aliens were among us at this time, then we would not have so much confusion to solve this problem."

"Why are we not in touch with them?" Godric asked.

"Their people are at war with the people of another planet, which is why they had to go back a few years ago. On the way back, they gave us strict instructions not to try to contact them in any way whatsoever," Aldous replied.

"But why? Why can't we contact them?" Godric asked.

The scientist replied, "They are afraid that our signal will fall into the hands of their enemy. If this happens, enemy may become our enemy too."

"Or could be a friend?" Godric speculated.

Aldous said, "Before helping us, they made a pact with us that we would not contact any alien civilisation other than his under any circumstances. If we remain firm on our promise, they will help us in every way, but if we break the treaty, then we will have to face destruction."

Godric questioned, "How do we contact them now when we really need them here?"

"They said that they would be back within a decade. Now we can wait for them or try our best to deal with this problem ourselves," Aldous explained.

MAIN TIMELINE – 1945

Next to the forest, a farmhouse lay in ruins, completely destroyed. Behind it stood a half-demolished barn, where Michael was tied to a chair. Harold, pointing a pistol at him, displayed videos of the future on a tablet mounted on a stand in front of Michael. The masters stood around with the guns in their hands and gazing at Michael with full focus.

Michael said, "You guys have shown me enough. Though it's hard to believe but I can trust you now. I have seen the work of your machine; it's just beyond everything I could imagine. How did you guys build such a miraculous mechanism? My shoulder is totally back to normal."

"Not only the shoulder, your whole torn body is back to normal because of us," Harold replied. "You have listened to your father's message. You are the only person we can trust. Now listen carefully to what we say."

Michael pleaded, "Our password matched, I have watched the videos and seen the miracle of science. Please release me now. Just give me the orders, and I am ready to follow. You can trust me."

"I think we should set him free now," Anselm suggested.

"What if he tries to attack us again?" Chodrak asked.

Harold turned to Gurbaksh Singh and said, "If he tries to be over-smart this time, just burst his head."

"Don't worry, Commander. Your beast is ready to die for the whole human world!" Michael spoke with great pride while smiling.

Harold said, "If that's true, then you need to go to the future to stop the third world war."

"What?" Michael exclaimed in great surprise.

"Don't worry!" Harold assured him. "You are not going to kill someone or raise an army against any country or countries for that. Just take this device with you and put it in the right spot to broadcast a warning from us to stop the third and last world war." He spoke while showing a black box one foot long, three inches wide, and one inch thick.

Michael asked, "How far into the future do we need to go?"

"Not we! Just you are going around seventy years ahead," Harold clarified.

"And you?" Michael inquired.

"We will wait for your return!" Harold replied.

"If something went wrong?" Michael questioned, concern etched in his voice.

Mansoor interrupted, "A lot of wrongs have already been done by the crazy team of your commander and the father. Now, don't you dare say anything negative."

PRESENT TIME BRANCH

Theo, Bella, and Godric are currently having dinner with Isla's family. Everyone is looking very happy.

"It's been months since I've heard his stories of World War," Isla's long-nosed father, Archer, a proud-looking man, said with a drunken grin.

"He must have come, but now his body is not as fit as it was in the past. He was fine in the morning, but we had to call the doctor in the afternoon," Theo spoke in a very respectful tone.

"Yeah! His steel-head body is now rusted by age; he may die soon," Godric added. His words shocked everyone at once.

"Oh God! Don't say that," Isla's mother said, suddenly surprised by Godric's words. The faces of both mother and daughter were quite similar.

"He is your grandfather! Why would you say such a horrible thing?" Bella exclaimed.

"Death is beautiful! It gives you freedom! Grandfather will go to heaven," Godric responded.

"Ha ha ha ha ha! And would have endless fun with beauties there," Archer said, laughing.

"Ha ha ha! Thank God! Someone has a sense of humour here," Godric said, laughing in agreement.

Bella and Isla's mother felt ashamed to hear both of them.

"How's your godly work going on?" Archer asked Godric.

"Faster than the speed of light! In the years to come, there will be no other preacher in the whole world equal to the preachers of the World Religion," Godric replied confidently.

Archer, looking puzzled, said, "I don't understand one thing: why all the fuss about something that doesn't even exist?"

"What do you mean?" Theo asked.

Archer elaborated, "The God! He doesn't exist! We all are the gods. We can do whatever we want. I think we need strict laws instead of making people walk in order under the fear of something like ancient times. Science has gone too far these days. Most of the people have become atheists like me. I just hate religions. I lived in North India during British rule, very close to a Sikh temple with Sikh soldiers. Even they could not make me a believer. But I liked their community meal. Ha ha ha ha!" He spoke quite boldly under the influence of alcohol as if the anger that had filled his heart for long had come out.

The angel next to Godric stood from behind with her arms around Bella's neck and looked at Godric like a child insisting on eating something.

"Oh God, he started again!" Isla whispered to her mother in a worried and embarrassed tone.

"It is not the fault of people who have become atheists; in fact, God has been presented for centuries as if He is the father of people. He is a father, but He is not the father like a father of a human being. That's why people think that when troubles come upon us, why doesn't Father God help us, why doesn't He destroy all the sufferings?" Godric explained.

At once, many angels came and sat around all of them.

"Absolutely! It is the duty of a father to provide all kinds of comfort to his children. What kind of father won't protect his children?" Archer said.

Theo placed a finger on his lips, motioning for Bella not to intrude.

Godric continued, "The only mistake we have made in our understanding is that the religious teachers called God the Father in another context, but the people understood something else."

"Father means only father! What else could it be?" Archer said with a chuckle.

Godric explained, "The God is the Father because he created the universe, but we simultaneously forget to understand that both gods and devils are part of the universe. Both powers are the creation of that one supreme God with a capital G. He likes an angel as much as a devil! If there is happiness in his right hand, there is sorrow in his left."

Archer asked, "God is the one who gives pain?"

"Yes!" Godric responded. "He is just playing. That is why it is said that kids are a reflection of God. If you give two soldier toys to a child, you will see that in a few minutes, he will start playing and make them fight with each other and destroy them. The game of creation is just that."

Archer smiled and said, "Theo! Your boy is really very good with words. But I can't believe in God until he stands before my eyes."

Godric countered, "Please tell me, in which religious book regarding the vision of God is it written that just by thinking once, one can see God or make someone see God?"

Archer admitted, "Reading scripture aside, I have never even turned my face to religious texts."

Godric sighed and continued, "Thank God. I also wonder how I missed getting this knowledge. Actually, like science tells us how to experiment again and again to discover something, and then how the final result can be achieved, religions also teach us spiritual experiments. To this day, no one who didn't walk on the path of devotion has seen God. So, if you want to see God, then you have to worship him day and night while following the spiritual teachings. And when you have seen God, you yourself will not be able to tell the people about that sight."

Archer raised an eyebrow and asked, "God cannot be described even by seeing him yourself?"

"God is so far away from the understanding of the human mind," Godric explained. "To this day, we haven't even been able to create a single language that can express our own feelings."

Archer shook his head and protested, "No, no! You are completely wrong here. All the poetry collections of the world only show human emotions."

Godric replied, "No, Sir! Till date, no poet has been able to describe any feeling!"

Isla jumped in and disagreed, "I don't agree with that! We all... can easily express our feelings very well. I am angry, I am sad, I am very happy! See? What is difficult in it?"

Archer grinned proudly and said, "See! My doll is also on my side. Thanks for supporting me, dear!"

Isla smiled and responded, "You're welcome, Dad!"

Godric smiled and suggested, "Let's pick any one emotion you can easily describe."

"Anger!" Isla replied.

Godric asked, "And you, sir?"

Archer replied confidently, "Same! Anger."

Godric nodded and said, "Okay! Then explain to me, what is anger?"

Archer responded, "When someone bothers me, I get angry. Simple!"

Godric smiled and clarified, "That is the reason you feel anger. But I want to know, what is the anger?"

Isla said enthusiastically, "When I get angry, my blood pressure increases, I can't resist acting, and I punch the person in front of me in the face until he passes out."

Everyone burst out laughing. "Ha ha ha ha ha ha!"

Godric then said, "Nice try, but that is just the explanation of the result of feeling angry! I want to know what is the anger itself. You both told me what makes you angry and what you do when you feel angry. So technically, these are the reasons and results. But there is a sole feeling of anger between these action and reaction. Explain to me that sole feeling. No reason, no action, only the feeling!"

Hearing Godric's words, both Archer and Isla fell silent, struggling to grasp how to express their feelings of anger. Bella and Isla's mother, sitting beside her, exchanged glances and smiled softly at the pair's quiet contemplation.

Theo said impatiently, "Oh come on! Just leave it. You guys are boring me!"

Archer turned to Theo and asked curiously, "When will I have the chance to see your father?"

Godric stared at Archer in great surprise as he fled without answering the question. But when his gaze shifted to Isla, he decided it was best to remain silent. Isla sat before him, her beautiful eyes blazing with anger as she glared at him, teeth clenched in fury.

Angel came after Isla and pointed the horns on her head with her fingers, teasing Godric mischievously and the other Angels sitting around looking at Godric very lovingly.

MAIN TIMELINE – YEAR 2026

Michael emerged from the wormhole onto the rooftop of a news channel's broadcasting building. His face was covered with a piece of cloth. He sprinted towards the nearby antenna, quickly placing the box Harold had given him. As soon as the box was set down, several mechanical legs unfolded from its sides, scurrying towards the core of the antenna. The box opened, releasing thin, almost invisible wires that connected seamlessly to the antenna's main circuitry. Nervously, Michael scanned his surroundings, vigilant for any prying eyes that might notice the machine at work.

All over the world, all TVs and mobile phones are connected to the broadcast of this Alien device within two minutes. The United Army of Human World logo is being broadcasted on every TV, mobile, in every government non-government institution, in common people's homes and on all the billboards worldwide.

SINNER AND THE GODS

PRESENT TIME BRANCH – BUNKER

Harold addressed the group, "What else could be the meaning of sending back the paper by writing 'all done'? Yes, he himself did not show interest to return, but I am confident that he must have done everything accordingly," he said, turning to all the people sitting at the round table.

All the masters, Theo, Aldous, three scientists, and Godric were currently meeting among themselves.

Aldous interjected, "Even though he is my boy, this kind of behaviour can't be justified for a soldier."

Chodrak leaned forward and speculated, "This is a common-sense thing, he must have been captivated by the beauty of the future that he didn't risk coming back."

Godric shrugged, "What's the problem for us if he stays there? He was already dead to everyone here. If he lives in the future, that's fine. If he dies with the whole world… well, I can't say that's fine, but it doesn't really matter to us. Only our mission matters, and I am a hundred percent sure he would have accomplished that successfully."

Aldous turned to Theo and asked, "Theo! What do you think about this?"

Theo nodded thoughtfully and responded, "We have a piece of paper written by Michael, and Godric's reasoning is plausible. I think we should consider this mission accomplished."

"Yes," Godric added, "One difficulty is that a device connected to the time machine remained with him. Can anyone misuse it?"

The scientist shook his head and reassured them, "We were already in danger of some kind of failure, so we could not take any kind of risk. That device was on self-destruct mode. We have no need to worry about that."

Aldous said, "I am very ashamed of my son's mistake."

Harold clapped Aldous on the shoulder and encouraged him, "No way, man! Why would you feel embarrassed for the heroic act of your son? He has saved two worlds today!"

Gurbaksh Singh smiled warmly and added, "We are all proud of you and your son."

Everyone began clapping in agreement.

Theo then turned to Godric, "Now let's move to Godric's plan. Son, where would you like to go first?"

Harold stood up, grinning, "Let's team up!"

Anselm burst out laughing, "Ha ha ha!"

Mansoor glanced at him, puzzled, "What happened to you now?"

Anselm, replied, "Ha ha ha! We went to the past to save the whole world so we can go back to the past to save him," he said with a giggle, pointing at Godric.

Chodrak joined in the laughter, "Ha ha ha! And the world doesn't even know everything was about to be extinct."

Gurbaksh Singh laughed as well and added, "Not everyone gets masters like us!"

Godric looked around at the group and said with a smile, "You all are my masters, and the master's duty is to save the disciple from all kinds of harm."

Vedant stood up and proclaimed, "Oh my Kalyugi Ekalavya. Give us the command. We would die for you."

"Ha ha ha ha!" everyone laughed.

EVENING TIME

Isla and Godric are standing in a garden. Between the two, Angel stands sadly, looking sometimes at Godric's face and sometimes at Isla's.

Isla glared at Godric, her frustration clear. "Do you even know what you were talking about? What was the need to do all that nonsense talk?"

Godric trying to defend himself said, "What could I do? Your father was speaking wrong about God."

Isla shook her head angrily. "It was a good opportunity to mingle with them. But you spoiled our best chance. Will God begin to deteriorate with the words of a normal man? Is God a child who would be harmed by anyone? Have you ever thought about both of us?"

Her voice began to crack, and she started tearing up while speaking.

Godric softened his tone, a little confused. "What is there to cry about now? Did someone say something wrong to you?"

Isla wiped a tear away and spoke in a trembling voice. "You are only busy with your own work. Sometimes you go to find masters, sometimes you get busy cloning subjects in the lab. You saved the timeline in the last few days, and now you'll be off somewhere else to uncover the secret of your dreams. Have you ever wondered how I am spending every single moment?" She took a deep breath, her emotions rising as she continued. "Why don't you understand? I can't live without you. I am worried all the time, thinking, when will we both be one? When will our little life begin?" She paused, her voice breaking as she cried, her frustration pouring out. "But you sit in my house and fight with my own father. Why did you need to do that? Have you ever learned to lose for someone that cares for you?"

Godric felt a deep sadness as he watched Isla cry. The angel standing nearby shared her sorrow. Silently, the angel raised a finger to her lips, signalling Godric to remain quiet. Without hesitation, Godric pulled Isla into his chest, holding her tightly. Within moments, Isla began to calm, lifting her face and resting her chin against his chest to meet his gaze. Godric's eyes were starting to form tears.

Godric leaned in and said with a kiss, "Let's get married!"

Isla frowned and replied, "My father won't agree! Even if they say yes to our marriage, they won't talk to me like before for the rest of my life."

Godric teased, "Then... let's kill him!"

Isla, with tears streaming down her eyes and speaking like a child, said, "I am not in the mood for kidding. I love my father so much!"

Godric, sensing her distress, asked softly, "What do you want then?"

Isla looked around and said, "Just see around. There is the whole beautiful world to see. Why can't you just take a break? Please, let's spend some time together."

Godric sighed and explained, "The world you are talking about—our team saved it from extinction last night."

Isla, confused and concerned, asked, "Why and how are you few guys doing all of this without telling anyone? There is a very strong government body in the world. They have the resources to fix this all. Why do you guys do this by yourselves?"

Godric spoke seriously, "My grandfather and a few of his other team members built this government. But this very self-created government will put them in prison if they get to know this world is not the main timeline anymore because of the actions of my grandfather and his fellas. We are living in a time branch, my love, and saving it was about saving the future of our relationship as well."

Isla asked, "How long will this all take to finish? I just want to be with you all the time."

Godric reassured her, "I will end it soon. Just a few more days, and I promise you, we are going to get married within this year. Don't worry about your father. He will accept my proposal happily."

Isla's lovely pink face lit up with joy the moment she heard about the marriage, and she hugged Godric tightly. The angel beside them, beaming with happiness, wrapped both of them gently in her wings.

MAIN TIMELINE— 746AD

TAMIL NADU, INDIA

A wormhole opened underwater on the seashore near a temple, from which Godric, Harold, and the five masters emerged. All of them were wearing clothes similar to the local people.

"Are you sure we have arrived in the right time frame?" Harold asked while walking along the beach.

Godric glanced around and replied, "Can't say for sure, but yes, the local people here can help us to reach the right timeframe."

Vedant asked, "Did you bring us to this age with a guess?"

Godric responded, "Keep cool, man. We will find out from the people."

Mansoor laughed heartily and joked, "Ha ha ha! Just make sure no one sacrifices us here."

Anselm looked curious and inquired, "What will you ask the people?"

Chodrak smirked and said, "This man never tells the whole truth before the time."

Gurbaksh Singh nodded and added, "I also find this habit of his very bad."

Godric paid no attention to the others as he suddenly began running towards a temple situated a short distance from the beach. The rest followed quickly in his wake. He came to a halt before two elderly men standing near the temple and bowed to them with his hands folded in respect. Moments later, the others caught up and gathered around him.

Godric instructed, "Vedant! Ask them if they have ever seen a person being sacrificed here."

Vedant replied, "Sorry, my foreign friends do not understand our language. My name is Vedant, and they all came from different places to visit the temple," he said, speaking very politely with folded hands.

"You're welcome. Tell me what we can do to help? If you are looking for food or accommodation, then I'll take you to an inn some distance away," the old man standing in front spoke.

Vedant declined politely, "Thank you! But we have no need of that. I have already arranged for the accommodation. Please introduce us to someone who has full knowledge about the history of this temple."

"I have been living near the temple my whole life. Ha ha ha! You can ask me anything you want to know," the second elder spoke.

Vedant asked eagerly, "Let's then hear about an incident related to this temple that you can never forget."

The elder grew serious. "Yes! Twenty years ago today, on the dark night of the month of Pausha, a sinner was sentenced to death by the gods themselves in front of this temple. I can't forget that incident till my last breath."

Vedant asked, "Did the gods themselves appear and announce the punishment?"

The elder nodded. "Yes! I saw them with my own eyes. There were ten gods, tall like palm trees. They had long shiny hair and skin like milk. All of them had four arms. When the intestines of that sinner were torn open by the priest, our hearts found great relief."

Harold, confused, asked Vedant, "What is he saying?"

Vedant held up a hand. "Wait a minute, let me hear the whole thing. Sorry, my friend is very excited. Can you tell us the whole story in detail?"

HALF AN HOUR LATER

At some distance from the temple, Godric is sitting on the beach, and all the masters and Harold are standing around him.

Godric sighed in disbelief. "I can't believe it. Of course that old man is lying," he said in an embarrassed tone.

Harold, annoyed, responded, "You killed baby Harold! That's why that baby is avenging his death again and again. Our mission is completed! And you all were making me sick by declaring me an ancient villain for this brat. Now we all know, I am a hundred percent innocent," he spoke with great annoyance.

Anselm, looking Godric directly in the face, said, "How could someone make a father kill his two-year-old innocent child?"

Mansoor, deeply troubled, added, "Such a poor use of Siddhi, that too for not getting a woman? This is an unforgivable sin. You have not only killed a child, but in his grief, his mother died within a few days. You are also responsible for her death."

Godric, defensive, argued, "We cannot trust an old man's words. How do you know that he's talking about me or someone else?"

Harold replied pointedly, "He only saw one person punished here in his entire life, and the temple is the one you saw in your dream. The meaning is direct and clear. You are a lowly person who eats children."

Vedant cautioned, "I think we should not be hasty about this. We now know that this incident took place twenty years ago on the dark night of the month of Pausha. Why don't we go to that time and see it with our own eyes?"

Harold agreed enthusiastically, "Absolutely! I would get a lot of relief seeing this sinner scream. It's been so many days that I haven't even been able to sleep."

Chodrak warned, "We cannot trust him completely, but even half the truth can be found in every single lie in the world."

Gurbaksh Singh agreed, "You said exactly right. Even if that person doesn't know the whole truth, it is clear to us that Godric's life is cursed. And one who has not made a mistake can never be cursed."

Godric, frustrated, asked, "Come on! Now I've become a sinner in your eyes too?"

Gurbaksh Singh shook his head. "Not you, but your past life is definitely tainted."

Harold, with great curiosity, declared, "Let's go and see this devil screaming live in front of our eyes."

70 CENTURIES AGO

"Bring a Vaidya. Her condition is not getting better," said Rashmi, sitting beside Prisha, who lay unconscious on the bed inside the hut.

Chaitanya, standing near the bed, replied anxiously, "How will a Vaidya come... No one wants to be expelled from the village for helping us."

Prisha's face had turned pale, and Rashmi sat next to her, clearly nervous. Chaitanya, seeing no solution, came out of the hut and began heading towards the village a few kilometres away from home.

TAMIL NADU – 726AD

It is midnight, and about 200 people are standing on the seashore near the temple. In front of the crowd, a man near the age of thirty, covered in injuries and resembling a Hindu ascetic, has his hands and feet bound to a sturdy wooden plinth driven deep into the ground. His body and torn clothes are soaked in blood. Several priests are gathered around him. Fifty metres away, ten towering gods hover above the sea, their white bodies glowing in the night. Each deity has long shiny hair and four arms, radiating a divine presence.

Anselm, looking bewildered, asked, "Are you seeing the same thing I'm seeing?"

Godric, with a nod of disbelief, replied, "I am seeing the ten big gods flying in the air on the beach."

Harold, wide-eyed, exclaimed, "Me too!"

Standing about 20 metres behind the crowd, they watched in awe as the gods manifested before the humans. The priests chanted mantras loudly, their voices echoing through the air.

Vedant remarked thoughtfully, "How kind-hearted people must have been in ancient times. Instead of one, ten gods used to appear in front of them. But in our times, we do not even get a glimpse of a god."

Gurbaksh Singh, shaking his head, muttered, "I think they are demons!"

Chodrak, surprised, asked, "From which side do they look like demons to you? After seeing such a charming scene, my whole life's education has come to an end."

Suddenly, one of the gods stepped forward with a resonant, heavy voice and declared, "This wicked man tricked our priestesses and her husband, killed their child with an illusion. Such a sinner has no right to live! We need his life taken away from this crippled mind right here and right now."

The crowd erupted with anger, shouting, "Kill him!! Kill him!!"

Another voice from the furious assembly cried, "This wicked man must be burned alive."

A third voice joined in, filled with hatred, "He made a father kill his child, this is not a human, he is a monster!"

The voices echoed from the gathering of angry, red-faced people, their fury palpable.

Suddenly, the deities merged with the sea, and the crowd began to drag the criminal, bound to a pillar, towards the temple, beating him and hurling abuse as they went. Harold walked alongside the people, while Godric, trailing behind, felt a deep sense of unease at the sight.

Harold said firmly, "Bad consequences for bad deeds!" He glanced at Anselm while they walked along.

Anselm sighed, his face looking sad. "Oh come on, man! How much more will you embarrass us?"

The people laid the bloodied criminal on a stone plinth as a priest emerged from the temple, carrying a strange weapon. At that moment, an ascetic in his early sixties approached and stood beside the criminal, bringing an immediate and profound calm to the crowd.

The ascetic stood before the crowd, his voice filled with bitterness and fury. "I could not even in my dream think that the person who was taking spiritual education from me in my Gurukul for the last fifteen years would turn out to be a snake," he said with a tremor in his voice. His eyes narrowed as he continued, "On the words of my wife who did not believe, now you have heard from the gods themselves that this monster is the killer of my child."

The Monk's expression darkened further as he raised his hand towards the sky in Abhayamudra. "Before his execution," he thundered, "I curse this evil one, taking the earth, the sky, the water, the air, and the fire as witnesses before all of you, that he will strive for moksha in every birth. And whenever he would come close to the moment, in every birth, the soul of my murdered son shall continue to kill him, and this monster will never be freed from the endless cycle of time."

"Jai Mahakal!!"

"Jai Mahakal!!"

"Jai Mahakal!!"

The people began chanting loudly in praise of Lord Shiva. The priest, holding a weapon, raised his arm high, and the blades of his weapon started to spin at lightning speed. With a swift motion, he struck the criminal's stomach, causing his screams to echo through the sky as his intestines were torn apart within seconds. Witnessing the gruesome scene, Godric closed his eyes.

NEXT DAY – EARLY MORNING.

Harold and Godric were laying alongside under a tree. The Masters were also resting. Everyone looked very sad.

Harold said, "Something is wrong. The weapon in the hand of that holy guy was very modern."

Godric frowned. "What do you mean?"

Gurbaksh Singh said, "I also have doubts about the gods. If they were gods, the fragrance of flowers would have been smelling all around. I think they are some kind of illusory demons who are making these people worship themselves by deception."

Chodrak looked thoughtful and said, "Harold! What's the big deal about people living so close to the gods having advanced weapons? As for the gods, I don't think they are monsters from any side."

Godric turned to Master Anselm. "Master Anselm! What do you think?"

Anselm replied solemnly, "You killed a child, that's it."

Vedant spoke up, "I think Gurbaksh Singh's doubt about the flowers is correct to a large extent! But why would a demon himself become a god and be worshiped by these common people of a poor village?"

Godric, deep in thought, said, "Don't you think we should meet my past life's family too? We need to find out the truth from the other side as well. He may have been falsely accused!"

Harold, looking uneasy, added, "I think those gods were aliens!"

Godric looked startled. "What..? What do you mean? Are these guys worshiping aliens?"

Everyone looked surprised at Harold's words.

Vedant, visibly offended, exclaimed, "No, it cannot be. You are insulting my gods."

Harold quickly clarified, "No! I am not saying that the Hindu gods do not exist. I am just saying that aliens have sacrificed a man in the guise of your gods. Aliens have always been in contact with our people since ancient times."

Gurbaksh Singh, narrowing his eyes, asked, "What is the benefit to them of doing all this?"

Harold explained, "The aliens who came in contact with my team told us they have been helping humans by projecting themselves as many types of gods. They consider us as backward class beings, and for our benefit, they visit our planet again and again in the guise of gods and teach us better ways of life. This work has been going on for centuries."

Anselm, deep in thought, asked, "So those aliens look like these gods we saw last night?"

Harold shook his head. "No! They were totally different, but that weapon was not made by human technology. I know the noise of alien machines, and that rotating noise was the same one."

Godric, with a sense of relief, said, "That means I'm not guilty! I knew that! I could not kill a child."

Harold, sternly, responded, "No! This does not prove your innocence at all. Aliens become gods and help humans like they did last night. They have also saved us from being destroyed by the third world war. I am the prime witness of this all."

Mansoor, concerned, asked, "What should we do now? Was our mission just that much? Will we not find the way to remove the curse? If we were seeing aliens instead of the gods, there might be another story behind the murder of the child!"

Godric nodded in agreement. "Absolutely! I was also thinking the same. There is definitely something fishy."

Harold suddenly blurted out, "Monster! You killed baby Harold! That's it."

Mansoor, calmly, said, "We all know that, but there could be a misunderstanding about that too. If you are getting rid of your sin by believing that, then it could be fine for you, but we can't let this curse go on. We need to find the solution. If Godric did such a grave sin, then he has already paid for it. You killed him many times. You both are even now."

Harold, still confused, muttered, "He said I killed him five times, but I did it only four times. The first time was that holy guy with an alien weapon."

Anselm, with frustration, said, "So what do you want? Want to kill him one more time to match the numbers? He has suffered a lot. We need to end this now."

Vedant agreed, "I agree with your point. We need to end this curse."

Gurbaksh Singh added, "And for that, we have to meet that master who gave the curse."

TWO HOURS LATER

Godric and all others are now sitting in the hermitage of the cursing ascetic eating a meal. Two young ascetics between the age of 15 to 18 are serving them food.

"We have sent a message to Master Kashyapa, but due to what happened in the past two days, many well-known people of the area are coming to see him. So Master is busy with them. You can rest here, and whenever there is time, he will definitely meet you," a boy explained.

Vedant replied, "Please tell the respected master that there is no need to rush. In fact, both my fair-skinned friends have come from across the seven seas. After many months, they have found a true divine saint. Where they have waited for so many months, they can happily wait for a few more hours."

"Thank you! I will try to get the master to come and see you soon," the boy responded politely.

Vedant asked, "Is the master's wife really a great devotee of the gods?"

"Yes, she is… and Guru Ma's mother was also a great devotee of the gods. She was blessed by the gods themselves that a divine baby girl would be born from her," the boy replied.

"And then?" Vedant prompted with curiosity.

"That's exactly what happened. A year later, she gave birth to our Guru Ma, and from birth, her hair was golden like the gods," the boy continued.

"Guru Ma's hair is golden?" Vedant repeated in amazement.

"Yes! They shine just like gold," the boy confirmed with a nod.

Vedant gestured toward one of his companions and said, "This white friend of mine is a good writer. He has started traveling the world to write a book on the great people of different countries of the world. If your master tells them about himself in detail, the name of this Gurukul will become famous even among the people living across the seven seas. Also, can we see Guru Ma too? We all would like to touch her feet and take blessings from her."

"I will tell my master," the boy answered. "If he thinks it is right, then Mother will meet you."

"What a difference! One was the evil one who killed Mother's only child, and the other is you, who wants to touch Mother's feet," the other boy, standing nearby, suddenly interjected.

Vedant spoke sympathetically, "We are very sorry for the death of the child. Whose strength goes before God's will? May his soul go to a better life next time."

AFTERNOON

"Tejas had been living with me for fifteen years, he himself did not know who his parents were. He had become quite adept in spirituality at an early age, travelling with groups of ascetics. When he came here, I felt that he was a very intelligent person, but I still find it difficult to believe that he could be so cruel to me. He learned how to acquire the shape shifter's siddhi and through that siddhi turned my two-year-old child into a dog and made me kill him with my own hands," the master Kashyapa said, sitting on a platform under a tree.

Sitting on the ground on the carpet in front of him, Vedant was writing his words on a wooden tablet. Godric and the others were also sitting around respectfully.

Vedant asked, "On which day and at what time did this event take place?"

Kashyapa replied, "The day before yesterday, the sun was setting, and I went to bring my wife back from her mother's house."

"How did you catch him so quickly after this incident?" Vedant inquired.

"If my disciple has the siddhi to shift shapes, then I am his guru! Do you think I would have become his guru without any siddhi?" Kashyapa responded confidently.

Vedant nodded and asked, "You mean you used Doordarshan?"

"Yes!" Kashyapa confirmed. "I had to use that siddhi to catch my child's killer. That monster was hiding inside a ruin in the forest."

Vedant questioned further, "Why do you think that evil person would have used siddhi to commit such a sin?"

"I came to know from my wife Arambha that before our marriage, Tejas had gone to her house to ask for her hand, but Arambha's mother refused him and sent him away," Kashyapa explained.

"Does this mean his misdeeds were the result of hatred born out of one-sided love?" Vedant asked.

"Absolutely! He had done all this with his own hatred," Kashyapa answered with certainty.

Vedant asked thoughtfully, "How did you get to know that this plot was his?"

Kashyapa said, "The ability to change the size of the body that he possessed is not held by anyone else here. Even I know the knowledge of attaining that siddhi, but I myself do not have that siddhi yet."

"Then he was bound to be caught," Vedant remarked.

"Absolutely!" Kashyapa said. "It was not a big deal for me to understand his tactics, but he had so much respect among the common people. So, I could not accuse him based on suspicion alone. That is why my wife and her mother prayed to the gods to appear and do justice. No one can escape the sight of the gods. What happened next, you and your friends saw yourselves."

Vedant asked, "When did your wife tell you that the evil one wanted to marry her?"

"Immediately after our marriage, when she saw him in the ashram," Kashyapa replied. "She immediately came to me and told me. I thought it was no big deal. Every person tries to build his own family, but I did not know that there would be so much hatred for us in that person's heart. My son..."

"Sorry to interrupt you!" Vedant said respectfully, pointing behind the monk. "Is she your wife?"

A short distance behind Kashyapa, a woman in her mid twenties with a strikingly beautiful face and figure walked between two middle-aged women. Her golden hair, contrasting with her fair skin, accentuated her beauty. Despite her face showing signs of grief, her allure remained undiminished. Godric and his companions watched in astonishment, feeling as though they were witnessing a supernatural encounter.

Kashyapa exclaimed, "Yes! She is my wife, Arambha!"

Arambha came to them all and sat on the left side of her husband, Kashyapa.

Harold whispered to Godric, "If you had killed this saint rather than killing a child for this woman, perhaps I would not have considered that act as your sin."

Godric replied, "Grandpa! You are the greatest lascivious creature of all time."

Harold warned, "Look carefully, because of your heinous deeds, this gentle nymph is going to die within a week."

Vedant respectfully said, "May I take your blessings."

Arambha smiled and said, "You are all my children. Mother's blessings are with you all."

Vedant got up from his seat and bowed at Arambha's feet.

Godric teased, "My grandfather would like to do the same."

Vedant urged, "Come, Harold. May you also receive the blessings of the Mother."

Harold hesitated but then, like Vedant, he too got up and bowed with his head on both feet of Arambha.

70 CENTURIES AGO

Chaitanya returned, his expression one of helplessness, with blood streaming from the left side of his forehead. Outside the hut, Arva played a short distance away. As Chaitanya entered, he found Rashmi seated against one side of the wall, while Prisha lay lifeless on the ground, her clothes soaked with blood.

Chaitanya cried out, "Prisha..!! What happened... open your eyes, my baby!" He suddenly ran over, holding Prisha's head on his lap and slapping her lightly on the cheek.

Prisha's breath had completely stopped. Chaitanya understood that she had said goodbye to this world forever.

"Why don't you say anything... how did all this happen?" Chaitanya asked Rashmi, his voice breaking as tears rolled down his cheeks.

Rashmi did not speak, simply pointing her right arm towards the front wall. Chaitanya looked at the wall, and suddenly his eyes turned red with anger.

TAMIL NADU 726AD

The sun was about to set, and Godric, Harold, and all the masters were hiding behind the bushes at some distance from a hut built in the jungle.

"Surely that monk and his wife are hiding something," Godric said, peering intently towards the hut.

Mansoor nodded, then replied, "Now let us see with our own eyes how true his story is."

"Kooh..! Kooh..!" echoed the voice of a Koel.

The door of the hut suddenly opened, and Arambha came out running in great joy. A man emerged from behind a tree and stood in front of Arambha.

"Shhhhh! Looks like Tejas has come," Chodrak whispered urgently, gesturing for everyone to stay quiet.

Now everyone was looking at Tejas. Being at a great distance, they couldn't hear the conversation between Arambha and Tejas at all.

"Oh! This doesn't look nice," Harold whispered to Gurbaksh Singh. "May they both have an extra-marital affair."

"Yeah! Her expressions and excitement explain everything," Gurbaksh Singh murmured in agreement.

"Shhhhh...!" Godric hissed, silencing them both.

Tejas was escorted into the hut by Arambha. Harold and the others sat in silence, their eyes fixed on the hut. After a few minutes, Arambha's husband came outside the hut, holding a bow and with a quiver of arrows slung over his shoulder.

"Arambha! Arambha!" Kashyapa called out loudly to his wife.

Arambha came out of the hut and started talking to Kashyapa. Vedant was trying to listen to their conversation but could not hear a single word of what Arambha and her husband were saying. Now a dog came out of the hut and began barking at Kashyapa.

"Look!" Mansoor said, pointing towards the back of the hut. "He is running," he added, as Tejas slowly came out of the open window.

Everyone's gaze shifted to Tejas, who, in a panic, ran into the forest. Meanwhile, the dog attacked Kashyapa, biting his leg. Arambha struggled to pull the dog away, while Kashyapa kicked the dog repeatedly. Instead of retreating, the dog became more aggressive. In the midst of the struggle, Kashyapa drew an arrow and, using it like a dagger, drove it into the dog's ear, killing it. The dog's body then transformed into that of a child, eliciting Arambha's anguished screams. Upon witnessing this, Kashyapa slumped lifelessly to the ground. Seeing the scene unfold, Godric placed his hand over his heart and bowed. Harold and the masters looked at Godric with confusion.

PRESENT TIME BRANCH – BUNKER

Harold, the five masters, Godric, Aldous, and Theo were currently sitting at a round table inside the bunker.

Theo said, "So after all this drama we have come to the conclusion that Aliens have indeed been in contact with our people since ancient times and my boy is a child killer. Godric! Never ever touch my machine again. Now the deal is done." He spoke the last word with much irritation.

Godric responded, "That girl was a mixed breed, you all saw that. She didn't look like the locals. So we do not know the full truth yet."

Gurbaksh Singh remarked, "How many more times do I have to repeat that you would not have been cursed if you were innocent?"

Aldous pointed out, "What's the big deal about that girl being an alien hybrid? Similar evidence is also found from the pyramids of Egypt that even at that time many humans and aliens had hybrid children. If you look carefully at the pictures carved on the walls, the kings there also seem to be alien hybrids."

Harold explained, "I have explained this to him a thousand times. That woman is a combination of Alien and human DNA, so tell me how your innocence is being proved with it? Whether the child is an alien mixed breed or a normal human, a child is only a child. You are a sinner! Just admit that, you stubborn bitch!"

Chodrak agreed, "I agree with Harold. Godric! You really did a grave sin. A child is a child. Don't be racist."

Godric protested, "Oh come on, master! I am not a racist at all. Master Gurbaksh! If we hadn't met, I would never have known about my previous births. Now when we have come so far, then why are you all angry about the sin of my previous birth? You are my masters. It is your duty to find a solution for me to get out of this trouble."

Gurbaksh Singh stated, "We are not angry with you because you committed a sin more than twelve hundred years ago. We may have committed even greater sins in previous lives. But our displeasure is that you are not fully admitting your mistake after seeing everything with your own eyes."

Godric questioned, "How do we know what happened inside the hut?"

Harold asked, "Really? Do we really need to go back there and see you doing something nasty with that hybrid? Shamelessness should have a limit. Just admit your crime and find a solution to your curse."

Godric replied, "Yes, I have made a mistake, but my intention was to run away from there, not to have her child killed by that monk."

Anselm said, "Even if you made that child a dog for any other reason, but if you had not done so, the child would have survived. If you wouldn't have done that, what could have happened to you? Most likely your and Arambha's illicit relationship could get exposed?"

Godric acknowledged, "Well! I admit I made a mistake. But I have suffered a lot for my sin. That child has killed me many times; don't you think that monk got angry and cursed me a lot more than my punishment?"

Mansoor agreed, "Yes! We all can agree with you on that point, but making a father kill his own son is a horrible sin. Yes, we want to help you, and now you need to see Vedant's master. Maybe he would be able to tell you the solution for this curse."

Vedant assured, "I will tell him the whole thing, and I'm sure he would have the solution. At least we know who can kill you again." He spoke the last words while looking at Harold.

Harold said, "I can't kill him. He is my grandson."

Chodrak commented, "You wouldn't do it intentionally. But it shall happen. Your soul is bound with that curse."

Theo argued, "If this is the matter of his soul, then no! He can't kill Godric."

Chodrak retorted, "Mr. Theo! You are no one to decide that. It's the curse."

Theo countered, "But as you said, the curse is bound with the soul. So it wouldn't happen."

Chodrak explained, "No one can deny that until Godric breaks the curse. The curse is a bond between the both souls."

Harold declared, "I have no soul."

Godric asked, "What??"

Harold revealed, "I am Harold's clone. He died in that car accident with your grandmother twenty-four years ago. Although I have his body, memory, and consciousness, I do not have the soul. Do even clones have souls?"

Hearing Harold's words, Godric and all his teachers were shocked.

Vedant said, "Yes! You have a soul, but you don't have the soul of Harold. Godric! Let's go with me. You really need to find the solution asap. Now we are totally out of options here."

Godric sat helplessly with his hands on his forehead.

Harold asked, "Godric! We all think, believe, and know you did an unthinkable sin. Do you agree with us?"

Godric replied, "Yes! I agree. Are you happy now?" He said this with a bit of sadness.

Harold answered, "More than happy! And now I want you all to stay close to this idiot. He needs a lot of guidance from you all. My farmhouse is free to live for all of you." He said this to all the masters.

All the masters faced each other.

Godric asked, "That's interesting. Would you all like to move in there? I really need you guys in this hard time."

Anselm agreed, "I have no problem. We have found the reason together, shall find the solution as well."

Mansoor confirmed, "Of course! We all will stick together!"

Gurbaksh Singh said, "How dare you think we would leave you?" He smiled as he grabbed Godric's wrist and shook it.

All the other masters also looked at Godric and smiled.

THE LOVE AND REFLECTION

FEW DAYS LATER

Isla stood outside the hut in the heart of the forest, hugging Godric tightly. His face was haggard, and his body appeared as if he had not rested for days. The angel, with a sorrowful expression, embraced both Isla and Godric.

Godric said, "I'm tired of thinking. How can I make a father kill his child?"

Isla replied, "I don't care what you were in past lives, I just know that you are my Godric, the love of my life. As for the curse, someone would kill you only if you try to attain moksha. Apart from this, that curse has no effect on your life."

Godric asked, "Should I remain stuck in the cycle of birth and death for eternity? Take birth, then go to school, then college, then university, then find a job or start a business, then get married, then have children and then start worrying about their future too, and then die in old age. And then take birth again and repeat the same. I can't live like this."

Isla responded, "I always think about settling my life with you, and you always talk about leaving the world. Life is not so bad. If we get the same kind of life forever, then what is the harm in taking birth again and again?" She spoke slightly resentfully while backing away from Godric.

Angel, standing next to her, hugged Godric's arm. Her facial expression clearly showed that she felt worried for Godric.

Godric remarked, "We can't be sure that we will always be born into a good or rich family."

Isla pointed out, "Good deeds lead to a good birth!"

Godric argued, "We have lived many lives. Our deeds of one birth alone are not enough to determine the next life and the happiness of that life. No one knows when an enemy from a previous birth will come before us to take revenge for his past life in a well-going, nice, and peaceful life. The cycle of Karma is very complex. Living in it, we can't claim to be happy forever."

Isla assured, "Don't worry, I will be your wife in every birth, and we will face every hardship together. Just keep in your mind, don't tell your mother about this curse." She spoke while hugging him again.

Godric said, "No! I won't tell her anything. I want to see your parents as soon as possible. Just tell them to come to our house for dinner on the last Sunday of this month. I will talk about our marriage sitting in front of both families."

Isla asked, "Really??"

Isla blossomed like a flower at Godric's words, and a spiritual glow came into both her eyes.

Godric confirmed, "Yes!"

Isla said, "I can't wait for that moment."

Godric replied, "I also can't wait anymore either. Tell me one thing! Will you always stand by me forever like today?" He spoke in a sad tone, pulling Isla's cheeks very lovingly.

Isla assured, "I will stand in front of you to face any problem. Every hard time will have to face me first before coming to you."

Godric thanked her, "Thanks, my love!"

Isla said, "You are welcome, my future husband. But what if Dad gets angry with your proposal?"

Godric replied, "I have a great plan to make your father agree with us. He must say yes."

Isla cautioned, "Just focus on our marriage only. Do not get stuck in any new mission again. I cannot make my children wait any longer."

Godric reassured, "Don't you worry. Now my mission is to marry you."

Angel immediately swung in happiness and hugged them both tightly.

70 CENTURIES AGO

Arva screamed in pain, "Mother…!!!"

Chaitanya ran out and saw that Pranja was holding his son by the neck, with four other aliens standing right next to Pranja.

Pranja demanded, "Hand over your daughter to me. Otherwise, I will kill this ugly son of yours right here…"

Chaitanya retorted, "You evil creature! You took advantage of my child's innocence… and now you want to take another child's life…"

One of Pranja's companions laughed and said, "Ha ha ha! He is not the only one who has tasted her innocence."

Pranja and all his companions started laughing, "Ha ha ha ha!"

Pranja said, "Humans can be so stupid as well as ugly. I had no idea about this… Let's get her out."

Rashmi shouted while coming out of the hut and crying, "Prisha is dead, you demon! You killed my doll!"

One of Pranja's accomplices immediately wounded Chaitanya and Rashmi with his laser gun. As Arva dashed towards his parents, Pranja struck him from behind with a large laser gun, reducing him to ashes. Chaitanya and Rashmi, witnessing their child's transformation into a pile of ashes, writhed in agony like fish gasping for water, yet they were immobilised despite their desperate efforts. Following this, Pranja and his companions entered the hut.

Pranja spat on Prisha's dead body in extreme anger and frustration and said, while looking at the half-human, half-alien baby fetus lying against the wall, "Ugly woman! You couldn't last even one more day!"

One of Pranja's companions said, "If you had taken her with you on the first day, we would not have lost her today."

Pranja replied, "If I had separated her from her parents on the first day, her sad mind would never have allowed her body to be worthy of us to produce our hybrid child."

Another of Pranja's companions spoke, "It will be better if we find only orphan girls from now on."

Pranja said, "We have to work on a new plan to solve this problem. Now set the whole hut on fire." He added as he came out of the hut, taking the fetus with him in a special kind of jar full of green fluid.

His accomplices placed a semi-oval device on the nearly lifeless Chaitanya's head, trapping his brain energy within it. They then lifted both Rashmi and Chaitanya, threw them inside the hut, and set it ablaze.

PRESENT TIME BRANCH – HIMALAYA MOUNTAIN

Vedant and Godric sat on the floor beside Vedant's elderly guru in a small hut. The thin old man, who appeared to be about 95 years old, had maintained a remarkably toned physique. Godric, sitting across from him, looked very weak, with anxiety visibly gnawing at him like a relentless worm.

Vedant asked, "Guru Ji, how much more punishment will he get for the sin he committed hundreds of years ago?"

Guru replied, "Whenever we do any sin, it is sown like a seed in the field of our soul. As time passes, this seed slowly starts to germinate. Before it starts its journey from becoming a plant to becoming a tree, we must start the process of uprooting it. The more time passes, the more the punishment will increase. Later, it becomes a tree of the old seed, and many new seeds are formed from that tree. Those new seeds also germinate and bring us to such a state that no man can eliminate our sin, but only God himself. According to the number of births he has taken, the seed of that one sin has become not only a tree but a whole forest."

Godric asked, "Could you give me any solution for this curse, please?"

Guru inquired, "How much remorse do you have for your sin?"

Godric responded, "If I have committed this sin, even if I die at the hands of that child's soul for thousands of lives, then the fruit of my sin would not be fulfilled. But I want to know what was the compulsion that made me let a child die like this at the hands of his father."

Guru said, "If you want to know the whole truth and find a solution to destroy the seed of this sin, then you have to awaken the consciousness of your own previous birth."

Godric asked, "Is that possible?"

Guru confirmed, "Yes! Probably, the memory of all our previous births is stored secretly inside our brain, and there is a way to unlock that door. But yes, there is also a big problem in using this method."

Godric insisted, "I would go to any length to know the truth. Please show me the way. Guilt for this sin is eating me like termites day by day."

Guru asked, "Are you married?"

Godric replied, "Not yet, but I will be soon."

Vedant asked, "With whom?"

Godric answered, "Isla!"

Vedant inquired, "Harold's Secretary?"

Guru interjected while speaking with sudden irritation, "Oh, shut up, Vedant! Are you planning to beat the drum at his wedding?"

Vedant apologised, "Sorry, Guru Ji." Then he suddenly put both hands together in panic and spoke fearfully.

Guru addressed Godric, "Godric! If you remember your previous births, not only would your memory come back, but you would also be more attached to all your past relationships than this birth. God veils our past births for a reason. There is a solution to every problem through Siddhi, but every time we have to pay a huge price. Can you separate feelings from your parents and life partner?"

Godric responded, "In my condition, I cannot love anyone even under this current weight of the realisation of my sin. What relationship matters to a corpse? Please help me. I am ready to sacrifice everything."

Guru said, "Vedant! You go outside and wait. I want to talk to him privately for a while."

Without saying anything, Vedant folded his hands, got up, and walked out of the hut.

Godric asked, "Suppose that I get to know the cause and that I am truly the guilty one. How will this curse of mine destroy the seed of my sin?"

Guru explained, "The curse can either be cut off by eliminating the cause of the curse or by receiving a greater Vardan, or you can say the boon. Liberation can be achieved from the path between the Vardan and the curse. And yes, repentance is also a big key to it. But as I have said earlier, this sin of yours is centuries old; it is not easy to get rid of it. Put your trust in God and get completely absorbed in his devotion. After all, everything happens according to God's will. He himself will definitely solve your problem in one way or another. But remember one thing: no matter how much the fury of difficulties breaks you in life, never ever question the will of God. Just submit yourself to Him one hundred percent."

FEW DAYS LATER

Godric sat on the floor in Padmasana, concentrating on his third eye. As he delved into his consciousness, he sequentially reviewed the memories of his entire life, moving from the present to the past. Gradually, he envisioned the scene of his birth, then imagined himself in his mother Bella's womb, and even further back, to the moment of conception. His imagination continued until he reached the point where there was no further memory to access, only an impenetrable darkness.

Thud! Thud! Thud! Suddenly, the door of the room was knocked.

Bella, sounding impatient, said, "Godric! How much longer will it take? They will be here in five minutes."

Godric, opening his eyes slowly, replied, "Coming!"

HALF AN HOUR LATER

Godric is now having dinner with Isla's family.

Archer said, "You should join hands with me in the robotics business. Although my design and programming is not of the end level, but because the price is low, we can earn a lot of money from middle-class families. Day by day, the demand for robots for domestic work is increasing."

Harold responded, "The offer is good, but I can't take any more tension. Now Theo and Godric see where else they need to invest their money."

Theo remarked, "We will definitely think about working on this side. After all, a friend is useful for a friend."

Godric stood up from his chair and interjected, "Sorry to interrupt you guys, I want to share something with you all."

Bella and Isla's mother both smiled at Godric and Isla sitting next to him. Isla's mother's eyes were shining a little more.

Theo said, "Please don't announce to baptize us in the World Religion now."

Everyone started laughing.

Godric continued, "Actually, I have two things to say. The first is that I am resigning tomorrow from the work I was doing as the operations head of the World Religion."

Harold exclaimed, "What!! Are you going mad?"

Upon hearing Godric's words, the smiles vanished from everyone's faces. Isla cast a downward glance and then looked at Godric's mother, Bella, with a questioning expression. Bella, equally perplexed, had no idea what was troubling her son.

Godric said, "I have done my part for the project. Now they don't need anything from my end. I just want a long leave for all this tiredness."

Harold replied, "We have a five percent stake in that project. You can take six months' leave if you want, but leaving everything behind like this is not the solution to anything."

Archer interjected, "Come on, Commander! Let him speak. What is the second thing you want to say?"

Godric addressed Isla, "Isla! Would you please stand up and stand in front of me?"

Isla got up and stood in front of Godric with a slight look of panic and amusement on her lovely face. Archer looked at both of them in awe.

Godric continued, "First of all, I want to apologise to you all for hiding my love life with Isla. We both have been in love since our high school."

Isla's mother said with a smile, "Isla! You are really a naughty girl!"

Bella spoke very happily, "I had an intuition about that for a very, very long time."

Archer said, while controlling his displeasure behind a little smile, "I don't know what to say but... I am happy to see you both together."

Isla, standing in a panic with Godric, breathed a sigh of relief after hearing her father's words.

Harold spoke with a light laugh, "You both are like Theo and Bella! They also hid their love from everyone."

Theo encouraged, "Go on, son! I am listening!"

Godric, kneeling on the ground and bowing before Isla, offered a diamond ring in his right hand very respectfully and said, "Isla! My high school sweetheart. Love of my life. Will you marry me?"

Isla responded with an overly condescending smile, holding out her hand for the ring, "Yes!!"

Bella and Isla's mother sprang to their feet in joy, embracing each other warmly. Harold and Theo also rose and greeted Archer. They then congratulated Godric and Isla, who shared a heartfelt hug and kiss. Standing behind his wife, Archer watched the scene with a thoughtful smile. Meanwhile, Harold stood off to the side, observing Archer with a furtive eye, thinking something.

NEXT DAY

Both Harold and Godric were standing at the back of their farmhouse.

Harold said, "You made such a big deal... Just for your marriage?"

Godric replied, "The deal would have been for marriage if I had made the deal in exchange for Isla's hand. Even his angels did not know that I was about to propose to Isla."

Harold asked, "What is the difference in that? You made a deal with him instead of asking Isla at first. So you just tricked him with the deal for Isla!"

Godric retorted, "What else could I do? Leave Isla? She is my childhood love!"

Harold remarked, "I was just thinking about setting you up and, sir, you have already raised the flags of vindication. You would have consulted me once."

Godric questioned, "What would happen by consulting? If you wouldn't like my plan, would I have given up the dream of marriage with her?"

Harold said, "Although Archer is my friend, I never got him into business with me. What do you think, he has put his offer of robots in front of us for the first time? He is an atheist. There is a canopy figure in our and his thinking."

Godric argued, "Being an atheist is not a sin; it is enough for everyone to live their life truthfully. An atheist who serves humanity is a million times better than those who pretend to believe in God and do nothing meaningful with their lives."

Harold responded, "I don't need your speech. It is not a sign of being wise to indulge every time. You have no idea how much I have struggled to get here. Looking at your habit of taking decisions based on your feelings, it seems that you will destroy our business within days."

Godric stated, "My world religion project is a million times dearer to me than your business. When I have left that, I can leave your money too. Don't bring your business into me and Isla's relationship. This is only a million dollars deal. In this way, their product will be launched and we would also benefit."

Harold said, "Let's complete the deal. I will tolerate this deal somehow for your love, but if you try to do any other deal with Archer after this deal, then I will understand that you really don't need my money."

Godric replied, "If you were truly my grandfather, you would never have said this."

Harold warned, "Say thanks to God I am not your grandfather; otherwise, this action of yours was more than enough for me to fulfil that curse again." He spoke very harshly and gritted his teeth.

Godric challenged, "Should I speak to your army chief about what you did with Michael?"

Harold shouted, "Shut up, you mental case! He was already dead to him. Getting rid of him after completion of the task was part of our mission."

Godric said, "Isla is half a part of me. Do not interfere in my personal life. You are not more than a lab-made subject for me."

Harold advised, "Your mind is not in the right state. Please find a good psychiatrist to fix you."

Godric said nothing and angrily went inside the house.

MAIN TIMELINE – 726 AD

TAMIL NADU

"I heard you got the power for shape-shifting," Arambha asked Tejas in a very attractive and sweet tone.

Tejas was cutting the grass around the flowers in the Ashram.

Tejas responded humbly looking at Arambha, "Sorry! You may have a misunderstanding."

Arambha inquired, "If my mother had agreed to the marriage that day, would you have hidden everything from me like this?"

Tejas answered, "You are now our Guru Ma. It is now a sin for me to even think about what we had between us."

Arambha said, "Loving is not a sin. If I had control over my life decisions, I would never have married this old man."

Tejas replied, "He is your husband. You should not talk about my guru in such a way."

Arambha argued, "When the duty of being a husband cannot be fulfilled by a man, then for his wife, he is nothing more than a clay idol."

Tejas said, "If there is devotion, even people can connect to Mahakal from the idol of clay."

Arambha retorted, "You still don't understand what I am trying to say."

Tejas stated, "I understand everything but the welfare of both of us is to stay away from each other. I can't think of anything wrong, even in my imagination, about my Guru's wife."

Arambha demanded talking in an irritated way, "Can you show me your shape-shifting ability or not?"

Tejas asked, "Why are you so stubborn?"

Arambha warned, "Look! If I want to turn your respect among all the people into dust, then one scream right now is more than enough."

Tejas replied, "Huh! Respect? This sparrow called respect is nothing but a superstition. Ignorant people like you consider fear and need as respect. Do you really think there is any dignity in this world? If you ask the truth, we do not even respect Mahakal."

Arambha threatened with regretful expression, "So you won't show me the Siddhi? It seems that I have to go to that old guru and say, 'Tejas looks at me in a wrong way.'"

Tejas pleaded, "No, no. Don't do that! My Guru is a very noble person. He will hurt a lot, and I will also be deprived of getting complete education."

Arambha said, "Huh! I knew that you don't have the guts you try to show around among others. I am going to my mother's house tomorrow. I will stay there for a few days. No one can see us in that forest. See you there the day after tomorrow. Mother goes to the temple for worship every evening. I will be alone at that time."

Tejas replied, "Guru ji can't let you go there alone. Surely one of the Sadhvis from our Ashram would be with you. It is difficult for us to meet alone."

Arambha said, "Don't worry about that. You just need to come on time. I shall be alone."

PRESENT TIME BRANCH – CHURCH

Godric and Isla, dressed as bride and groom, looked stunning as they stood before the priest, fully prepared for their wedding. Their families and approximately 200 guests were seated before them. Additionally, hundreds of invisible beings had gathered to witness the ceremony. Every corner of the church, from floor to ceiling, was filled with angels. Godric's angel was perched on two steps between the church floor and the platform, close to the couple.

Bella said, "Both look exactly like us."

Theo asked, "Can we both marry each other again according to the Bible?"

Bella laughed, "Ha ha ha! Ask the priest... I am ready!"

Archer, who was sitting with his wife near the two, looked at Isla's face, his eyes slightly wet.

The priest began the marriage ceremony and consummated the marriage by having the bride and groom exchange vows to support each other as husband and wife in every way.

The priest said, "Now you can kiss each other."

Isla remarked, "At last we have become one."

Godric replied, "I never break my promise."

Both of them kissed each other.

"You are my God!" Closing his eyes and kissing Isla, Godric heard the voice of his previous wife, Shamshir Kaur, and her face appeared before his closed eyes.

Isla said, "Now you are 100% mine," and hugged Godric after kissing him.

Godric replied, "I was always yours, my love," kissing Isla's forehead and speaking lovingly.

All the guests present and the parents of both were congratulating each other while clapping. All the angels were flying in the air around the newly-wed couple, expressing joy.

MAIN TIMELINE - 726AD

TAMIL NADU

Arambha walked through the dark forest at night with her mother, Advika. Advika has dark skin and sharp features. As they approached a ruin, they found a large patio in the centre, overgrown with vegetation. Advika pressed a gem-like button tied around her wrist, causing a secret door on the ground to open in front of her feet.

Advika asked, "Are you sure he will come?"

Arambha replied, "How many more times will you ask? I think you don't believe me either. You just stay out of the house all evening. Don't let the sadhvi come back from the temple too soon."

Advika said, "Your father was waiting for this time for a very long time."

Arambha explained, "The person who brought my mother out of a life like hell and blessed her with so much respect among all the people, I would go to any extent for him."

Now, both had reached an underground alien facility. Numerous flying saucers were parked in front of them, and many advanced tech weapons were also seen around.

"Wow! My daughter is getting more beautiful day by day," said Pranja, as the door of a UFO opened and he got down from it.

Arambha ran and hugged Pranja. Her mother moved forward and touched Pranja's feet with great respect.

Pranja, who was seven feet tall and looked like a giant in front of Arambha and Advika, said, "After all, the first pray finally has come to you."

Arambha replied while speaking like a child, "Please don't call him pray. I like him so much."

Pranja advised, "Control your emotions, my girl. The time you spent with him is a lot. Now you only need to focus on your mission to protect your own clan."

Advika commented, "Sometimes I think she really lost her heart to that bastard."

Arambha insisted, "No! I just like him. My love is my Rakshasa clan only."

Pranja said, "Now the time has come for us to take revenge for our disgrace from the Brahmans that they have been doing to our clan for centuries. I have not forgotten the painful death of your elder mother, Prisha, till today. I wish she would have immediately left her parents and gone with me."

Advika remarked, "She was naive. You should not have chosen such a young girl to destroy the Brahmins."

Pranja said, "Stop the nonsense! She was my first girlfriend who healed my wounds and supported me in every way. If it wasn't for her, I would be dead today."

Arambha said, "Oh come on! You two have started this fight again. Mother! When will you stop being jealous of her?"

Pranja said, "Leave it! She keeps talking nonsense. Tell me, how's my little one?"

Arambha responded excitedly and with a smile, "He's very naughty. He makes me and the sadhvi both tired every day. It's hard to look after such a brat."

Pranja laughed, "Ha ha ha ha! He's the same as you were."

Advika said irritably, "Give us the Sarp Mani to capture her lover's power. Sadhvi would be looking for us if we don't head back soon."

Pranja said, "Oh, your anger! What do you worry about? Even though she came into my life before you, she was neither more beautiful than you nor could she give me a child. You are my best partner." He grabbed Advika by the arm, pulled her towards himself, and hugged her in a romantic manner.

Advika shyly said, "Stop it! Your daughter is here."

Arambha said, "Awee... mother! You look so beautiful with a shy face."

Hugging Advika, Pranja looked at an embryo placed in a very large jar on one side of the wall, lost in his old thoughts.

Prisha and Pranja stood inside the UFO, and a hologram of the Asian subcontinent was visible on a table in front of them.

Prisha asked, "Will our kingdom be over this entire area?"

Pranja replied, "Yes! From the Himalayas to the sea, the entire area will be ours, and you will be my queen."

Prisha said while hugging Pranja, "And our child will be a prince!"

Pranja vowed, "I will not leave a single Brahman alive. As they forced you and all the rakshasas to live in the jungles, when I rule, no Brahman will even have a place in any jungle."

Prisha said, "Once they beat my father a lot in front of us. How can it be a sin to take knowledge of a Veda! You are right, my father is a naive person."

Pranja urged, "We don't have much time. You have to go with me as soon as possible. If your parents find out, then our whole plan will be ruined."

Prisha replied, "Just stay half a month more. I don't know when I will get a chance to meet them again."

Pranja said, "After winning the war, we will take your mother, father, and your brother with us to the palace. We will welcome them by showering flowers in the assembly of all the great Rakshasa kings of the empire."

Prisha said excitedly, "Mother likes flowers very much! We will lay flowers at her feet too."

Pranja said, "Ha ha ha! I will do as you wish."

"Please give us the Sarp Mani now; we are getting too late," said Advika lovingly while moving back from Pranja's hug.

Pranja said, "Oh! Sorry, my love. I was just lost in our old romantic memories. Just wait, I'll bring it as soon as possible."

NEXT DAY

Tejas reached near a hut built in the forest. He looked around, stood hidden by a tree, and made two sounds same as Koel with his mouth.

Arambha said while coming out of the hut, "There was no need to do so much drama. No one is watching us."

At the sound of Arambha's voice, Tejas emerged from behind the tree. The sight of Arambha before him, appearing like a celestial being, momentarily stunned him. Regaining his composure, Tejas took a deep breath and walked towards her.

Tejas asked, "When will your mother come back?"

Arambha replied, "Don't worry. It will take a while." She was looking at Tejas in a lustful manner.

Tejas continued, "Come on, tell me which creature you want to see changing form?"

Arambha said, "Let's come inside the hut. I will see that after worshipping the Sarp Mani placed in front of the idol of my father."

Tejas urged, "Do whatever you want, quickly."

Arambha led him inside the hut, where her two-year-old child lay in a swing, milk dribbling from his mouth. On one side of the hut, an idol of the deity was placed on a three-foot-high pedestal. In front of the idol, an earthen lamp burned on a plate, alongside a small golden box, four inches in size, containing items for the Aarti. Atop the box, a diamond-like stone cast a soft glow throughout the hut. Arambha took the plate, performed the Aarti for the idol, and then set it down on the ground in front of Tejas.

Arambha said, "Let's show Siddhi now."

Tejas asked, "Whose form do you want to see shifted? You should have brought a living being for that."

"You can change your own form!" Arambha suggested.

Tejas hesitated. "If I couldn't come in my real form, then? I'm not that much of an expert in this Siddhi."

Arambha replied, "Your guru used to praise your education a lot. Why are you afraid now?"

"Siddhi is not child's play," Tejas said cautiously. "I can't use it on myself at all. Can I use it on you?"

"No, not on me," Arambha responded quickly. "Don't use it on yourself. What if he turns you into an animal and runs away?" The thought crossed her mind.

Tejas pressed, "What are you thinking now? I have no time to waste."

"Alright," Arambha conceded, "you can try it on my son. Turn him into my beloved dog, Moti."

"Are you kidding me?" Tejas exclaimed. "The use of a Siddhi on a child? I think you've gone mad."

"I am completely fine," Arambha retorted. "Come on, show me, otherwise I will start shouting."

Tejas protested, "Why are you insisting? I can't just use it directly on anyone! He is just a child."

Arambha, growing irritated, snapped, "Just shut up and turn him into Moti!" She spoke harshly as she picked up the child from the swing.

"I'm asking for the last time. Are you sure about this?" Tejas asked, one final time.

"Show the Siddhi, you idiot!" Arambha demanded harshly.

Tejas sighed. "Alright," he said reluctantly, "put him on the ground."

Arambha placed the baby beside the Sarp Mani in front of Tejas. Tejas cupped water from the plate in his hand and closed his eyes. Chanting a mantra, he sprinkled the water over the child. As soon as the water touched the child's body, the baby transformed into a dog. Arambha, standing beside him, was stunned by the sudden transformation.

Arambha said lovingly while hugging the dog, "Wow! You really turned him into my Moti."

"Arambha! Arambha!" her husband called from outside the hut.

Tejas ran and hid under the bed positioned on one side of the hut. Arambha, unsure of what to do, took a moment to collect herself. Not understanding the situation, she composed her thoughts, opened the door, and stepped outside.

Arambha said, "Swami! You here?"

Kashyapa replied, "I saw sadhvi and your mother in the temple, so I was worried about you. Why didn't you go with them? What if any animal comes?" His voice was filled with concern, clearly expressing his worry.

He carried a bow and quiver of arrows with him.

"I was born and brought up in this forest," Arambha responded. "I am used to live in the jungle. There is no danger in being alone here."

Kashyapa frowned. "Some wild dogs killed a man a week ago."

"Boef! Boef! Boef! Boef!" The dog suddenly appeared from behind Arambha, immediately catching her husband by the leg.

Kashyapa struggled to free his leg.

"Moti! Go away! Moti!" Arambha shouted, trying to control the dog.

"It has rabies," Kashyapa said, his eyes widening as he noticed the foam coming from the dog's mouth. He kicked the dog away from himself, trying to fend it off.

Taking advantage of the commotion outside, Tejas quickly emerged from under the bed and, without looking around, dashed out through the back window of the hut.

"No! No! He's fine!" Arambha screamed, seeing her husband kicking the dog. "Moti, stop! Moti!"

The dog, however, was relentless. In the struggle, it bit Kashyapa's leg several times. Despite Arambha's best efforts, she couldn't control the frenzied animal.

Finally, Kashyapa drew an arrow with his right hand and struck one of the dog's ears with such force that it pierced the dog's brain, passing through the skull.

Witnessing the dog's suffering, Arambha's entire body shook with terror. She shrieked and recoiled instantly. The dog's form soon transformed back into that of the child. Seeing his own son's lifeless body before him, Kashyapa's heart was shattered. He collapsed to the ground, crying out in anguish. Meanwhile, Arambha cradled the child's body in her arms, her grief overwhelming as she tugged at her hair in a frantic display of despair.

Kashyapa said in a trembling tone, "What kind of illusion is this?"

Arambha cried out loudly, "I don't know. He was just sleeping inside. I want my son back. Oh, my baby."

PRESENT TIME BRANCH

It is morning, and the first rays of the sun spread their golden light all around. Surrounded by many angels, Godric sits in Padmasana by the pool in a beach house. He fixes all his attention on his third eye, visualising the events of his life in a sequence from present to past. He revisits moments with the masters and Harold, learning in the research centre, meeting Isla secretly, travelling to various countries to select the five masters, beginning his search for the masters, studying neurology at university, enjoying time with friends in college, and the mischief of school days. These memories unfold one by one, and now he recalls himself sitting on his mother's lap, listening to stories.

"Muaah!!" Isla sat on Godric's lap and kissed him on the cheek.

All of Godric's attention was broken, and the angels sitting around them expressed their regret by hitting their hands on their foreheads.

"Why have you become an enemy of my devotion?" Godric asked lovingly, pulling Isla's cheek as he opened his eyes.

Isla pouted and teased, "Now you should worship me only."

Godric smiled and said, "When a person is meditating, never consider him alone. Many other spiritual beings remain around that person all the time and..."

"What about me?" Isla interrupted, her voice playfully challenging.

Godric continued patiently, "And if they get angry, that would not be good for us. So never bother me again when I sit in meditation."

"No..! We won't do anything like that," Angel said in a cute manner, placing her chin on Godric's right shoulder from behind, expressing surprise at his words.

Isla frowned slightly and said, "It was fine until the time machine, but trying to see the past life through meditation, don't you think it's too much?"

Godric spoke very politely, with seriousness in his tone, "It took more than two decades for the makers of the time machine to complete their project, and without alien tech, it would have been impossible even in the next fifty years. Here I've only started working on the method of seeing past lives a few days ago, and your doubts have already begun."

"I didn't mean that," Isla said softly. "I'm just worried. Isn't there any other way?"

Godric sighed. "Apart from that, it can be done by going back to my past life with the time machine and asking Tejas why he killed the child."

"I was thinking the same myself," Isla replied, "Can't we use the time machine again?"

Godric hesitated, "I can use it, but what if people catch me with Tejas? It is also possible that he won't tell me the truth. Moreover, if Tejas considers me to be an elusive person and turns me into a dog or a cat, then what would we do?"

"Hee hee hee! How cute you will look as a cat!" Isla said mischievously.

"This is no joke, my love," Godric replied. "He can truly do that. I have already discussed all possibilities with the masters. The only last resort I have is to see my past through meditation. Now, you should also start chanting the name of Akaal, so no demon or evil soul could get inside your womb. It totally depends on a mother's aura what kind of soul will be born from her."

"It means that if the child does not turn out to be a good person, then mister has already made an excuse to blame me?" Isla mocked, her eyes wide in exaggerated indignation.

Godric smiled. "If the child turns out to be great, then you are the only person who would get all the credit. My love, I am not kidding! The soul does not enter the woman's eggs through the man's semen; it directly enters the fertilised egg inside the woman's womb during or after the act of sex between man and woman. But sometimes it can take a few months for the soul to enter the child's body during pregnancy. The man is only responsible for the biological structure of the child, but the type of soul depends solely on the spiritual level of its mother."

Isla looked amazed, "Does this mean my child will choose me as a mother? That's so cute."

"No! We cannot take birth by our will, but yes, we are born only through a mother with the same aura or spiritual level as us. So whenever man and woman have sex, they are not alone; they are surrounded by countless souls. But nature itself decides which soul, similar to the mother, will enter the womb."

"Okay," Isla said with a nod, "I will start meditation as soon as possible. At least I can do that for our future child. Tell me one more thing, can I also see my past lives?"

"Yeah, that's possible for you too," Godric replied thoughtfully. "It is very important for a person to be mentally mature. Otherwise, you might get lost in past lives."

"How could I get lost by seeing my past memories?" Isla asked, frowning in confusion.

Godric explained, "Through the method I am using now, births are not only seen but we also live them mentally at an emotional level. We fall in love with the family and friends of our past lives, just as we did at that time."

"And what if you fall in love with a girlfriend from one of your past lives?" Isla asked with a teasing grin.

"Ha ha ha ha!" Godric laughed. "I can't guarantee that."

Isla's face paled at Godric's laughter. "Don't make fun of me like that! Now I am your wife," she said, putting a finger to his lips and speaking softly.

Godric kissed her forehead and asked gently, "Do you really want to see your past lives?"

Isla shook her head. "I don't need to get into that mess."

"Oh come on," Godric teased, "you might find your past life boyfriend."

"Nice try!" Isla shot back with a smirk. "But you can't get rid of me that easily."

"Nah! I am serious," Godric insisted. "If you want, I can teach you."

"No," Isla said, smiling. "I just want to learn love. Could you teach me, please?"

"The God is love!" Godric said, his voice full of affection.

"And you are my God!" Isla replied, hugging him tightly.

Godric smiled. "I shall create heaven for you, my angel."

"I am already in heaven," Isla whispered back.

Godric didn't say anything, gazing deeply into her eyes, full of love.

RESEARCH CENTRE

Harold and all the masters were currently sitting on a bench in the park in front of the World Religion wing.

"My wife was a very religious woman," Harold said, his voice quiet with reflection. "But I never understood anything about spirituality until today. Godric is in so much pain after learning about that curse. I can't bear to see him like this. Do you think there will be a solution?" Harold asked, his tone full of respect.

"Don't worry!" Vedant replied calmly. "One solution or another will definitely be found, but it is very important for a person to be tormented in the fire of repentance by realising his own sin."

"What are you talking about?" Harold asked, his brow furrowing. "You are his teacher! How can you speak like that?"

Chodrak interjected, his voice calm but firm, "If spirituality were so easy, then everyone would have become Brahmgyani. We have no enmity with him to see him suffer. In fact, it is very important to break his ego."

Harold said, "I don't see any ego in him. I have never seen him hurting anyone."

Mansoor said thoughtfully, "The act of hurting others is done by those whose own hearts have been burned by seeing others rise high, but why should that person hurt someone who only considers himself to be above all?"

Gurbaksh Singh nodded slowly and replied, "There are many types of arrogance. Although spiritual knowledge gives us liberation, many people become proud of this knowledge. The matrix of nature is very complex. If it does not lead us to the negative path, then along with the positive path, it gives us such a hug that instead of walking forward, the person stops at the same place and starts digging his own grave."

Anselm added, with a serious tone, "And Godric had started digging the same grave. Thanks to God, the secret of his curse has been revealed; otherwise, after a month, he might have come to us and said that we all should sit quietly on one side and get knowledge from him to attain the nectar of spiritual peace."

"Ha ha ha ha!" All the masters burst out laughing.

Harold asked, with concern evident in his voice, "Has anyone seen his condition? Don't you feel sorry for him? It is your duty to break his curse."

Anselm shook his head and said firmly, "We were, are, and always will be with him! But it is his job to find out what the solution to the curse is. If we cooperate more than this, then his curse will take us too."

Harold frowned and said, confused, "I do not understand. How does his curse affect you?"

Anselm leaned forward and explained, "If an unruly bull is running towards me, should you stand in front of me?"

Harold sighed and asked quietly, "So from now on, you can't support him at all?"

Mansoor spoke in a calm tone, "The master shows the way to the disciple but does not carry him to the destination. If Godric is burning in the fire of remorse, that is best for him. With this, his soul will be further purified. As far as the curse is concerned, the Guru of Vedant has shown him the way. What your grandson does next with that knowledge will depend on his own understanding."

Harold said, with growing concern, "Although his habit of talking nonsense is increasing nowadays, he is my grandson! I'm really worried about him."

Vedant placed a reassuring hand on Harold's shoulder and spoke encouragingly, "My friend, finding the solution for everything does not work all the time. Sometimes some work should be left to God. Have some faith, man."

Harold didn't say anything further and sat silently, looking at all the masters as if a mother's child was lost in a fair.

AN ANCIENT CONSPIRACY

FEW DAYS LATER

"The plane carrying one hundred talented preachers of World Religion to the headquarters of UG is still missing. It is worth mentioning that a few days ago at one o'clock in the afternoon at the headquarters of UG, these preachers were planned to give the first speech of World Religion in front of all the major leaders of the world. But the security agencies said that the plane had been hijacked by the Anti-World religion group. The head of...," A middle-aged news channel journalist of African origin is speaking on TV while presenting a news report.

"It's so sad, In what kind of situation would be all the poor souls right now." Isla said in a pitiful voice as she sat anxiously on the sofa in the lobby, watching TV.

Godric spread some mustard on the sandwich and glanced at Bella, who was busy cooking beside him. "I think the plane has crashed somewhere," he said casually. "If AWR had hijacked it, then by now some demand would have come from them. Whenever UG gets a chance, they just start playing with the blood of their enemies."

Isla, who was leaning against the counter, frowned slightly. "But the search team did not find any debris from the area where contact was lost," she pointed out.

Godric shrugged, taking a bite of his sandwich. "It is not necessary that the plane become a victim of an accident as soon as communication with the control room is lost," he responded. "Maybe they lost their way after losing the signal and crashed somewhere in the sea."

"Godric! Let's go. We can't be late today." Harold's voice interrupted the conversation as he hurried down the stairs, quickly straightening his tie.

THE MOUNT EVEREST

Deep within the mountain lies a multi-storey Alien intelligence base, a hidden fortress where hundreds of warships are stationed. On the uppermost floor, a large hall looms ominously. Lining one wall are various metal structures where a multitude of World Religion's preachers are imprisoned, their faces etched with despair. Towering over them is a massive, 70-foot machine resembling a pendulum, its presence dominating the space. At its apex, a human brain still attached to a spinal cord and webbed with delicate wires, beneath it, a golden crystal the size of a tennis ball glows faintly, is disturbingly on display.

As the prisoners are being lifted out of the cell one by one by two robotic hands, heart-rending screams fill the air as the laser machine removes their flesh and their internal bodies with all their nerves and organs are being hung around the large machine. As the robotic hands are hanging their fleshless unconscious bodies on the hangers, many wires are being connected to all their veins and organs from the back side of the hangers. Even though the entire body is separated from the most mass muscles, the body of any prisoner is not dying. Due to the life support provided by the alien machine, each person's breathing is running at a normal speed.

Twenty metres from this ominous device, Pranja and several of his fellow commanders sit around a circular table, their expressions cold and unyielding. The cries of the captives fill the air, their desperate pleas for mercy echoing off the metal walls. Yet the aliens remain unmoved, their eyes devoid of sympathy as they gaze upon the prisoners with chilling indifference. They all are expressing great joy at seeing this bloody scene. Their expressions resembled that of a customer standing outside a butcher's shop, salivating at the sight of fresh meat being carved from a slaughtered animal.

Pranja said, "As soon as my plan to open the tenth gate is completed, you can attack this entire planet at once."

"Don't let us down this time too," Alien 1 replied sternly. "Our king has long stopped us from attacking humans just to see one of your plans come to fruition. Their life energy is very important for us to go to the next galaxies."

Pranja responded confidently, "If my plan A doesn't work, then I have to destroy this entire planet to carry out my plan B. I never cheated on you, and I won't cheat on you today. Be ready to attack. Save as much life energy as you want, but be patient for a few more hours."

Alien 2 pointed to the screaming prisoners in front and asked, "What do you think their life force would be enough to open the tenth gate?"

"I have not met so many people with as much energy as these hundred men have," Pranja said thoughtfully. "I hoped that these would be sufficient to complete our work."

Alien 2 looked puzzled as he questioned, "How did you finally find this characteristic of these humans? I have destroyed many planets to date with my squad, but we have never thought about such an ability of the creatures of any of those planets."

Pranja explained, "Connecting to the entire universe, eliminating the grip of time, and even going beyond creation can only be possible by the body of these human beings. When I came into contact with humans, I came to know that they could achieve such powers which are beyond the reach of our science. But thankfully, I managed to sync the two frequencies of their bodies by making a few changes in our life energy storage technology, which is why today we have the understanding of generating force against gravity without any fuel for our ships. And we can also change the shape of our body."

"This planet is a big one, millions of people are living here," Alien 3 remarked. "But you got only two frequencies in all those years?"

Pranja shook his head as he explained, "All humans are not intelligent enough to understand the capabilities of their bodies. Most of them just live dumb lives like animals. I went to hundreds of places, but to date, I could not find any other supernatural men except two. Human scriptures say that the state of being enlightened is the kingship of the entire universe. I searched a lot for such a spiritual person so that I could record every frequency of the entire universe at the same time, but every time I found a person who succeeded in achieving that state, the state of enlightenment had already come and gone on him."

"The frequency could have been obtained even by imprisoning them," Alien 4 suggested.

Pranja sighed, "No human being can achieve the Godly knowledge by force. It is their recognition that the energy needed to achieve that state has to be stored for many births, and no one knows when that energy will be completed or when the tenth gate of a human will be opened."

Alien 1 frowned and asked, "If such humans are so difficult to find, then according to this, we will have to wait for thousands of years more. Can we achieve this level of power with your machine?"

"I had prepared a great plan to achieve this characteristic for our people," Pranja said, his voice filled with determination. "Along with my team at different places, by pretending to be the gods of these humans, I bred with their women and produced hybrid children. We have had great success in producing hybrid babies in a place called Egypt. There, we made humans the most stupid by the frequency that destroys gravity and also ruled over them through our hybrid children for a long time. But unfortunately, none of our hybrid children could achieve that characteristic of the human body through which we can rule the entire universe. Some time ago, the person who acquired the frequency of shape-shifting was caught in our trap through my hybrid offspring. But even that child of mine could not completely work for me."

"This means we can never achieve this power by ourselves," Alien 1 concluded with a hint of frustration.

Pranja nodded slowly, "Unfortunately, our body can never achieve this feature, but I found the solution to this problem a thousand years ago and worked day and night to make this machine. Although our plan with hybrid children had failed miserably, I had definitely learnt by living among these humans that they are very hungry for power. Just as in the olden days we bred them with their women by becoming gods, in the same way, in the new age, we presented our science to them and made them disciples of the power of our technology. We convinced them to make one government for the whole human world. These hundred chickens that have come to us today are all the miracles of that plan. Now, we will get the strength to use all the frequencies of the whole universe according to our own will by opening the tenth gate with their life force through our science."

Alien 5 got up from his chair and spoke to Pranja with a hint of displeasure while glancing at his watch, "How much longer do I have to wait to complete this mission? Only because of this plan of yours, my soldiers have been waiting for a long time."

Alien 4 smiled and replied, "Patience, my friend, patience! As soon as our partner's plan is completed, we will start hunting these humans together around the whole planet."

Pranja looked at Alien 5 with a confident smile and said, "If the tenth door opens this time, one word from my mouth would be enough to complete the missions of your entire life."

UG HEADQUARTER

The UG Headquarters stands as a colossal, 100-storey pyramid-shaped structure, its triangular form dominating a sprawling three-square-kilometre area. Surrounding the building on three sides is a vast expanse of greenery, featuring a meticulously landscaped garden and two artificial rivers winding gracefully through the grounds. Two kilometres away on each side of the headquarters rise towering fort walls, 100 metres high and 60 metres wide, bristling with automatic cannons and guns. Human and robotic soldiers patrol both the interior and exterior of the fortress-like complex, their movements a seamless blend of organic vigilance and mechanical precision. The building extends just as deeply into the earth as it does above, with subterranean levels descending to a heavily fortified bunker. In this secure chamber, the 6-foot-tall, 60-year-old President of UG, a man of Irish descent, sits at a round table alongside five high-ranking army officials, each between the ages of 50 and 60, representing diverse global backgrounds. Around them, like the tiers of a stadium, are rows of additional round tables, providing seating for around 500 chairs. Apart from the men sitting by the main round table, there are more than 200 Viceroys and around 200 army officials representing UG in different countries of the world are present at the moment. Each representative has a patch of their country's flag on the left side of their chest.

The President said, "All of us, the representatives of the world power who have gathered here this week to listen to the first speech of the world religion, have lost the plane carrying our own hundred preachers?" He leaned forward, glaring at the room. "Did you see... how much we are being made fun of all over the world? Representatives of all countries, intelligence agencies, and army generals could not protect their own preachers!" His voice rose in anger. "Do you even have any idea how much this can increase the morale of the rebels in the whole world?"

"Mr. President!" A fifty-year-old commander of Chinese origin spoke hesitantly, standing as he addressed the leader. "Our team has found some clues that make it hard to believe this is even possible!"

The President narrowed his eyes. "What do you want to say?" he asked sharply.

The commander took a deep breath. "This work could be done by aliens," he said, almost in a whisper.

After hearing the word "aliens," the whole hall erupted into whispers, nervous murmurs filling the room.

The President's expression darkened. "What kind of aliens?" he demanded, his voice cutting through the noise.

"The same ones who attacked us three decades ago," the commander replied, his face pale.

The President frowned. "And what evidence do we have for that?" he asked skeptically.

"When the plane disappeared," the commander explained, "we checked all the signals that we received before it vanished. The way our signal was breaking—it was similar to all the recordings of plane crashes that happened during the first alien war."

The President stared at him in disbelief. "Why would they hijack a plane full of preachers?" he asked, incredulous.

"I have no idea about that," the commander admitted, shaking his head. "We have more than fifty similar recordings from the past attacks, that is the only reason my team thinks this could be the work of aliens."

"Maybe some of our enemies got their hands on the alien tech and are using that against us," suggested another commander, this one of African origin, his tone cautious.

The Chinese commander shook his head firmly. "Our spies can't be this weak. Not even one of our enemies has man-made modern weapons, how would they have any kind of alien tech and understanding of using it?"

The President sighed heavily, rubbing his temples. "I need more information about this," he said firmly. "If you are right, we will have to declare a global emergency!"

MOUNT EVEREST

All the subjects were now suspended from hangers surrounding the alien machine. A golden electric current flowed from the nails embedded in their heads, connecting each of them to the crystal atop the machine. Resting above the crystal, the spinal cord threaded with countless wires, absorbing energy directly from the crystal through numerous delicate wires extended from its lowest vertebra and channelling it into the brain at the top.

"Commander! Their energy level is too low. Only one percent of the energy we need is being replenished," an alien scientist said urgently, his eyes fixed on the energy bar visible on the screen in front of him.

Pranja said, "I already had doubts about that."

"I think we shouldn't have done it all so quickly," Anne said as she emerged from behind a machine, her voice soft but regretful. "Where we waited for so many years, if ten to fifteen years had passed, would it have been too late for us?"

Pranja frowned, irritation creeping into his voice. "I made your father the king of the whole planet in the main timeline, and yet his daughter is struggling to fulfil her father's promise."

Anne stiffened, her eyes narrowing. "I did my best to look after all these subjects," she snapped. "You just couldn't hold yourself back and came here before the given time."

Pranja's eyes blazed as he turned to her. "Someone from your government found a way to reach the main timeline and tried to warn the humans about the nuclear war."

Anne's face paled. "How can that be possible?" she asked in disbelief.

Pranja shrugged, his expression hardening. "Maybe they stole some of my assets, or someone really does have a sharp enough brain to build a time machine. Your father sent me the message to accelerate everything."

Anne bit her lip, anxiety etched on her face. "As we both expected, these subjects won't be enough to complete our task," she said, her voice laced with frustration. "Do you have another plan for that?"

"I am not a dumb human being," Pranja replied, his voice dripping with sarcasm. "Of course I have a Plan B!" He raised his voice. "Commander! Raise the army. We shall complete both our dreams simultaneously! Kill as many humans as you wish!" he ordered, his voice filled with cold determination as he turned to Alien 5.

Alien 5 grinned widely, a devilish smile stretching across his face. "Now you're speaking my language," he said, placing a proud hand on Pranja's shoulder.

Pranja smirked, stepping forward. "Soldiers…!" he roared, pressing a button on a device strapped to his left wrist. "We are going to war!"

As soon as his words echoed through the base, all the soldiers stationed in various parts of the army base stood up. Wild, frenzied cries started echoing all around the base.

THE INVASION

FEW HOURS LATER

In the remote forests, mountains, deserts, and seas across the globe, the doors of hundreds of concealed alien military bases began to open. From within, thousands of warships emerged, taking their positions in the sky like eagles poised to strike. These ships were divided into three distinct classes by size. The largest vessels were as vast as football fields, while the mid-sized ones stretched to the dimensions of a tennis court. The smallest, though still formidable, were roughly the size of a semi-truck.

All these warships first targeted villages and towns around the world, including America's Stowe, Meredith, Galena, Magnolia Springs, Deadwood, India's Hampi, Gangotri, Velankanni, Kedarnath, Auroville, Russia's Kinerma, Suzdal. , Vyatskoe, Rostov, Ples, England's Port Isaac, Bibury, Castle Combe, Polperro, Grasmere and Egypt's Sharm El-Sheikh, El-Alamein, Marsa Alam, Dahab and Abu Simbel. Apart from these specific villages and towns, alien warships began encircling hundreds of other villages and towns worldwide, casting a shadow of terror over the entire globe.

A mid-range warship launched its first strike on Port Isaac. From the weapon at its bow, a blinding white energy surged forward with lightning speed, like a relentless wave crashing over the land. In a single devastating blow, half the village was obliterated. Destruction was visible everywhere. The area struck had been reduced to rubble, with bricks shattered into hundreds of fragments. Among the blood-soaked debris, human remains lay scattered, bones, veins, and organs, gruesomely torn apart, not merely from external force but as if they had been violently ripped from within by the explosion. In the part of Port Isaac, which is safe, there was a cry among the people to save their lives. Around 8 small alien drop ships landed around the village. Three aliens from each ship came out and surrounded the whole town and started moving forward to attack the humans. The spider Machines, with their elongated bodies four feet long and two feet wide, skittered behind them on eight legs.

Tuk! Tuk! Tuk! Tuk! Tuk!

Two male and one female police officers came out of their cars and started shooting at the aliens.

Broooom!!!

An eight-foot-tall alien lunged at the police with a weapon that looked like a bazooka, scattering both the cars and the police officers standing in front like sand. The aliens then ran quickly into the houses of the village. They began searching every corner of every house, beating every man, woman, child, and elder hiding inside, without using any weapons to kill them. The screams of the victims echoed throughout the village. Those over forty years of age were repeatedly beaten by the aliens, slammed against the walls and roofs of the houses. As soon as a person became unconscious, the aliens fired a gunshot at the top of their head, inserting a three-inch long and half-inch wide probe two inches into their skull. Fine wires emerged from the probe and penetrated the human brain. Every child below the age of fifteen and every person above the age of forty was treated in the same way. After piercing the humans' skulls, the aliens stored their life energy by attaching a device six inches long and two inches wide to the top of each probe.

The spider-like machines that accompany the aliens are relentlessly hunting every man and woman between the ages of 15 and 40. These machines capture their prey and bind them to their metallic bodies. Once secured, they begin the grisly process of removing the skin with precise lasers, exposing the internal organs and veins. Delicate, thread-like wires extend from the machines, connecting to their victims' bodies, just like the larger machine stationed at Mount Everest.

The men and women with guns are shooting, but they are not having any effect on the aliens. These aliens are hitting everyone with laser guns who tries to fight them, turning their skin into a sand-like material. After that, they go to each person who has become a pile of veins and organs and store their life energy by inserting a probe into their head.

Across the globe, hundreds of villages and towns like Port Isaac were being systematically obliterated by alien warships. Young men and women were captured, skinned alive, and hung on poles besides the streets and the telecommunication towers by the spider machines. These machines drained their life energy, sending it as a golden, lightning-like thread directly to the hovering warships above each devastated village. From there, the energy was channelled to a towering, 100-metre-high alien antenna atop Mount Everest. Amidst the chaos, videos and photos of the invasion began flooding social media, unleashing a global panic. People everywhere were horrified by the images and videos of skinned humans suspended on the towers and poles, still breathing and attached to the spider machines.

UG HEADQUARTER

The President of UGHW stands behind the lectern in a white room that is twenty feet wide and thirty feet long. A camera is positioned ten feet in front of the lectern, and behind the camera are about fifteen screens, on which the reporters from various news channels are visible.

The President said, "At present, more than five hundred villages and towns across the world have been attacked by aliens. We will fight these insects till our last bullet. Our forces are ready to destroy them," he said boldly, his voice carrying a serious tone.

"Was our army completely unaware of this attack? Should we consider it a failure of our government's intelligence?" a female journalist asked from the front, her face appearing on the number one screen.

The President's gaze hardened. "This is not the time to throw mud at each other but to save the entire human race from this alien attack," he replied firmly. "I hope all of you will support us during this world emergency."

"But someone will have to take responsibility for this failure!" another journalist pressed, his voice rising with frustration.

"What do these aliens want? Are you in contact with them right now?" a third journalist interjected urgently.

"This attack seems hundreds of times bigger than the one that took place three decades ago. Will our army be able to fight them?" yet another journalist asked, sounding deeply concerned.

Seeing the President avoiding direct answers, the journalists began shouting their questions simultaneously, their voices overlapping in the room.

The President raised his hand and the room fell silent. "The guidelines we have issued for people living in every corner of the world, please broadcast them on your TV channels repeatedly as much as possible," He said with diplomatic finesse. "Keep yourselves safe. Thank you." With that, he quickly left the room, leaving behind the barrage of unanswered questions and frustrated journalists.

FARM HOUSE

Harold, Theo, Bella, Godric, and Isla got out of a big four-wheel-drive vehicle and quickly ran from one side of the farm house to the bunker at the back.

"Come on! Hurry!!" Anselm said, standing by the bunker's hatch and gesturing urgently with his hand.

They all reached the bunker and quickly got inside.

"These toys are not gonna work on them!" Godric said seriously as he entered the bunker last, speaking to the masters standing in front of him.

Gurbaksh Singh, Chodrak, Vedant and Mansoor stood nearby, holding machine guns as if preparing for war.

"What else can we have?" Harold asked Godric, a little annoyed.

"Don't we have any high-tech army weapons?" Bella asked, looking around the bunker.

Harold shook his head. "Nah! We have these machine guns only."

"The time has come," the angel whispered lovingly, hugging Godric from behind.

"How much food storage do we have?" Isla asked, her voice tight with concern.

"We have enough food to feed all of us for a year," Theo replied confidently.

"How in the world did those aliens attack us?" Godric demanded, turning angrily to Harold. "Did you guys mess up with them? Please tell me if you are still hiding something from all of us."

"I have no idea why they did that," Harold said, shaking his head. "We had a deal, and we never did anything against their will."

"Maybe they were doing all those favours for their own purposes," Theo suggested. "By being part of the government for the last three decades, no secret of our military is hidden from them. Now they know everything about our world."

Godric frowned. "It makes a lot of sense! Maybe that time branch was also a part of their plan."

"Get ready! We will all be on your side!" the angel said softly, hugging Godric's right arm.

"Why do they put that nail in the head of every human?" Bella asked, puzzled.

Harold sighed. "They can't eat anything grown or born off their planet, so they developed a technology to store the life energy of any kind of living being. Later, they use it to feed themselves and live longer without any food."

"Dad! Did you guys make any deal with them regarding this?" Theo asked, eyeing his father suspiciously.

Harold shook his head firmly. "Nah! Never! But we had to make some arrangements for them to live here."

Godric's eyes narrowed. "Did you guys feed them humans? I mean... did you arrange any human energy for them?"

Harold hesitated, then sighed. "Unfortunately, we had to use the prisoners for that."

"Oh, come on, Harold!" Gurbaksh Singh exclaimed. "Do you have any idea how powerful human life force is? They must have found it very useful to them."

Vedant, who had been listening quietly, finally spoke up. "Looks like our world has become a chicken farm for the aliens."

NEW YORK CITY, USA

The city of New York is being attacked from all sides by around forty first-class alien warships. Missiles from these warships shatter large buildings as if they were made of glass. Meanwhile, spider machines are leaping from numerous second-class alien ships hovering over downtown and landing on the rooftops of buildings.

Thousands of alien drop ships cling to the sides of buildings. Four aliens from each drop ship enter the structures and using scanning machines in front of their left eye to search for hidden humans. Once found, they brutally beat and break their victims' bones, throwing them out of the building from windows for harvesting their life energy in a merciless manner. People who have been thrown out of the buildings and those who are running for their lives on the streets are being captured by the second-class alien ships hovering over the buildings by eliminating the pull of gravity. Thousands of people can be seen floating upward everywhere in the city.

As soon as any civilian between the age of 15 to 40 approaches the roof of a building, the spider machines on the rooftops grab them with their long, rope-like advanced tech arms. Another robotic arm tears the bodies apart. After that, the spider machines connect the human remains to themselves and then hang around the edges of the buildings and stab the probes into the heads to transmit their life energy live to the Everest. All the people less than the age of 15 and over 40 are having their limbs torn apart on the spot. The machines then store their life force in energy storage devices.

Tokyo, Paris, London, Amsterdam, Beijing, İstanbul, Los Angeles, Rome, Singapore, Berlin, Chicago, Dubai, Bangkok, Barcelona, Madrid, Hong Kong, San Francisco, Antalya, Brussels, Cairo, Delhi, Mumbai, and including

Seoul, hundreds of other cities around the world have been badly tortured and destroyed by Aliens. Civilians are crying for help but there is no escape from the devils of an unknown world.

LONDON, UK

UAHW's 100 warships are approaching the city of London to eliminate the aliens.

"Target locked! Waiting for your orders, sir!" the pilot of a human warship said, his voice tense as he and his fellow pilots flew toward a massive alien warship hovering 2,000 metres above the city, surrounded by many other small alien ships.

"Fire!" the general's heavy voice commanded over the radio.

All human warships launched approximately 200 rockets at the alien ship. As the rockets entered London's airspace, they abruptly disappeared and reappeared on the opposite side of the city, continuing in the same direction. Upon impact, the rockets struck a large area adjacent to the city, destroying numerous buildings and killing many civilians who were taking refuge inside.

"What the heck was that?!" a pilot exclaimed in great surprise.

"Sir! It looks like they have a teleportation shield! We missed the target!" the pilot said urgently to the general over the radio.

The general's voice crackled through the headset. "Our ships can go inside the shield. Just enter inside and then hit them as hard as you can," he ordered firmly.

"Yes, sir!" the pilot responded with determination, gripping the controls tightly.

Now all the human warships have entered the airspace of the city to attack the alien ship from close range. However, they were immediately teleported to the far side of the city, outside the airspace. In response to UAHW's air force, hundreds of drop ships emerged from the alien ships and began attacking with laser guns while pursuing UAHW's vessels. The controls of the teleported warships ceased functioning, leaving them vulnerable as the alien ships destroyed them mid-air. The destruction was swift and relentless, like a hawk striking a flying pigeon and chopping off its neck with lethal precision.

UAHW AIRBASE

Fighter jets are taking off from the runway, and many soldiers are busy preparing the jets for the take-off. There is chaos all around.

"Sir! We are using all types of frequencies, but their pattern changes within every ten seconds, we could not destroy even one alien ship anywhere in the world." One of the air force controllers sitting in front of many computer screens in the control room, a thirty-year-old British girl, said to a very tall African general in his 60s standing on her right.

The general paced back and forth, frustration etched on his face. "First, they locked our nuclear weapons, and now we are not capable of breaking their shields. How do they...?"

"Sir! The president is on the call," a middle-aged man of Arab origin interrupted, handing the phone to the general.

The general grabbed the phone, putting it to his ear. "Yes, Sir?" he answered briskly.

"I just got word that we have lost more than 1000 warships and 10,000 jets all around the world within an hour!" the president's worried voice crackled over the line. "Their teleportation shield is beyond our understanding! Please stop your men from fighting in all the cities around the world. We need a solid solution before the next attack!"

The general, ignoring the president's plea, looked at the radar screen in front of him, his expression tightening. "Mr. President, some of the giant alien ships are heading towards the headquarters," he said, his voice filled with concern.

Twelve large dots were seen on the screen, moving rapidly towards the UG headquarters from three directions.

"What?" the president gasped in shock.

"Please lock yourself and all other officials inside the bunker!" The general speaks very seriously, with a very worried expression on his face. "I am sending the maximum air force to protect you."

"Oh God," the president whispered, his voice trembling. "May the judgement day have come upon us!"

SYDNEY, AUSTRALIA

Including thousands over the edges of the buildings and from poles throughout the CBD, approximately 2000 people have been hung by the spider machines on both sides of the Harbor bridge. Two ships hovering in the air on both sides of the bridge and hundreds of other ships over the city are drawing energy from all these people and transmitting it to Mount Everest.

In addition to the thousands of alien warships already present on Earth, the main alien army is now landing in various locations around the globe. More than 500 thousand alien ships fill the skies, creating an ominous presence over the entire planet. No major city remains untouched by the alien onslaught. To harvest life energy, the bodies of hundreds of thousands of people have been skinned and displayed on the edges of the buildings, along electricity poles, network towers, and bridges. Within a few hours, the world has plunged into complete lockdown. The alien forces, numbering in the millions, are invading residential areas, killing humans indiscriminately, and collecting their life energy as if they were insects.

MOUNT EVEREST

"The energy level has now increased to eighty per cent, but despite the fact that we have received the energy of 160,000 more people in the last hour, this energy is not increasing at all," said one of the old alien scientists sitting next to Anne.

Pranja folded his arms, his tone firm. "How many humans in total are we using right now?"

The scientist glanced at the data on his screen. "More than eight hundred thousand from all over the planet," he reported.

Pranja's eyes narrowed. "Our king is about to arrive! Our work should have been done by now," he snapped.

Anne turned to a seven-foot-tall alien commander with an ugly, imposing face standing next to Pranja. Pointing at the subjects of the world religion hanging around the machine, she commanded, "Commander! Find their masters! Maybe they can give us the best solutions. I need all five of those old monks alive and with their full flesh."

Pranja nodded in agreement. "Just do as she said," he ordered.

The alien commander grinned wickedly. "Don't worry, Commander! Soon they will be at your feet!" he said confidently.

Pranja waved him off impatiently. "Go now! I need them within five hours." he demanded.

The commander bowed slightly, his arrogance evident. "You shall have them even before that," he replied, his voice dripping with confidence.

Anne's expression softened as she turned back to Pranja. "I need to see my father," she said, almost pleading. "Please tell your men to take me to the main timeline. It's been a while since I last met him."

Pranja sighed, his tone shifting to one of appeasement. "Oh, come on, just wait a few days. I really need you here. Once we're done with our work, you'll be free to go anywhere, future queen of the human world!" he added with a smile, his voice taking on a buttering tone.

Anne crossed her arms, frowning. "Not more than three days," she insisted.

Pranja smiled, raising his hand in assurance. "No worries! You have my word," he promised.

BUNKER

All the masters are seated around the table, engaged in serious discussion. With his back against the wall, Godric watches videos on his laptop, depicting the oppression of humans by the aliens. Meanwhile, Harold and Theo stand in front of Bella and Isla, who are in the nearby kitchen.

"Why can't we escape through the time machine?" Bella asked Theo.

Theo narrowed his eyes slightly, suspicion creeping into his voice. "Who told you about the time machine?"

Bella smiled coolly. "Your daughter-in-law told me! And I am happy to see my son is obeying his vows. You hid it from me, that's totally fine according to your so-called protocol, but now there is no protocol outside this bunker. So please answer me. I don't want to waste our time."

Theo glanced sharply at Isla. "Isla! Did Godric really tell you about that machine? I think.."

Harold cut him off abruptly. "Yes! We can use the time machine, but that bunker is far from here," he said, his voice firm.

Bella's eyes flicked from Harold to Theo. "Then we shall go to wherever it's hidden from the world! Am I right, Father?" She asked, directing her question to Harold with a sharp glance at Theo.

Isla hesitated, then spoke up gently. "Sorry to interrupt my elders, but I think this is not the best time to fall out with each other."

Theo sighed, his tone softening. "I won't fall out with anyone here," he said calmly. "But people must understand the difference between obeying the vows of marriage and the vows we have with others." He turned to Isla, then glanced at Bella with a respectful expression.

Harold cleared his throat and nodded subtly towards the door. "Isla! I think we both should talk outside," he said quietly, his eyes signalling for her to slip away.

Isla caught the hint and nodded. "Okay! Let's go. I need a word with my dearest husband as well," she said lightly, speaking like a sensible child, pretending to understand the gesture without showing any emotion.

Both Harold and Isla hurried out of the kitchen. After they left, the sound of clattering crockery echoed from the kitchen, followed by Bella's loud but muffled voice, shouting angrily at Theo.

From across the room, Godric suddenly called out. "Masters! Come here and look at this!" he said excitedly, eyes fixed on his laptop as he beckoned the others over.

Godric placed the laptop on the table in front of the masters. Harold and Isla joined and stood behind them. On the laptop screen, a drone-captured video played, showing hundreds of skinned and hung bodies scattered across the Eiffel Tower. The life energy from these victims was being transmitted to the alien warship hovering above the tower.

Mansoor shook his head in disgust. "These creatures are very cruel. They have no humanity."

Chodrak raised an eyebrow. "They should have some alienality."

Mansoor looked puzzled. "Is that a word?"

Chodrak smirked. "Like a human needs humanity, an alien needs alienality."

Isla spoke nervously, her eyes wide as she watched the people hanging in the video. "Are they all alive?"

Anselm turned to Harold, concern etched on his face. "Harold! Do you have any idea about this? What are they doing to them?"

Harold shook his head, frowning. "I don't know. Normally, they just put that nail in the head and absorb the life energy. I've never seen them doing this to any prisoner."

Godric pointed to the laptop screen, his expression grim. "Look at these videos. They're doing this all over the world. Every human who is hanging is alive, and there are ships hovering over every group. I think these aliens are using our planet like a life energy grid."

Vedant gasped. "Oh God! If this is true, then these devils will never leave our planet."

Gurbaksh Singh sighed heavily. "We can't stay inside this bunker forever. We need to find a permanent solution as soon as possible."

Isla spoke up, determination in her voice. "That's why we need to go to the other side of the city. The time machine is the only solution to save us."

"Who told you about that machine?" All the masters spoke in unison, their voices filled with surprise.

Godric, standing next to Isla, glanced at her nervously, like a mischievous child caught in a lie.

Isla stammered, blushing. "Um… the vows! My marriage… I mean, the vows that my husband and I exchanged on our wedding day… that made him tell me about… everything! I know the machine is in the bunker behind the farmhouse of our ex-army chief."

Chodrak threw his hands in the air, astonished. "So you just told her everything? Even the exact location?"

All the masters looked at Godric in disbelief.

Godric shrugged defensively. "What's wrong with that?"

Gurbaksh Singh shook his head. "Leave it, masters. This is not the time to teach him."

Harold raised a hand to calm the group. "Guys, guys! Let me explain it to her." He turned to Isla kindly. "Dear, it's impossible for us to cross the city. These aliens aren't going to let us go anywhere. And even if we succeed, we can't stay in the past forever."

Godric stepped forward, his voice defiant. "What if we cross the city and go into the past, not to live forever, but to stop you from making any deal with these aliens?"

Harold looked at him sternly. "Then you'd end the world even earlier! Do you really think these aliens just landed with hundreds of warships a few days ago? They've been coming and going for centuries. But… I still don't understand why they waited so long for this day." He scratched his head, confused. "They could have done this decades ago."

Godric's eyes lit up. "Population! Maybe they needed more population for their plan. Now our population has almost doubled since the first contact with them."

Isla nodded thoughtfully. "Yeah, that could be the reason."

UG HEADQUARTER

Approximately 1,000 large alien warships have encircled the UG headquarters, establishing a perimeter of 3 kilometres from all sides. An army of 500,000 aliens stands ready at a distance of 1 kilometre from the headquarters' main gate. Outside the gate, 300,000 human soldiers and 100,000 heavily armoured fighter robots, each about 7 feet tall, are prepared to engage in battle. On top of the walls and at the main building's doors, around 100,000 human soldiers are stationed. Despite the presence of modern tanks and guns, the alien machinery vastly outmatches UAHW's capabilities. Human warships patrol around the headquarters, and hundreds of guns mounted on the walls are aimed on the alien vessels.

"General! What are they waiting for?" spoke on the radio, looking at the live video of the battlefield on the front table in the hall inside the bunker under the HQ.

"I have no idea, Mr. President, maybe they are waiting for more enforcement!" the general answered on the radio.

The President did not say anything further and tried to calm his nervousness by taking a long breath.

"What is that?" A soldier standing on the wall of the HQ said to his comrade, watching the commotion in the clouds above.

Now many more soldiers started looking up, their faces reflecting growing fear. A 3000 metre long and 1000 metre wide triangular shaped golden and black giant alien war ship is slowly descending beyond the clouds.

"How did our radars miss such a mountain-sized ship?" said an old man of British origin while watching the video of the ship on the screen in the control room of the HQ.

Zeh REE dee ah!!

Zeh REE dee ah!!

Zeh REE dee ah!!

Zeh REE dee ah!!

A haunting, ethereal war cry that chills the blood starts echoing around the battlefield.

All the Aliens are shouting war while shaking their right and left punches enthusiastically.

The king of Aliens, about 8 feet tall, sits inside the golden ship hovering near the clouds above the HQ. A very beautiful crown full of shining stones made with a combination of golden and black colours is placed on his head. There is a wide 20×20 metre wide hologram of many planets on the left side of the king. Each planet revolves on its path along with its duplicate planet, and some alien numbers are also visible along with each planet. The king is standing on a 50×50 metre wide transparent floor through which he can see the battlefield with his eagle eyes.

"My king! Do we really need to waste our time on this? Why don't you just kill them all in one shot." Standing beside the king, a six-foot-tall, thin, old alien advisor spoke.

The King replies, "Nothing is more intoxicating than seeing the soul of my enemies trembling in front of my warriors. When melodic cries full of pain echo through the battlefield, then, and only then, I feel the piece of victory."

Zeh REE dee ah!!

Zeh REE dee ah!!

Aliens are leaving cheers in full swing. Looking at them, it does not seem that there will be any fear of war within them.

King's ship started the war with a huge siren.

Aliens waved their heavy swords in the air and started running towards the HQ to attack. Their heavy bodies are shaking the earth like an earthquake. It seems as if the long-hungry lion hardly found any prey.

Meanwhile, the soldier robots in the front rows surged forward aggressively to counterattack the aliens. Behind them, human soldiers stood ready to roar in the battlefield, clutching their weapons tightly.

The alien King watches with satisfaction as the aliens and robots charge towards each other like bulls. In stark contrast, the President of UGHW is gripped by panic. The robots, armed with laser guns, are attacking the advancing alien army from the front, but the lasers seem ineffective against the aliens. The aliens continue their advance, seemingly unconcerned and not returning fire.

Alien King spoke very arrogantly to the aliens standing next to him, "Ha ha ha ha! Do they really think they can kill us with the tech that we donated to these crippled mind lowborn creatures?"

President, looking at the screen, said aloud, "Oh God! Help us."

As the warriors on both sides closed in, they collided with immense force. The aliens scattered the robots like shards of glass in this initial clash. Instead of attacking with any gun, the aliens used the swords, spears, and axes, which are very big, just like the aliens. The robots' limbs were shattered and twisted by the aliens as if they were empty tin cans. Heads and the severed legs of the robots were seen flying through the air. Within five minutes, the aliens had reduced the robots to a pile of debris. They then climbed atop this wreckage and began challenging the soldiers stationed at the gates of the HQ walls.

Instead of moving forward, the Human Army started pushing each other back. The fear can be smelled in the bones of the whole human army. Aliens have started moving towards the HQ, which is in full swing for the attack. The guns mounted on the walls of the HQ and the warships of the Human Army fired thousands of rockets at the Aliens, but all the rockets were destroyed by the alien ships in the air. Along with this, the Alien warships simultaneously destroyed all the human warships with a joint attack and their debris was scattered inside the walls of the HQ. The soldiers outside the HQ are shivering like lambs, but there is no way out except to fight to save themselves. Aliens approached them like hungry wolves and kicked the first row of the human army like a football. The already scared human soldiers tried their best to fight back and opened fire, but they could not escape from the wrath of bloodthirsty aliens. These giants are hunting the entire army as if a wolf has entered the chicken coop. In just ten minutes, they tore the bodies of all the human soldiers like envelopes and scattered them all around. The legs, arms and head are separated from each soldier's body. Many aliens even put their legs on the soldiers' chests and separated their heads from their torsos like farmers digging carrots out of the ground.

King speaks excitedly to the advisor standing beside him, "See! Did you see that? Where can we have such an entertainment? This is what I want to see!"

"I am glad to see you happy after a very long time, my lord! Soon, this whole planet will produce an unlimited life force for our whole army!" The alien standing by spoke.

Now, the alien army faced the walls of the HQ and began forming a ladder, climbing on each other's shoulders. In their fear, many soldiers leaped inside the HQ for safety. The aliens constructed the makeshift ladder with lightning speed and swiftly scaled the walls. Within minutes, they tore through the entire human force stationed on top, roaring like lions.

"Don't worry, Mr. President! They can't enter the bunker!" said a viceroy of English descent standing next to the President.

At this time, in the hall built in the bunker below the HQ, all the representatives are standing in a group with the president and watching the war situation on a huge cinema screen in front.

All the alien warships had now gathered near the walls of the HQ. The human soldiers stationed at the main doors of the building panicked and fled inside after seeing the horde of hundreds of thousands of aliens cross over the wall and charging towards them. Along with the staff and civilians already taking refuge, they hid wherever they could find space, desperately seeking safety from the impending attack.

Now, suddenly, the buzz of aliens stopped from all around. From the bunker to the top floor inside the HQ, this time is looking worse than a nightmare for all the humans present.

After some time, many alien ships came near the main building and landed on the ground. Thousands of spider machines came out of them, and they started digging into the foundations of the headquarters. These machines started crawling around the foundation of the entire building like worms, and soon, the foundations of the bunker under the HQ were also hollowed out. Meanwhile, all the pillars used to strengthen the HQ have been cut by spider machines with the help of lasers. After excavation, the spider machines took out thousands of devices of a specific type of one-foot size from inside their bellies and installed them all around the foundation of the HQ. Even from the bottom of the building, soil has been removed from many places, and devices have been fitted.

The King's warship hovering over the HQ now started descending towards the main building and slowly came down. It stopped at four times the height of the building.

The souls of the people and soldiers hidden inside are trembling. Some women have even fainted due to fear. The president and all the other representatives present in the bunker are looking full of anxiety.

The president looked around in shock. "What is happening? Are we dead?" he asked in surprise, feeling weightless.

Every person inside the bunker seems lightened like a flower and does not feel the gravity at all.

"My feet are not touching the ground! What are they doing to us?" a viceroy of Arab origin shouted loudly in panic.

The huge cargo hatch of the king's ship hovering above the HQ opened. A dim light came out of it and spread like the first rays of the sun on the entire building of the HQ.

Now, the HQ has left its grip on the earth and slowly started rising, and every person inside it cannot feel gravity. Along with humans, computers, tables, chairs, pens, printers, etc. They are all flying in the air.

Zeh REE dee ah!!

Zeh REE dee ah!!

Zeh REE dee ah!!

Zeh REE dee ah!!

Seeing the multi-storied building of the HQ moving upward in the air, the Alien army started shouting loudly.

In five minutes, the entire building, along with its foundation, rose out of the ground, to a height of 1000 metres, floating between the alien ship and the ground. The spider machines were crawling around its walls like flies on molasses.

The King's warship shifted the entire HQ building southward, away from its foundation pit, and began lowering it slowly into the midst of the alien army. Once the ship placed the HQ on the ground, the spider machines drilled into the underground walls and the alien forces climbed up the building. Including spider machines, hundreds of aliens poured in through the holes and thousands more aliens broke through the doors and windows of the upper floors, resuming their relentless hunt.

FARM HOUSE – BUNKER

"Boom.!!!" A strong wave of energy vibrated the entire bunker and shocked everyone inside.

Vedant looked around in confusion. "Is that an explosion?" he asked, his voice tense.

Harold shook his head. "It's not an explosion, it's a lightning strike from an alien warship," he replied.

Theo rushed towards the group, his face pale with urgency. "Hey guys! We need to go to the bottom. I think there's a war going on outside the bunker," he said hurriedly.

Bella is also behind him.

Godric said, "Let's go, masters!"

Now, all these people started descending towards the lower floor of the bunker through the stairs built in a corner.

An alien ship the size of a football field is flying over the bunker, and due to its attack, the farmhouse has been scattered far and wide.

"Let's dig them up! But no one should get hurt!" Said the alien commander while seeing Godric and his fellows descend the stairs on a screen of a scanner inside the ship.

As soon as the Commander's signal was received, about 50 drop ships came out of the Alien ship and landed around the hatch of the bunker. Many spider machines came out of these drop ships along with the aliens.

"Make sure you get the whole bunker!" The alien commander put the radio on his left arm near his mouth and said to his companions.

As soon as they heard the Commander's words, all the spider machines started digging into the ground.

Inside the bunker, Godric is present on the lowest floor with his companions, and all these people have no idea what is happening outside.

The spider machines very quickly removed all the soil around the four walls to a width of four feet. They also removed the soil from many places under the bunker and installed many anti-gravity devices around the whole structure.

The alien ship hovering over the Bunker started pulling the four-story bunker up with its anti-gravity power just like the HQ, and as soon as the Bunker slid up a little, the knees of all the people on its lower floor bent down a little, and they felt a slight jolt as if they were in an elevator.

Bella gasped, "Oh my God! Are we flying?"

Everyone's feet have now risen above the floor.

Harold's eyes widened in panic. "Oh God, they have found us!"

Theo looked around in alarm. "Are they pulling this bunker out?"

"This is the time, my love! Get ready for the war," Angel whispered into Godric's ear.

The aliens standing outside cheered with glee as they watched the four-story bunker rise from the ground and move towards the ship. They crowed like animals, revelling in the sight.

"Let's pick up our guns!" Gurbaksh Singh shouted, floating towards the stairs.

Anselm nodded in agreement. "Let's go!"

Harold's voice was filled with regret. "Sorry, guys! My friends and I made a huge mistake!"

Mansoor, his tone grim, replied, "If sorry could fix every mistake, then Allah would have had no need to create hell."

"Shut up!" Harold snapped back.

Godric addressed Bella and Isla, his voice firm but caring. "Mom! Isla! You both stay here. No matter what happens, do not come out."

Bella and Isla, floating nervously in the air, hugged each other tightly.

Isla's voice trembled. "Are they going to kill all of us?"

Godric gently kissed Isla's forehead. "They can't touch any of you as long as I am alive."

The bunker floated slowly, entering the ship through the cargo hatch. The hatch closed behind it with a heavy clang.

The commander turned to a large spider machine behind him and ordered, "Cut the bunker piece by piece."

The Alien Commander is standing on a high deck near the bunker, and around 100 aliens are standing around the bunker with many spider machines.

The spider machine said something in alien language to other spider machines, and all these machines started cutting the uppermost floor of the bunker with the help of lasers.

Harold stood with a gun in his hand, his voice brimming with excitement. "Get ready!" he shouted.

Godric, standing at attention, responded, "Yes, sir!"

On the top floor inside the Bunker, Godric and others with guns in their hands standing in a circle. Everyone is looking around with sharp eyes.

Alien machines started cutting the top floor from the centre in one direction from all sides. All the walls inside the bunker are showing rapid cracks. The machines cut the upper floor in a couple of minutes, and a crane placed inside the ship caught half of the upper floor of the bunker in its claws from all sides and started lifting it.

As soon as the crane lifted the severed section of the bunker, the upper floor was found empty. The crane set the removed section aside, and the spider machines immediately began cutting through the remaining floors. One by one, the crane lifted the top three floors and placed them aside. When it reached the fourth floor, Godric, Harold, and the masters opened fire in every direction. Isla and Bella stood between them, nervously covering their ears.

"Ha ha ha ha ha ha ha ha ha!" the demonic laughter of the aliens began to echo around.

The bullets hit the aliens' bodies but shattered like glass upon impact, leaving the aliens completely unharmed. Amid the continuous gunfire, the crane lifted the remaining half of the fourth floor and placed it aside with the other three floors of the bunker.

The Commander looked around at the chaos and said, "Come on, masters! Your guns can't save your ass," he joked, observing the firing all around.

Godric and the others had run out of bullets, and Gurbaksh Singh had drawn his Kirpan (sword), while the others brandished their pistols. Yet, no one fired a single shot.

The Commander addressed them again, his tone more serious. "Masters! You have no need to fight with us. We are here to take you safely with us without any harm."

Harold, eyes wide with concern, demanded, "What do you want from us?"

The Commander grinned, his gaze fixed on Harold. "Hello, my friend Harold! I still remember that excitement in your eyes when you agreed to build a government for the whole world, a vision that led to the deaths of thousands of your own people. But today, I don't need anything from you, old bitch! I need only these five masters of your World Religion."

Harold's face flushed with embarrassment upon hearing the Commander's words.

Godric stepped forward, his voice trembling with anger. "What do you want from my masters?"

The Commander replied, "One of my crazy friends would like to have a word with them."

Mansoor's confusion was evident as he asked, "Why? Why would an alien want to speak with five old men?"

The Commander's smile widened. "Because you have something important that he wants. I would have killed all of you on the spot with one shot if you weren't so important to us."

Gurbaksh Singh spoke firmly, "I will go with you, but you will have to leave this family behind."

The Commander shook his head. "They will all have to remain under my custody until you five masters fulfil your task."

Anselm interjected, "No! We can't go with you like that! You will have to leave them in a safe place without any custody. None of you should come close to them."

At that moment, the spider machine standing next to the Commander whispered something in his ear, which elicited an evil smile from him.

Vedant, holding a pistol to his jaw, declared, "Leave them, or we will kill ourselves!"

The Commander held up his hand, signalling for silence. "Stop! You have a deal! I won't kill them or harm them in any way. But I need that young man too."

Harold's voice was filled with desperation as he said, "No! You can't take my grandson! I offer you myself instead. You can kill me right now if you want."

The Commander's eyes narrowed. "Then get ready to die!"

All the aliens aimed their guns at them. Just as the aliens prepared to fire, Godric's angel suddenly appeared, positioning herself in front of him. Her eyes blazed like lightning, and her entire body glowed with a spiritual white light, radiant as a full moon. Her fangs, sharp as knives, extended six feet on either side.

Wait!" Godric said urgently. "I will go with you. But don't touch my family."

"No!" Isla cried, her voice trembling. "You can't leave us. They will kill you."

"If he doesn't," the Commander growled, "then I will kill each one of you right now."

"Don't worry, Angel," Godric said soothingly, looking at Isla. "Just calm down. I need to save them all."

"These aliens are going to kill all of us," Harold said with desperation. "Don't make any deals with them."

"If they're going to kill all of us," Mansoor replied, his tone slightly irritated, "then why shouldn't we try this deal? We are the masters of World Religion; they would really need us for something important." He turned to Harold as he spoke.

"We accept it!" Gurbaksh Singh said it decisively. "But you will have to drop this family close to another bunker! That's on the other side of the city!"

"Show us the way," the Commander instructed. "We will do as you wish."

"We will surrender ourselves after you drop them safely," Vedant said, speaking through a pistol held at his earlobe.

"We shall do whatever you devils want!" Chodrak said vehemently. "But don't you dare lay a finger on this family!"

"I will release them as you wish, masters!" the Commander promised. "You have my word! But don't try to be too clever. Otherwise, I'm going to hang you all like the other worms all around the globe!"

Isla and Bella both had tears in their eyes. Isla was holding Godric's arm very tightly, while Bella and Theo held each other's hands. All the masters and Harold looked around in disappointment, unable to find a way to rid themselves of the aliens.

UGHW HEADQUARTER

After tearing the bodies of the President, Army commanders and all the viceroys, they were hanged outside all around the main walls of the HQ by installing live life energy transmitter machines. Thousands of ordinary people and soldiers had been strung up like their leaders, hanging from the main building from the ground level to the top. Their life energy was being siphoned away by three alien ships, hovering 1000 metres above the ground between the main walls and the main building. The Alien King stood triumphantly atop the HQ, arms raised high in the air, proudly claiming his victory over the Human World.

Zeh REE dee ah!!

Zeh REE dee ah!!

Zeh REE dee ah!!

Zeh REE dee ah!!

Outside the HQ, hundreds of thousands of aliens are facing their king, waving swords, spears and axes in the air, cheering loudly.

About 40% of the cities and villages of the entire Earth have been badly destroyed by Aliens. UAHW has been defeated everywhere. There is hardly any place left on the entire planet where they have not oppressed humans. Millions of people are being enslaved by aliens and can be seen chained up around many alien camps near the big cities. Everything that happened at the HQ is being broadcast by the aliens on every single mobile phone and TV channel on the whole planet, as well as on the billboards everywhere.

TEN DAYS AGO – MAIN TIMELINE 2026

In an opulent modern palace perched on a mountain, Oscar stood in a spacious room adorned with beautifully painted walls. In his hand, he held a locket, his gaze fixed on a hologram displaying the main timeline and its parallel time branch moving forward. The year 1976 was visible on the time branch, while 2026 appeared on the main timeline. Behind Oscar's left shoulder stood Anne, dressed elegantly like a princess.

Oscar spoke solemnly as he hung the locket around Anne's neck. "When all the aliens have landed on Earth along with their king, press the diamond on this locket five times. With this, the virus will spread through all the systems. You will then have five full hours to come back."

Anne looked at him, her brow furrowed. "But what if Pranja's machine works before the five hours are up?"

Oscar shook his head reassuringly. "What he hasn't found in thousands of years, where will he find it so soon? You just need to wait for the entire alien army to land on Earth, and then press the button five times."

Anne's voice was laced with concern. "By any chance, if his machine works after his king's arrival and he gets all the frequencies of the universe that he dreamed of, what will we do then?"

Oscar's expression remained calm. "Just press the button and come back to me!" he said firmly.

Anne's voice wavered slightly. "Father! Don't you know how powerful a person can be after opening the tenth gate?"

Oscar reassured her with a confident smile. "He won't be able to find people with that much energy in such a short time frame. You're just overthinking this. Now go back to your time branch, and I will wait for the future queen of this whole planet with the crown in my hands."

PRESENT TIME BRANCH - MOUNT EVEREST

Godric and his five masters were imprisoned in chambers built into the wall. Their eyes burned with fury as they gazed at the bodies hanging on the machines before them, yet they remained silent, their mouths sealed by silencers. Just a short distance away, Pranja and Anne, along with other alien scientists, observed a hologram of Godric's energy projected by the large spider machine. Surrounded by aliens inside the bunker aboard the alien ship, the holographic image revealed the power within Godric's body. He was enveloped in a golden aura, glowing from head to toe.

Pranja looked at the hologram with a triumphant smile. "Yes! Finally, I found what I was waiting for. Why didn't you tell me about him before?" he asked Anne.

Anne's face was filled with great consternation and surprise. "I had no idea about his power. He never discussed any of this with me," she said, her voice tinged with distress.

Pranja's gaze turned intense. "I need to know if you are telling me the truth, my love!"

Anne's tone grew a bit irritated. "What do you mean? Do you really think I can betray you?" she asked, her eyes flashing with annoyance.

"I just need a small test!" Pranja declared.

Suddenly, the spider machine standing next to Pranja grabbed Anne and restrained her, wrapping numerous wires around her head, heart, and various other parts of her body.

Anne cried out, "Stop! Are you going mad?"

Pranja's expression remained cold. "Now tell me if you knew anything about that man's power."

"I didn't know anything about his powers!" Anne protested, her voice laced with a pretence of great fear and panic.

Pranja turned to the machine. "Is she telling the truth?" he asked.

The machine released Anne from its embrace.

Anne kicked the machine in frustration. "I will talk to my father about this!" she said, clearly annoyed.

Pranja smirked, his voice full of satisfaction. "Thanks for your loyalty! I have been searching for a being this powerful for thousands of years. Ha ha ha ha… Finally, I found him! You and your masters are more than enough for me to attain an artificial moksha!" He gestured triumphantly towards Godric and the masters.

In her mind, Anne thought, "Oh! Father! You were so wrong!" She looked at the machine absorbing life energy from the entire world.

AWAKENING

THE BUNKER

Aldous, one scientist, Theo, Isla and Harold are standing in front of the time machine. All of them are facing Bella, who is looking at them in full anger and disappointment.

Harold said, "Listen! No one had any intention to hurt you or disrespect you. Even Godric insisted on telling you the whole thing."

Isla, shedding tears, replied, "Mother! None of us wanted to create any situation after knowing the truth. A mother's love is always above all for her children. Godric was too invested in his mission."

Bella, with a mix of frustration and urgency, asked, "As you all are experts in science, spirituality, religion, politics, and tricks, now tell me how we can save them. Do your sharp minds work in real-life situations or not?"

Theo intervened, his tone firm, "Bella! This is not the time to yell at anyone. All of us were bound to our duty."

Bella's voice rose with distress. "What kind of duty puts your own son in danger? So much happened right under my nose and I don't even know one percent of that! My son went to the past! He is cursed! The person who killed him in last four lives is his own grandfather in this life! Really?"

A scientist spoke up, "Ma'am! Your love for him and your anger towards us are understandable, but your son is very stubborn. He made a deal with us, so we had to help him with this whole thing."

Bella turned to the scientist, her frustration palpable. "Alright, sir! Now tell me, what solution do you have to save my son and his masters?"

The scientist was at a loss for words.

Aldous, speaking with empathy, said, "Look, I lost my own son as well. I can understand your pain, but all the people here also care about your son. We are just running out of ideas. Those creatures are just too clever and powerful. I am so sorry, but..."

Bella interjected, her voice determined, "I have an idea."

Harold asked, "May we know what kind of idea you have?"

Bella replied confidently, "Never underestimate the power of a God-fearing woman. Now listen to what I am going to teach you all, over-smart, modern, and Godless humans."

ONE HOUR LATER

MAIN TIMELINE – WWII 1945

Harold, Isla, and Aldous emerged from a wormhole, tumbling to the ground like soldiers amidst a dense forest. Aldous lay in the centre, Isla to his left, and Harold to his right. All three were clad in British WWII military uniforms. Harold and Aldous gripped rifles, while Isla held a tear gas launcher. The distant roar of gunfire, the hum of planes cutting through the air, and the booming echoes of bomb explosions filled the atmosphere, heightening the tension and creating an overwhelming sense of fear.

Isla frowned at Harold. "If you could not have shot yourself in the leg at the perfect timing, will we have to shoot you direct in the chest?"

Harold's eyes were filled with despair. "I live or die, it doesn't matter anymore! The curse has already shown its colours again."

Isla looked at him, puzzled. "But how?"

Harold gestured vaguely. "Couldn't you see that? My deal with the aliens, my five percent stake in The Great World Religion, my farmhouse, my bunker! All of that leads death closer to my very own grandchild again, even without any intention."

Isla stepped closer, trying to comfort him. "Don't worry, Grandpa! That curse is not your fault. I know how much love you have for Godric."

Harold shook his head in frustration. "Even after trying so hard, we are still at the edge of the end. Maybe if we had never met those aliens, neither they would have shown us the end of our world, nor would we have listened to any of their nonsense."

Aldous interjected firmly. "Come on, Harold! This is not the time to think about all of that."

Isla turned to Harold with urgency. "Grandpa! Why didn't you give me the real video of that nuclear destruction?"

Harold's expression was defensive. "That was the real one! Real like that Harold in the battlefield!"

Isla shook her head. "No! That wasn't real! Even Godric tested it in the lab, and it looked like movie scenes with very high-tech cameras and graphics!"

Harold's face turned serious. "No! That was the real video! I swear to God! That was the original one!"

Isla was frustrated. "Did you ever test it?"

Harold called out. "Hey, Chief! Did we test that video?"

Aldous shrugged. "Nah! I think the excitement of the moment clouded our rational thinking."

Isla glared at them, her voice trembling with frustration. "Again? Even at a time when the whole world is about to end, you guys are trying to hide things from me. Why do you still need to hide that video? You know! You're all just full of lies! Now I don't know who I should listen to!"

Harold shook his head, his expression serious. "Why would we hide that from you? I have no reason to lie about it."

Isla's eyes narrowed. "I am one hundred percent sure you're hiding something. And why not? The people who can lie to the whole world about the first alien attack—how can they be serious about just one girl?"

Harold's face grew more intense. "Once your very own husband said to me... a truth and a lie are not about the words; it's about your intention! If your intention is negative, then a true word becomes a lie. But if your intention is positive, then a word that seems like a lie is actually the truth. So whatever we say to the world, don't focus on our words, look at our intentions!"

Isla's frustration grew. "Nah! You guys didn't watch your steps, and now my husband is in danger because of you both."

Harold's tone hardened. "No! He is in danger because he killed Baby Harold to get involved with someone's wife thirteen centuries ago. Yes, I made a mistake, but it's all happening because of the curse."

Isla raised an eyebrow, her face reflecting naïve curiosity. "Was she beautiful?"

Harold's eyes widened in disbelief. "Really? He was cheating on you with that girl centuries ago, and you're just measuring her beauty?"

Isla shrugged. "That was his past life. What do I have to do with that?"

Aldous, clearly annoyed, cut in. "Can you both shut up, please?"

Hearing the army chief's words, both Harold and Isla stopped arguing and turned their attention to the front line.

Harold leaned towards Aldous, his elbows resting on his left side. "We need to get closer; that idiot is about to leave the fortification very soon!"

Isla looked at Harold, her voice filled with concern. "If you couldn't save him from the other one, will we be able to come back and try again?"

Aldous nodded firmly. "Yes! And we shall try again and again!"

Harold glanced through the telescope with urgency in his voice. "He's leaving; let's move closer!"

About 100 metres in front, Zoraver is coming out of the front. These three got up quickly and came to a distance of 50 metres from the front line. All the soldiers are marching out of the front towards the enemy but Zoraver is walking quickly back from the front.

Isla, observing Zoraver's mysterious expressions, said, "He's not running away from the war. It looks like he's really seeing something, like he's chasing someone."

Harold, focused on aiming his gun at his past self, instructed Aldous, "Focus on me over there. I am about to shoot him. When you see me looking back at Zoraver, just shoot me in the legs."

Aldous, watching Harold through the scope of his gun as he advanced with the soldiers, replied with a grin, "Oh man! I am about to tear at least one of your knees today."

Harold looked back, shouted at Zoraver, and started moving forward, firing at the enemy.

Isla's focus is on Zoraver. He stopped a short distance away, drew his rifle forward and fired. Now, Zoraver is being walked forward again, but his gestures are pointing to an inner sense rather than an external meaning.

On the other hand, the past Harold's attention turned to Zoraver again. He pointed his gun at Zoraver and put his finger on the trigger.

Thak!

Thak!

Both Aldous and Harold shot Harold's legs simultaneously.

AAAHHH!! Harold let out a pained sound and fell to the ground.

Isla fired three rounds of tear gas at Harold. Two soldiers quickly restrained him, while the rest continued firing at the enemy ahead. As the two soldiers turned their attention to Isla and fired at her, she swiftly dodged the shots. Harold and Aldous then reacted, swiftly shooting both soldiers in the chest, killing them instantly.

On the other hand, Zoraver took a few steps forward and stopped. Both his hands were joined, and his feet lifted off the ground for three feet. Time stopped, and suddenly, all around, silence, like a cemetery, spread everywhere. Even the leaves of the trees stopped moving, and the bodies of all the soldiers fighting the war stuck to the ground. The guns, the bullets coming out of the barrels and the planes fighting in the sky above, everything has stopped moving at once. Everyone is trying to move from their place, but they can't even move for an inch. Even the bullets can be seen freezing in the air. Fighter pilots are also surprised to see their frozen aircraft and their shells.

Isla's eyes widened in amazement. "Wow! He is flying!"

Harold glanced up at the sky, where Zoraver was hovering three feet above the ground. "Hopefully, there is no alien ship up there," he said, his tone cautious.

Aldous, breathing heavily and speaking in a drunken manner, sniffed the air. "What kind of fragrance is this? It smells like flowers I've never encountered in my whole life."

Isla nodded, her expression serious. "Godric told me about this smell. We are not alone right now! Angels and gods have arrived here to see him achieve moksha."

The warzone was now filled with the fragrance like flowers instead of the stench of ammunition.

Harold looked around, puzzled. "What will happen next?"

"He is becoming the whole," Isla replied cryptically.

Aldous frowned. "What do you mean?"

Isla explained patiently, "A drop is merging with the sea."

Harold scratched his head. "Did Godric tell you anything in simpler terms about this?"

Isla smiled slightly. "If you ask a drop of water what it is, it would say, 'I am a drop of water!' But if that drop merges with the sea, will it still be just a drop of water?"

Harold thought for a moment. "No! It will become the sea."

Isla's eyes sparkled with satisfaction. "Yeah! You got the answer!"

Zoraver's face radiated with a spiritual light, and his brows lifted as if under the spell of divine intoxication. His body felt numb, as if life were ebbing from his extremities toward his head. From the center of his head, a golden light surged, connecting with the particles of the cosmos. Zoraver seemed to merge with infinite universes, trillions of galaxies, countless worlds, gods, angels, devils, and demons, flowing through all and encompassing them all within himself. One consciousness was weaving the entire order, and a profound stream of joy surged beyond human endurance. Zoraver Singh had become one with the whole existence, and an invisible white light emanated from him, spreading in waves across the entire universe.

Aldous glanced at the wild animals gathering around Zoraver, his voice tinged with confusion. "No one is able to move even an inch, but how are these animals gathering around him at this very moment?"

Isla, observing the scene with a serene smile, replied, "Don't worry! They are not here to disturb him. Actually, animals can sense his purity. We are a few of the luckiest people in human history who have the chance to see someone being enlightened."

Harold shook his head in awe. "Looks like animals are closer to God than humans these days," he said, his tone reflecting a mix of admiration and disbelief.

PRESENT TIME BRANCH – MOUNT EVEREST

Below the primary antenna that receives human life energy atop the mountain, numerous smaller antennas, each 25 feet high and 4 feet wide, encircle the peak. Atop these antennas, crystals emit a faint yet impenetrable shield around the entire mountain. Godric's angel battles tirelessly against this formidable barrier, attempting to breach the alien base, but every effort proves futile. The protective shield, reinforced by the human life force, remains resolutely strong.

Pranja and Anne, along with an alien scientist, stand before Godric and the masters who are imprisoned in chambers. All the masters and Godric are looking at Anne in great displeasure.

Pranja said, "I need every single life energy particle of their bodies to be connected with him."

The scientist nodded. "No worries. Everything will be done accordingly."

Anselm spoke with frustration, "We told you everything! There is nothing more that can be done with the help of your machine and our bodies."

Vedant added, "It doesn't matter how much energy you use. A normal human brain can't bear that, and it will either explode or fail to function normally again."

Pranja asked, "You guys can't open the tenth gate even if the energy is at its peak?"

Gurbaksh Singh shook his head. "Nah! That's impossible. That's the reason many people go mad when they push themselves too much for meditation or a meditative state. If you want to connect with God, you would need to be like God. Brahmgyan is not about gaining power; it's about leaving everything behind and being ready to become zero."

Godric glared at Anne with rage. "I am sure someone fooled you, Mr. Alien!"

Pranja retorted, "Then how did I gain anti-gravity and shape-shifting powers with the help of a human body? Do you really think you can fool me?"

Godric replied, "Supernatural powers are avoided by all saints. Using them means you are the reason for the leakage of a fuel tank that will take your car to its destination. Attaining those powers and opening the tenth gate are incomparable."

Pranja asked, "What if I help you open your tenth gate by giving you all the energy and then scan all the frequencies around you to control the universe?"

Mansoor said, "The universe is already controlling you. Your wish to control it is also the doing of the universe! Couldn't you find a true guru in thousands of years?"

Chodrak added, "Maya is playing with you. I admire your intelligence, but it's causing destruction instead of building something better."

Pranja sneered, "Don't teach me, dog! Just tell me if you have any solution for me. Otherwise, we will destroy the whole planet and move on to hunt another one."

Gurbaksh Singh asked, "Why should we let you destroy other planets to save ours? It doesn't make any sense to me."

Pranja commanded, "Commander! Send some of your best soldiers to bring their families as well. I would love to tear their flesh with my own hands."

The commander spoke while patting the head of the big spider machine standing next to him, "As you wish, my friend."

Mansoor said, "You are not a man of your word."

Pranja laughed and said, "Oh, come on, you stupid monk. I am no man. I am an alien, a super-intelligent creature from another world. The most advanced race of warriors in this entire universe."

Godric countered, "But you are not speaking like a warrior. A warrior never kills innocent people."

Pranja laughed again. "Ha ha ha! Again, why don't you understand? That's a human thing to say. It does not apply to me. One more thing: you all humans act innocent until you have power. As soon as you get some, it shows your real face, hiding behind the mask of humanity. Do not teach me; I know very well how terrible you humans are. And now it's time to kill your so-called innocent family, too, like others. But I can stop if you fulfil my wish."

Godric replied resolutely, "Do you really think I would put millions of people in danger to save my own family? The entire human race is one family, and that is the language of a warrior."

Pranja's voice was cold and commanding. "I want him on the top! Make sure you connect his whole body to the machine. I need the energy from every single inch of his mass, and hang all the masters like the others!"

The scientist looked up, concern evident in his eyes. "Don't we really need them whole too?"

Pranja shook his head dismissively. "No! I changed my mind. Just take their flesh off."

Anselm's voice was filled with rage as he shouted, "You monster! May you face the punishment that makes you feel the pain of those millions of souls you've made suffer in your entire life."

Pranja turned his gaze towards the scientist, his expression stern. "Shut their mouths and finish him first," he said firmly.

As soon as the scientist heard Pranja's order, he sealed the mouths of Godric, Gurbaksh Singh, Chodrak, Vedant, and Mansoor as before after a few finger touches at the screen of the tablet in his hand, and the machine's robotic hands started moving towards Anselm's chamber.

Godric and all his masters are trying hard to free themselves from the machine to help Anselm, but they are not succeeding at all.

Alien machine hands dragged Anselm out of the chamber, while Pranja and the commander beside him watched with keen curiosity. Godric and the other masters looked on with intense anger, but they were powerless to assist Anselm despite their desperate attempts. As Anselm faced his impending doom, he stared into the eyes of death and prayed to God. Pranja signalled to the scientist beside him, and the machine began to tear Anselm's body apart with lasers. Anselm's screams of pain filled the air, but there was no trace of fear, only the raw agony of his suffering. Pranja, inhaling the scent of burning flesh like a macabre perfume, wore a devilish expression, reveling in the darkness of his evil deeds. Anselm's flesh and blood falling on the ground made Godric even more angry than being scared of aliens. All the masters are praying in their minds for Anselm in their own traditional ways. Now, the unconscious Anselm was hung by the Alien machine on one of the hangers of the big machine at the top row and started absorbing his life energy by putting the probe on his head and applying life support to all his organs through the fine wires.

BUNKER

"How long will they take? Its been almost two hours," asked the scientist to Bella.

Bella, Theo and the scientist are all sitting around the round table near the time machine.

Bella looked troubled. "I have no idea. He must be enlightened. Otherwise, we're all doomed," she said.

Theo shook his head, his frustration evident. "Half of the world is already gone. They destroyed everything. I have no idea why you put so much interest in this plan."

Bella's voice was tinged with irritation. "What is Brahmgyan, Moksha, or enlightenment?" she asked.

Theo shrugged. "How would I know about any of this?"

Bella's eyes narrowed. "Then you have every right to be quiet!"

Theo sighed, exasperated. "Again? Can't you just move on? The world is dying, and you're just finding every reason to fight with me?"

Bella crossed her arms. "Yes! Anything else?"

The scientist, who had been observing silently, interjected calmly, "No worries, Professor. We're all on the same page. They all have a hive mind."

Bella turned to the scientist. "Sir! May I ask what you mean by 'hive mind'?"

The scientist glanced at Theo and smiled.

"Go on! Answer her," Theo urged.

The scientist addressed them both. "Can someone answer me this?" he asked, gesturing to a pen flying in front of him an inch above the table.

As he spoke, four other pens and three tablets lying on the table began to float in the air.

Theo's eyes widened in alarm. "They have come for us!" he exclaimed.

Suddenly, everything and everyone lost gravity and started floating.

Theo, hugging Bella as they floated, looked in her eyes. "My love! I have no knowledge about your voo-doo stuff! Just tell me one thing, can an enlightened person make us time travel?" he asked.

Bella is looking at Theo's face in a bit of anxiety. The scientist also came close and hugged Theo's left leg.

Outside the bunker, a massive alien ship hovers ominously in the air, pulling the bunker steadily towards itself using anti-gravity devices. Surrounding the bunker, numerous drop ships, alien soldiers, and spider machines stand vigilant. Inside the ship, the alien commander stands beside the big spider machine, intently studying the three figures visible inside the bunker through a scanning device.

"Where are the others?" the Commander asked the spider.

The spider responded with a series of electric signal-like noises.

"Didn't they keep an eye around the bunker?" the Commander enquired, frustration evident in his voice.

The spider machine replied in its mechanical rhythm.

"How can that be possible?" the Commander snapped, his irritation growing. "If they didn't come out, where are they hiding? Our scanner shows only three people."

The spider machine resumed its scanning, examining each corner of the floating bunker. But there was no one present except Bella, Theo, and the scientist.

"I have already checked everywhere, you idiot!" the Commander shouted, slapping the machine's head in frustration.

The machine emitted a loud, rhythmic noise in response.

The alien immediately checked its tablet and conducted another scan of the entire bunker. There was no sign of any biological presence.

"How can this be possible?" the Commander exclaimed, his voice a mix of anger and disbelief. "Where did they go? Pull the bunker inside as fast as you can and tear it apart piece by piece. I need all of those worms alive!"

MAIN TIMELINE – WWII 1945

Near the front lines in the forest, Theo, Bella, and the Scientist emerge from the wormhole, weapons in hand. The entire war zone is illuminated by a divine, fragrant light. Bella's gaze shifts ahead, where she spots a group of fifteen soldiers and numerous animals standing at a distance, their figures bathed in the ethereal glow.

Bella smiled happily at Theo. "I think we got what we wanted with the grace of God," she said.

Theo looked at her with a hint of doubt. "Are you sure?" he asked.

The scientist, observing the soldiers from both armies standing together, nodded in agreement. "I think she is right. No human effort can gather enemies together like this," he said.

All the soldiers and animals stand motionless, as if suspended in time. Bella silently approaches them, with Theo and the Scientist following closely behind. As they near the group of animals, the creatures and soldiers part, making a path for them. In the centre of this gathering, Zoraver Singh sits cross-legged on the ground, his face radiating a spiritual light that fills the hearts of those present with peace. In front of him, Harold, Aldous, and Isla stand with folded hands, their expressions reverent. Bella, Theo, and the Scientist quietly join them, standing side by side.

Isla looked around anxiously. "Mother! Why did you guys come here? Who is with the time machine?" she asked, her voice filled with concern.

Theo shook his head, his face tense. "The machine is gone. They took the whole bunker, and we barely escaped in time."

Harold's eyes widened with fear. "Oh God! Does that mean we are stuck here forever?" he asked, his expression showing his anxiety.

"Her Chhin Naam Ridhe Jin Dhyana, Chritr Roopantr Akaal Smana, Smapt Bhramn Moorat Hoae Raakh, Boond Smundrn Rooh Brahm Vismana. How can you be stuck somewhere if you are everywhere?" Zoraver spoke in an intoxicated tone, slowly opening his mystical eyes.

Everyone bowed in respect and sat on the ground in front of him.

Harold looked up at Zoraver, his voice apologetic. "Hello, Zoraver! Firstly, I am so sorry for my attempt to kill you. That was just a misunderstanding on my part."

Zoraver waved his hand dismissively. "No worries. I am more than alive now. Anything else?"

Harold nodded, looking hopeful. "Could you help us, please? We came here to fix my mistake, and now we are stuck with no way to return to the future."

Zoraver's gaze was contemplative as he spoke. "We are trillions of quadrillions of pearls in one thread, a thread that has no beginning and no end. Just try to look inside; you are the whole. Past, present, and future all happen at once, under the one, through the one. You have never been stuck and shall not be ever."

Theo turned to Bella, whispering, "Did you understand anything?"

Bella shook her head slowly. "He's telling us about experiencing the power that we are all capable of."

Zoraver looked at Bella and Isla with a serene expression. "Finally, I can't doubt any curse given by a pure soul. It always serves a divine purpose," he said.

Bella and Isla exchanged puzzled glances after hearing Zoraver's words.

PRESENT TIME BRANCH – MOUNT EVEREST

Pranja, with a smile expressing surprise, said, "So they used our tech to complete their stupid project and tried to warn the whole human world about the third world war. I'm impressed! They really have some brains."

Pranja, his partner Alien Commander, the Alien Scientist, and Anne were standing next to the time machine made by Theo.

The Scientist chuckled and remarked, "And the whole human world would have laughed after watching a clip of a newly released movie along with the warning message."

Anne raised an eyebrow. "So there was no one to question how the entire world's network was hacked to show just a movie clip as a prank?"

The Commander explained, "Your father had to kill a few hackers to ensure that everyone believed it was just a nasty prank."

Pranja nodded thoughtfully. "I would like to meet that brilliant mind who made this time machine with our advanced technology. Commander!" he said, turning to his partner. "Check their location, where they are hiding right now, and drag them all to me as soon as possible. Meanwhile, I will finish my business with these fleshless monks."

Pranja turned his back to the time machine, his gaze now fixed on Godric, who was suspended atop the machine. Godric was entirely unclothed, bound by an advanced technological mould that locked him in place, his body covered in fine wires from head to toe. A helmet filled with sensors encased his head, with a needle poised just half an inch from the space between his eyes. Every pore of his skin was embedded with delicate wires that pulsed faintly. Under his feet, the crystal absorbed the life energy siphoned from the fleshless breathing bodies of five masters, their subjects suspended below, and a million people from across the world. The atmosphere was charged with tension, as the machine continued its relentless extraction. The energy is floating through the probes on everyone's top of the head. While absorbing from others, simultaneously, the crystal emits this whole energy under the feet of Godric.

Pranja takes a look at his tablet to check Godric's energy level, and it looks at its peak. Standing aside, Anne looks nervous after seeing Pranja has enough divine energy to open the tenth gate.

The scientist spoke urgently, "We must finish this right now. Our king has won this planet, and it's time to show him what you dreamed of seven thousand years ago."

"It's time," Pranja agreed. "Let's do it, my friend."

Anne interjected, "Excuse me! Don't you think that by doing this, you are giving the same power to Godric as well? If I'm not wrong, he is being enlightened because of you. What if he destroys everything after attaining moksha?"

Pranja's eyes narrowed. "You used to work in the research centre on spiritualism, but I don't see that you've learnt anything from it."

Anne looked puzzled. "So he's not being enlightened?"

Pranja shook his head. "Yes, he shall be enlightened, but enlightenment has two types: Sunn Samadh and Jagrat Avastha. Sunn Samadh means your body is like a dead person, but you are transcendent, mixed with the whole energy and consciousness of the creation and beyond it. On the other hand, Jagrat Avastha is when your body is fully awakened, and you are connected to all the surroundings as a human being, as well as mixed with the consciousness of creation and beyond it. Both states are similar, but the difference is that during Sunn Samadh, the enlightened person's body does not react or feel anything a human feels or does. Godric is about to achieve Sunn Samadh very soon. I just need to sync my machine with his power. That's it."

"But he would know that you are doing something wrong!" Anne argued, her concern evident. "If he merges with the whole consciousness, wouldn't he stop you with his supernatural powers even if his body is not working?"

Pranja's expression was firm. "The whole consciousness has nothing to do with right and wrong. It's the joy beyond the limited human brain. Everything that is considered good or evil happens under the command of the consciousness. The concepts of right and wrong are merely human limitations. Godric will not react while he becomes one with the whole because there will be no Godric; he will not exist while he is connected to the whole. He will be floating within the oneness. Only a person with Jagrat Avastha is dangerous for us. That person can disconnect himself from the oneness and play the role of both a human and a god simultaneously; that's called the fifth role. But no one is here to play that fifth role, my love."

The commander announced, "I've got their location! They are in the past."

"I'm proud of you, my friend!" Pranja said with a smile. "While you chase them, I will be gaining and decoding the cosmic powers for our race to make us rulers of the entire universe."

Anne appeared deeply curious about the unfolding situation, but Pranja was focused solely on realising his long-held dream. He moved to a deck, positioned ten metres away from the machine, and settled into a chair encased within five concentric rings. Wires from the helmet fitted on Godric's head were connected to the chair. Pranja placed a similar helmet on his own head, its needle hovering half an inch from the centre of his eyebrows, mirroring Godric's setup.

Pranja said, "Start it!"

FRAGRANCE OF THE DEATH

MAIN TIMELINE – WWII 1945

Aldous stands a few metres away from Zoraver and the others, accompanied by his son, Michael. Isla and Bella are seated with Theo and Harold directly in front of Zoraver. Each of them, including Zoraver, is armed with a gun. A handful of soldiers, weapons ready, are stationed around them, maintaining a vigilant watch. The surrounding animals, calm and subdued, move quietly among the group.

Isla said, "I wish Godric would be here to see you."

Zoraver replied, "How long you gonna chase the same soul? Its time to work on yourself to be enlightened rather than wishing to be with the person you could not live a whole life through many births for centuries."

Isla asked, "What do you mean?"

Zoraver replied, "Maya plays accordingly. Your mind and the universe, both are in sync together. Whatever you think, the whole universe knows that well and plays its part in not letting you out of the cycle of time."

Isla sighed. "Can't you say anything in simple words?"

"Yes, I can but I won't," Zoraver said with a smile. "The human mind follows only what it does not understand. It takes entangled words as a challenge.

If I tell you everything in a simple way, then you won't take it seriously. It's a very basic human psyche."

Isla turned to her mother. "Mother! Could you explain his words in some simple way? Please."

Bella responded, "He says Godric is an illusion for you. He is a distraction. Am I right, Mister Zoraver Singh?" she asked in a slightly unpleasant tone.

"Soldiers!! Look to the north!" Aldous shouted loudly.

A wormhole began to open a hundred metres away from them, rapidly expanding in size. As the wormhole widened, animals scattered in fear. Zoraver stood up, gripping his gun tightly, his eyes filled with awe. The alien commander emerged from the wormhole, accompanied by ten spider machines and twenty alien soldiers. Despite the looming threat, the human soldiers displayed no fear, standing ready to fight.

Commander snarled, "Harold! Even if you fly to the other side of the universe, I shall find you and tear the bodies of your whole family one by one while singing a song in front of your eyes."

Harold whispered to Zoraver, "Are you able to kill them all?"

Zoraver stepped forward, emerging from the circle of soldiers, and shouted, "Hey!! Go back where you belong! Your one move against any single person here will become the grave of your entire world."

The spider machine moved behind the alien commander, chittering something in its gibberish language.

The commander turned to the machine and asked, "What do you mean? Is he the one?"

The spider machine responded.

The commander laughed menacingly. "Ha ha ha! Let's see how much power an enlightened human can have. Come forward and fight like a warrior. I will kill you all in the old ways," he said while tossing his gun aside and drawing a four-foot-long heavy sword from the scabbard on his back.

The other aliens followed suit, discarding their guns and drawing their ancient weapons.

Zoraver took a step forward, speaking in a mysterious and aggressive tone, "No worries! I will fulfill your wish in the old way too."

All the spider machines, along with the aliens, ran away and began hiding among the trees. This sudden retreat instilled a wave of fear among the commander's companions, but it inspired a surge of courage in the humans standing behind Zoraver.

Commander, with aggression, stepped forward quickly to attack. "I will tear you apart like I did with all their so-called masters."

The Commander's words about the masters stirred anger in everyone rather than fear.

Aldous shouted, "Soldiers! Fire!"

All the soldiers and others started firing, but aliens were coming forward like bulls. Zoraver alone is standing still without firing, looking sharp at the commander. He put his gun aside and took his two and a half feet long Kirpan out of its scabbard and started running forward to attack.

Commander and Zoraver charged towards each other with incredible speed. As they closed in, the commander began to swing his sword overhead, aiming to strike Zoraver. However, Zoraver moved with lightning speed, delivering a swift, powerful strike with his Kirpan. Within two seconds, he chopped off the commander into multiple pieces, scattering the remains across a ten-metre radius. Enraged, the remaining aliens attacked Zoraver, but none managed to land a blow. Within moments, all the aliens lay defeated, their bodies in disarray. Zoraver stood triumphantly atop a mound of their chopped off limbs and heads.

"Bole so Nihaal! Sat Shri Akaal!" Zoraver roared the war slogan, and the whole jungle echoed.

Isla, Bella, Aldous, Harold, Theo, the scientist, and all the soldiers looked at Zoraver in bliss. A divine feeling of peace ran through their bodies, and their minds had no words to say.

Harold said to Theo, "Now I understand why your son was so fascinated to be enlightened."

PRESENT TIME BRANCH - MOUNT EVEREST

Pranja sat encircled by an array of sensors attached to his head, back, shoulders, and feet, his eyes closed in concentration. The rings revolved steadily around his chair, while Godric's helmet was connected to Pranja's through a network of wires.

The scientist came close to Anne with his tablet, filled with excitement. "Princess! Look at him, he is about to be enlightened," he said eagerly.

The alien scientist showed all the energy flow from Godric's feet to his head.

Suddenly, the head of the alien commander flew out from the wormhole of the time machine and rolled to the feet of the scientist.

Seeing the head of his commander, the scientists began shaking in fear.

"We are under attack! Soldiers! We are under attack!" Anne shouted in panic as she ran away.

Ten alien soldiers approached the wormhole on full alert, prepared to attack, waiting for what was on the other side. All the spider machines burst out of it and quickly scattered.

The alien scientist hid in a corner behind a small dropship, intently watching the screen of his tablet. As the energy level reached 100%, the needle positioned between Godric's eyes began to spin at thousands of RPM. Simultaneously, the needle between Pranja's eyebrows started rotating at the same speed. A white spark emerged from the upper part of Godric's nose, between his eyes, and reached out to touch the spinning needle.

Anne said, "Sorry, Godric! I have to do it for my kingdom!"

Hidden behind a chair, she took her pistol out of her jacket, checked the bullets, and loaded it. All the alien soldiers advanced towards the wormhole, ready to shoot with their laser guns. Godric and Pranja were both synchronised and the tenth gate of both was vibrating.

Anne came out of the cover and aimed at Godric's head.

Click – Boom! Anne fired at Godric.

The bullet came out of the pistol but stopped a foot away. Time had stopped. Everyone and everything around was frozen in the moment.

"Na guddi na!" said Zoraver, throwing the floating bullet away with his left moustache, like a hockey stick hitting a ball.

Anne stared at him as if she had seen a ghost. Zoraver smiled at her, seeing a golden thread crawling around Anne's whole body.

After a few seconds, everything returned to normal. Gunshots from the wormhole blasted the aliens' heads. As soon as she could move, Anne ran away. Meanwhile, Zoraver didn't stop her and moved toward the machine.

Isla, Bella, Theo, and Harold emerged from the wormhole alongside their companions, looking at Godric as they rushed to the machine.

Aldous, speaking to himself in excitement after killing one of the aliens, said, "I love my supergun!"

Zoraver saw his father's fleshless body hanging with the others. He chopped all the main wires of the machine. As soon as the machine stopped working, the energy flowing to Mount Everest from all over the world lost its connection to the main antenna.

Isla, Bella, Harold, and Theo reached the deck closer to Pranja. Harold fired at the wires connecting Godric to Pranja, disconnecting the entire process.

Click – Thak! Click – Thak! Click – Thak! Isla fired three precise shots at Pranja's head, shattering the helmet. But the bullets had no effect on Pranja. His eyes remained closed, his body numb and unresponsive, impervious to the attack.

"Zoraver!" Isla shouted. "My bullets aren't working on him!"

"Isla!" Harold yelled while climbing up to the machine. "Stay away from him!"

Theo and Harold reached Godric and began taking the wires off his body. Zoraver came up onto the deck and stood in front of Pranja.

"Come on. Open your eyes, you devil," Zoraver said. "It's been thousands of years, and you're still fooling the entire civilisation of these aliens."

"This demon killed all the masters, including your father," Bella added, her voice filled with emotion. "They were godly men. He must burn in hell-fire for eternity."

Zoraver, with calm resolve, replied, "Don't worry. They merely paid the price for playing with spirituality."

"What do you mean?" Bella asked, clearly displeased. "They were excellent masters!"

Zoraver shook his head. "Only an enlightened Guru, a Masiha, or an Avatar can start a religion. These five forgot their limits because of their egos of knowledge, and now they're hanging like dead goats up there for their sins."

Isla exclaimed, "Come on! One of them was your father!"

"Shut up, you child!" Zoraver snapped.

"Excuse me?" Isla retorted.

Zoraver's voice hardened as he said, "Nah! You are not excused."

Isla didn't speak further. Zoraver stared at Pranja, his gaze unwavering and aggressive.

"Just kill him!" Bella urged. "What are you waiting for?"

"Shhhhhhh!" Zoraver silenced her. "Now go down and take care of your son."

Isla and Bella exchanged no further words with Zoraver and descended from the deck. Meanwhile, Harold and Theo brought Godric down from the machine with the help of other soldiers. Above them, the angel hovered anxiously, her gaze fixed on Godric.

Zoraver turned his attention back to Pranja and said, "What should I call you? Pranja? Chaitanyasura? Come on, open your eyes, you ugly Asura. Haven't you learned anything in your thousands of years of life? You can't outplay God. He's the only one who plays with everyone and everything."

"How did you find me?" Pranja growled, his voice dripping with anger as he opened his eyes.

"Find you? Huh!" Zoraver replied. "I've never been away. You just don't have the eyes to see me."

Bruuummm...!! A drop ship hit the deck with a strong beam, spreading smoke around Zoraver and Pranja. The alien scientist flew the drop ship above the machine, closer to the deck.

Pranja broke free of all the rings around the chair and swiftly leapt onto the machine. He picked up the crystal and ejected it into a receptacle in his armor, positioned in front of his belly button.

"I'm going to wipe out this entire planet before your very eyes!" Pranja shouted as he got inside the drop ship.

Below the deck, everyone watched Zoraver and Pranja. The soldiers fired at the drop ship, but Pranja and the scientist escaped.

Godric, lying in Harold's lap, slowly opened his eyes.

Zoraver jumped from the deck and came to Godric.

Harold, puzzled, asked, "Why didn't you kill him?"

Zoraver replied, "I shall kill him along with his clan. It's been a long time since I saw them on the battlefield."

The angel came closer to Zoraver, bowed in respect, and then hugged his right leg with a sad expression on her face.

Harold pressed on, "What are you talking about?"

Zoraver turned to Godric and said warmly, "Hello, Godric! How are you?"

While caressing the angel's head with his right hand, Zoraver smiled. Godric gave him a thumbs up in response.

AN HOUR LATER

Both Pranja and the scientist are flying in the drop ship, and at a distance of three kilometres, they can see the headquarters of UG, which has come under the control of the alien army.

The scientist says, "Although I have been with you all the time in completing your project, I truly never had full confidence in the idea that a human being really could possess so many powers!"

"Huh! At least I found someone who believes me," Pranja replies.

"What do you think? Will he attack us again?" asks the scientist.

"We will capture him before he attacks us," Pranja states firmly.

"But he Is very powerful," the scientist remarks, concern evident in his voice.

Pranja smirks and says, "Not more than our entire army. He can kill some of us but not all."

Beep! Beep! Beep! A sound comes from the drop ship, and its engine stops working.

"We are losing control!" the scientist exclaims, anxiety and fear creeping into his tone.

"Prepare for emergency landing!" Pranja orders sharply.

Both of them eject themselves from the ship. They land safely with the help of parachutes, but the drop ship explodes 400 metres away from them after crashing to the ground.

The scientist, irritated, says, "This is the most shitty day of my life."

"Don't worry! We are close," Pranja reassures him while looking towards the King's ship atop the HQ.

"Did you see the princess?" the scientist asks.

"Nah!" Pranja responds casually.

"We promised her father to keep her safe!" the scientist reminds him, concerned.

"Shit happens! This is the nature of war," Pranja responds nonchalantly.

"But our king would take it seriously!" the scientist points out.

Pranja smiles mysteriously and says, "So we have one more reason to raise the army against that enlightened human."

"I love that smile," the scientist says.

MAIN TIMELINE – 2026

Oscar sits on his throne, and Anne stands beside him. No one else is present in the court except the two of them.

"Are you sure Pranja escaped from him?" Oscar asks.

"Yes! He did," Anne confirms.

"I know that stubborn alien very well," Oscar says thoughtfully. "He shall come back to that guy and capture him to get what he's been craving for thousands of years."

"Nah! He can't dare to face that enlightened man," Anne replies confidently. "I saw him running away from him. Even if he tries, they only have a few hours left. I hope every one of them dies there as we planned." She hands her necklace to Oscar as she speaks.

Oscar nods, "I hope everything goes accordingly."

"Father, you have no need to be afraid of anyone," Anne assures him. "Whether our plan works or not, they won't find out anything about our mission."

PRESENT TIME BRANCH

Across the globe, the alien army has ravaged cities and thousands of villages. Only a few remote areas remain safe, but the hunt for survivors continues unabated. No human military forces or soldiers are visible; every airbase lies in ruins, reduced to ashes. The fleets are gone, leaving no means to confront the aliens. Humanity is left to hide while spider machines crawl relentlessly across the land. Thousands of humans are enslaved, forced to construct bases around the world for the alien soldiers.

PANJAB, INDIA

Amidst the fields of ankle-high wheat, an alien dropship sat nestled within an acre of sugarcane where Harold, Godric, Aldous, Theo, Bella, Isla, scientist, and soldiers gathered. The angel is perched atop the dropship, overseeing the scene.

Godric said, "I will do whatever I have to do to avenge my masters. They were true heroes, martyrs who sacrificed their lives instead of giving away the secrets of human spirituality to that devil."

"Why didn't Gurbaksh Singh use the army of martyrs against these aliens?" Harold asked Godric.

Godric shook his head. "That was an illusion! He never had that power. Sorry he had to trick you, otherwise, you wouldn't have listened to me or any of us."

Harold sighed irritably. "I don't know who to trust. Everything is beyond my understanding. I couldn't even comprehend my grandson to this day. How am I supposed to know what those aliens are going to do?"

Theo turned to Zoraver. "Zoraver! Why did you bring us all to this place?"

Zoraver responded, "Have you ever wondered why most of the spiritual literature was written in this country?"

Theo shrugged. "Sorry! I know nothing about spiritual literature, but my wife is good at that stuff."

Bella said, "Many people who are interested in spiritual knowledge believe this is the holy land of Rishis, saints, gurus, and Avatars!"

Zoraver raised an eyebrow. "Holy land? Really? Do you think that too?"

Bella nodded. "Yeah! Holy people live in holy lands."

Zoraver smirked. "Nah! That's not true."

Isla asked, "Then what's the truth?"

Godric interjected, "A cancer hospital must be built in the area where most people have cancer."

Zoraver looked at Isla and asked, "Understood?"

Theo crossed his arms. "So, you call your motherland an unholy land?"

Zoraver replied, "Whole earth is my motherland. I've taken many births on different lands, with different religions, different ethnicities. There is no land that is holy or unholy but the people."

Theo sighed in frustration. "Except for Godric, no one here understands you properly. So just tell me in simple human words, why are we here? We could have hidden anywhere in the Himalayas or any other remote areas. Why did you bring us here?"

Zoraver replied firmly, "You can't hide from them! We all will have to fight!"

Harold frowned. "They are millions! We have no army to tackle them. UAHW doesn't exist anymore and millions of people have already died. I know you're powerful, but being here to fight instead of hiding from them seems like a joke to me."

Zoraver's eyes darkened. "All the saints who ever walked this land, their energy still exists, and their spiritual footprint is too strong here. Soon, the

Song of swords will be whistling in the wind, devils will dance with angels, and the whole world will witness the fragrance of death."

Harold leaned over to Michael and whispered, "Whatever that was, I just feel like a soldier again."

Michael smirked. "Why do I have a feeling he's kind of enjoying this whole scary thing?"

Zoraver called out, "Godric!"

Godric responded, "Yes?"

Zoraver said, "Your guilt about that centuries-old sin is binding your energy! Let me release it."

Godric shook his head. "No worries! I will have to carry that weight."

Zoraver insisted, "Nah! You deserve to know the truth. Even guilt is a kind of attachment to the world. Our feelings work both ways. If falling in love is an attachment, hate is also the same thing. Whether it's negative energy or positive, both keep us wandering far from the truth. To escape the matrix of nature, you need to stand in between both. Then you will be able to enter into nothingness."

Zoraver gazed into Godric's eyes with a mystical smile, and Godric became instantly numb. His eyes rolled upwards toward the third eye.

Isla, her voice tinged with anxiety, asked, "What are you doing to him?"

Zoraver calmly replied, "Just trying to show him who the real sinner is."

UG HEADQUARTERS

Pranja and the Scientist stood in front of their King inside the ship at his court. A few other commanders and soldiers were also present.

The King scoffed. "Why should I fear a human who has some power to kill a few of my soldiers?"

Pranja spoke earnestly. "He can stop time. It's a great power."

The King waved his hand dismissively. "I can play with time too. We will get whatever we need from this world and leave all the ruins behind for that so-called superhuman."

The Scientist interjected, "Suppose he appears here, stops time, and kills all of us. How would we stop him? I think he kidnapped the future queen of the Earth as well. What would we say to Oscar about that?"

The King laughed. "No human can kill me. Not even your so-called enlightened one."

Pranja said, "He killed our one of the most valuable commanders, and the daughter of our most important ally is missing. Do not take it as the nature of war. If we leave him behind, then our act can become a loophole. For the sake of my father, please listen to me this last time. I would never ask for anything again."

The advisor came close to the King and whispered something inaudible.

The King asked, "How many men do you need to capture him?"

"I need the whole army," Pranja responded earnestly.

The King, startled, got up from the throne and exclaimed as he moved towards Pranja, "Are you mad? You need the most powerful army in the entire universe to catch a human?"

Pranja bowed deeply, taking a crystal from his armour and presenting it to the king. "This crystal holds the life energy of more than a million humans. If you compare it with the people of any other world, we would have to conquer at least a hundred times more civilians from any other planet to gather this much energy. But he is not just a human being. Do not see his body. He is connected to the whole of existence. That human has a flow within the universe and beyond. Even if we have to make a call to all our allies, we must not hesitate for that."

The King, thoughtful, ordered, "Scan it and compare it with the data of total storage."

The advisor carefully placed the crystal atop a three-foot-tall pole positioned in the centre of the holographic projection of the planets. A scientist, using a laser gun mounted on the roof and precisely aligned with the pole, fired at the crystal and initiated a scan. After the procedure was complete, the advisor retrieved the crystal from the hologram and gently returned it to Pranja's hands.

Just in a few seconds, the hologram of the crystal appeared among all the planets and connected with each of them with a golden spark. Suddenly, the glow of the whole hologram increased many times over, surprising everyone present in the court.

"Marvellous!" the King exclaimed. "I am surprised, my soldier. But still, I can't allow you to command the whole army for one human."

"But..." Pranja began.

The King interrupted, "I can understand he ruined your project. You must be disappointed in him and want revenge. You can have one thousand of my soldiers and five ships to catch him. I can't do more than that."

"My lord! You need to see this video clip. Many of our soldiers retrieved it from the humans from different places around the world. All the humans are calling him the alien slayer!" a soldier reported as he hurried into the court.

"What is that?" the King asked.

The soldier handed his tablet to the King. The video displayed the entire scene from Mount Everest.

"My King! Few of our ships are failing all around the world, but the reason is unknown as yet!" said an alien dressed like an engineer, rushing into the court.

"See! It could only be his work," Pranja argued. "Let's gather the whole army and kill him in front of the entire human world."

"My lord, I agree with Pranja! We need to kill that enlightened one as soon as possible!" one of the commanders declared in an aggressive tone.

"This kind of video brings shame upon our entire army. We must crush him in front of his whole race!" another commander added.

"How did they send this video around the whole world?" the King demanded.

"He has superpowers!" the scientist suggested. "Maybe he hacked our system to mock us with this video among all the humans."

"That bastard will have to pay a big price for this action," the King said, his voice cold. "Commanders! Make sure your soldiers double their efforts to kill these worms all over their planet. I shall show them the consequences of this kind of mockery."

Pranja looked at his fellow scientist and smiled.

PANJAB

All the soldiers sat together outside the ship. Inside, Zoraver sat in deep meditation, with Godric and the others seated around him.

"How could Anne betray us?" Isla asked. "She was like a sister to me."

"Her father was an ambitious man," Aldous replied. "I think she just tried to go one step further."

"The way Oscar was obsessed with alien technology," Harold said, "he could have brought this disaster much earlier."

Godric added thoughtfully, "I saw something when I was connected with Pranja. He's not even an alien, and Anne is not just a scientist."

"Then who are they?" Bella asked.

"Pranja is something else," Godric explained. "I mean, the vision was like... he changed his form. He is very powerful and has a strong tie to another kind of civilisation that used to live among humans on this planet in ancient times."

"Oh God!" Isla gasped. "Now I understand. The other aliens died even with single shots of our bullets, but when I shot him three times, he didn't even get a scratch!"

"It looks like Godric's destiny is bound with these aliens," Harold mused. "Poor masters, they had no idea what they were dealing with."

"Those aliens would have never found our planet," Godric remarked. "I think Pranja is the reason they're here."

"Tell us everything you saw," Theo urged.

"I need to know about Anne first," Isla interjected.

"She belongs to a royal family from the future," Godric replied.

"What the fu.." Isla began before Bella quickly interjected.

"Behave, girl!" Bella reprimanded.

"Sorry, mother," Isla apologised. "I'm just surprised!"

"What else do you know about her?" Harold asked.

"I don't know everything in detail. They were just visions. I think we are not the present. We are the past, and these aliens are from the future. Pranja is the one playing a double role in this whole thing. He has some kind of hidden agenda that I couldn't discern," Godric said.

"So, he's not an alien?" the scientist asked.

"No!" Godric replied firmly. "He's another kind of creature… or, we could say, an entity."

"They're coming. Get ready for the war!" Zoraver suddenly opened his eyes, speaking with courage.

"How many?" Harold asked tensely.

Four hundred metres away, an alien was relentlessly hunting a middle-aged Sikh man. Desperate to protect his wife and their two young children, aged five and ten, the man sought refuge beneath a Kupp (a storage of chopped straw fodder, shaped like a crude shelter, standing about 20 feet tall). Just one hundred metres away, the alien, with an arrogant, predatory smile, began to close in on them.

"Khar teri bhain nu!" shouted an elder man as he struck the alien from behind on his butt with a hoe.

With one strike, the handle of the hoe snapped. The alien swiftly kicked the old man, sending him flying ten metres away. Without hesitation, the alien closed in on him. Struggling to his feet, the man lunged forward and tried to stab the alien with the broken handle, but his skin was impenetrable, as hard as stone.

"AAAAHHHH!!" A bloodcurdling scream tore through the air, trembling the people hidden in the Kupp.

"Bapu? Lagda salea ne bapu nu fad lya," the man whispered to his wife.

The alien inserted a probe into elder's head, draining the life energy from his brutalized body. Now, he was walking towards the family hidden in the chaff.

"Don't go anywhere, they will kill all of us," the wife said in a panicked voice.

"Shut up! I need to save my father!" the man replied.

Suddenly, a hand like a hawk's claw pierced through the wall, spearing the man's stomach from behind and lifting him up like a crane, dragging him out of the Kupp.

"AAAAAGGGG!!" The man's agonising wail shook both his children and his wife to their core.

The woman and the children screamed in terror and fled. Having absorbed the life energy of the children's father, the alien began moving steadily towards them. The children, shaking with fear, cried out as two spider machines suddenly appeared in front of them, capturing the terrified pair as they ran. The mother froze in her tracks, paralysed by fear, unable to approach the monstrous machines. The alien stepped forward, positioning himself between the two spiders that held her children captive.

"You have killed every member of my family! Please, leave my children alone! You can kill me instead! Please, please, don't hurt them. They are just kids," the mother, sobbing with folded hands, pleaded helplessly from a distance.

The alien, with a cruel smile, relished the sight of the trembling family, consumed by fear.

The spider machines hurled the children into the air, and the alien standing between them drove his nails through their stomachs. He then lifted them high above his head like a trophy of victory.

Aaaahhhhh!

Eeeehhhhh!

The screams of both kids like razor-sharp shards, shaken the mother's soul with unimaginable pain. She screamed and collapsed, witnessing this heart-wrenching nightmare. A spider machine swiftly attacked her, tearing her body apart.

A gunshot rang out, striking the alien and blasting his head apart. He collapsed to the ground, his lifeless body falling next to the children. Almost instantly, both spider machines, sensing the disturbance, began scuttling towards the source of the shot. Before they could advance further, two more gunshots echoed in quick succession, hitting the machines squarely and destroying them on the spot.

"Maybe we could give these guns to our whole army before they attack our planet," Aldous said, standing among the soldiers after killing both spiders with his gun.

100 CENTURIES AGO

Inside a cave, a six-and-a-half-foot-tall old Asura with a hunchback was methodically severing the heads of three monks and placing them into a bag. Outside, a seven-foot-tall young Asura stood with his sword slung over his shoulder. Snow-capped mountains surrounded the cave. Both Asuras had prominent horns, blackened bodies, and broad, pig-like noses.

"Chaitanyasura! Come inside," the Asura inside the cave called to the one standing outside.

"Yes, master Vigyanasura?" Chaitanyasura replied as he stepped inside.

Vigyanasura held out the head of a monk and commanded, "Open its jaw and tell me what you see inside its mouth."

Chaitanyasura took the head in his hands and opened its jaw. "Are you seeing something special?" Vigyanasura asked.

"No, master! All the teeth and tongue are visible like any other human," Chaitanyasura answered.

"Really! Do they look normal to you?" Vigyanasura pressed.

"Can I see the other two heads as well?" Chaitanyasura requested.

"Take them and check all of them carefully," Vigyanasura instructed, handing his bag to Chaitanyasura.

Chaitanyasura placed the bag on the ground, took out the remaining two heads, and opened their jaws to inspect inside. "Strange thing! All three have their tongues stuck to their palates," he remarked.

"Do you know why?" Vigyanasura inquired.

"Oh! I see," Chaitanyasura exclaimed eagerly, smiling. "Is this what you were talking about a year ago? Do they have Amrit in their heads?"

"Yes! You identified it correctly," Vigyanasura confirmed. "There is a hole in the palate of every human being from which the Amrit flows down into the mouth, spreading throughout the body. But these monks closed that hole with their tongues through meditation, storing all this Amrit in their heads so that their third eye could be opened with its power."

"Can we extract their Amrit and become immortal by drinking it?" Chaitanyasura asked excitedly.

"This Amrit is not the divine Amrit one experiences during the enlightenment," Vigyanasura explained. "But yes, it is the source through which the enlightenment is attained and the great divine Amrit is experienced which make someone immortal. When humans start practicing repeating a mantra continuously, sometimes their tongue starts to feel sweetness because of the increased amount of this Amrit coming into the mouth through their palate. However, without understanding anything, some fools consider it as the achievement of the divine Amrit. But that divine Amrit is not any kind of fluid. Divine Amrit is beyond human taste, emotions and imagination. Humans can get it and be immersed in wonder, but no human can explain that experience. Only the human body has the ability to attain enlightenment with the Amrit in its head. Why only human body? I don't know! So... this fluid present in the heads of these monks has no use for us to attain enlightenment and become immortals, but yes, we will definitely find a way through this rare treasure toward a shining future for our entire Asura race."

"What could be more shiny than being immortals? What's the use of this so-called rare treasure for us if we can't be enlightened?" Chaitanyasura asked.

"Ha ha ha! I know how much you're obsessed with attaining immortality. However, the important question at this time is how we can establish our strong relations with those golden warriors to combine our science with theirs. I am at the brink of fulfilling the dream that our entire race has craved day and night for thousands of years. And yes! Their science could be useful to find a solution for attaining the enlightenment too. I will try my best to help you for that." Vigyanasura said.

"Really, master? Will you really do that for me?" Chaitanyasura asked joyfully.

"Yes, I shall definitely find a way for that," Vigyanasura reassured. "But first, help me with the necessary work. Now, put these heads in the bag and assist me in extracting their Amrit."

PRESENT TIME BRANCH – PANJAB

Aldous, Harold, and others stood in a circle around the dead alien, looking around, fully alert.

"Who is he? I am totally confused!" Godric said. "After seeing those visions, it feels like I was connected to something more than an alien."

"His name is Chaitanyasura," Zoraver responded gravely. "He is an Asura, an ancient being. He has a great master whose intelligence is far beyond any other creature of this universe that gave him the ability to blend the principles of spirituality and physics together perfectly. These aliens came in touch with him around ten thousand years ago, when the general of the alien army, the brother of the king was dying with an incurable disease. Vigyanasura cured his disease in exchange for being an ally of aliens. After that, with the combination of his spiritual science and the alien science, he invented the soul-absorbing technology and a device that can transfer the consciousness of one person's mind to another's. However, his inventions were not for the aliens. He had his own evil deeds. He knew it wouldn't be possible for him to use his tech at high scale by being alone. So he began manipulating the alien king's brother to use his inventions for alien soldiers to live without any kind of food on other planets and store the consciousness of intelligent beings of other planets. The alien thought it would be smart to kill Vigyanasura and store his whole intelligence in his own mind. But he was a fool. Even that thought in his mind came because of the manipulation by Vigyanasura. So that overly smart general killed Vigyanasura and used one of Vigyanasura's inventions to enhance his own intelligence. He used a device that was not only designed to store knowledge or intelligence but also to absorb souls. This misguided action resulted in the alien king's brother falling under Vigyanasura's control. Now, that very individual has become the current alien king, driven by a desire to eliminate us all and capture our life force."

Godric asked, "That means the alien king is an Asura?"

"Yes!" Zoraver confirmed. "And he's the main character of this whole story."

Isla inquired, "What about Pranja?

Zoraver explained, "Chaitanyasura is even one step ahead of his master. He wants to be enlightened, but not like a human being. Instead of absorbed by the Oneness, he wants to control the whole universe by creating a sync between his mind and all the universal frequencies while maintaining his individuality at the same time."

Bella exclaimed, "That's even worse! We won't be able to control him if he succeeds in that. How did these intelligent beings come under his influence to help him create such an evil tech?"

Zoraver responded, "That's why his name is Pranja! He successfully scanned and decoded the frequencies of supernatural powers of human beings, and then used them as evidence to convince the aliens to let him work on a project to get artificial moksha with human life energy. Otherwise, the aliens were seeing us as weak creatures and had been using our planet as an army base for thousands of years."

Harold asked, "But how did they not get to know about human superpowers for thousands of years by themselves?"

Zoraver replied, "Actually, these 'thousands of years' are just thirty-six years and six months of their time zone. So basically, they didn't take too long to know about the potential of human body. Furthermore, Pranja is also behind the idea of creating a time branch for each planet they've attacked in recent years."

Aldous questioned, "What's his plan behind this idea of creating the time branches?"

"To get what he wants while maintaining the balance of the whole universe and making strong allies with the main timelines of every planet on their way," Zoraver explained.

Godric asked, "What is the benefit for Pranja and his master in attacking other planets for these aliens?"

"So that they could make a big storage of souls for their own Asura army to rule over all the three Loks. This is the most ancient dream of the whole Asura race," Zoraver said gravely. "The life energy that aliens are absorbing in their devices, they transfer it back to their planet in real-time. But the secret is, that energy is not just energy; it's the storage of billions of souls from different worlds."

Aldous exclaimed, "Oh God! Now this whole alien thing has totally gone out of my mind. Just tell me one more thing, how can these both Asuras create an army with those souls that they captured with their voodoo science?"

"Your soul is divine energy, and your consciousness drives it," Zoraver continued. "Vigyanasura has been conducting his experiments to create hybrids on many planets for thousands of years. Once he got the perfect hybrid DNA to produce creatures for his army, he's going to create billions of hybrid subjects and possess all of them with the souls that he has under his custody. After that, he's going to put his own consciousness into each of his hybrid subject and create a hive mind."

Zoraver's explanation about Vigyanasura's plan left everyone shocked.

"If he plans to create a hive-mind army, then we would only have to kill their leader," Michael suggested. "Just kill him right now, and it would be over forever."

Zoraver shook his head. "No, no, no! Just don't get stuck on the words. When I say 'hive mind,' that means those billions of soldiers would be one consciousness. They all will become Vigyanasura! Moreover, that alien king is also a body under the control of Vigyanasura. Just killing that body would not be the best idea to stop him."

Aldous asked, "Is he trying to outplay God?"

Zoraver smirked, "Good. Now you got this alien thing!"

Michael looked sceptical. "You were just a soldier fighting in the British army a few hours ago. How did you come to know everything about our enemies?"

Zoraver replied cryptically, "I have countless eyes, ears, and memories. Been in wars since the beginning. It was just part of my journey to fight alongside you to be here at this very moment."

Harold inquired, "What if we surrender ourselves to them and run our government as their ally?

Zoraver answered, "They had already found an ally in the main timeline decades ago, and as a result, this time branch came in existence. There is no diplomatic way to stop this invasion."

Zeh REE dee ah!! Zeh REE dee ah!!

Suddenly, the terrifying sound of the alien war cry began to echo all around them.

The cry echoed loudly, but no one could be seen. The terrifying sound rumbled the whole atmosphere and made the ground vibrate for miles.

Aldous shouted, "Soldiers! Take your positions. Today is the day when we shall fight as one."

Everyone made a circle and lay down on the ground, pointing their guns in every direction. Zoraver remained standing in the middle of the circle.

Zeh REE dee ah!!

Zeh REE dee ah!!

Theo asked in confusion, "Why can't we see anyone?"

Zoraver, ignoring the question, asked, "Are you ready to die for the sake of the whole human race?"

"Yes!" they all replied.

Zoraver smirked, "Yeah! Of course you would die here."

Isla gasped, "What?"

Zoraver grinned mischievously. "Prank!"

Harold groaned, "Really? Is this the time for jokes?"

Michael whispered to Harold, "I told you! He's enjoying this whole thing. Sure, he has some kind of beef with those two ancient things and the aliens."

Zeh REE dee ah!!

Zeh REE dee ah!!

Over five hundred thousand alien soldiers suddenly appeared, surrounding the area in every direction, standing just 500 metres away. Each one was poised for attack, with over a thousand warships hovering ominously in the sky behind them. Towering above all the other ships was the king's warship, a massive, imposing presence. From its helm, the alien king glared down at Zoraver, his eyes burning with rage, filled with a wrathful intensity that seemed to pierce through the battlefield.

Aliens were broadcasting the battlefield live across the entire globe. All the humans hiding in various places, gutters, basements, tunnels, bunkers, or caves who had access to mobile phones, TVs, or any device, were watching and listening to the scene unfold.

Bella said in a shaking voice while looking around, "I think this is judgement day for all of us."

"Zoraver! Could you stop the time right now?" Theo asked urgently.

Zoraver replied, "Yeah! But I won't!"

Harold, confused, asked, "What? Why won't you do that?"

"What's the fun in killing thousands of these devils after freezing them?" Zoraver responded. "Jaat got Singhan ki danga, danga in Satgur te manga."

"Is he crazy?" Isla said irritably to Godric.

Godric hushed her, "Shhh..."

"No! You shhhh!" Isla snapped. "Zoraver! We can't fight them. You need to freeze the time!"

"Do you really think Vigyanasura isn't aware of what I can do to his whole army?" Zoraver replied calmly.

Isla, still anxious, retorted, "As you've told us about his intelligence, he knows more about you than any of us! But still, you..."

Zoraver cut her off, "Then why would he come here to attack us?"

Harold interjected, "You hurt his ego! That's it. Now go ahead and stop the fu... time!"

Zoraver shook his head and said, "Nah! Ego works on shit minds only. Actually he wants to get everything at once what he was searching for thousands of years and I won't let him take that."

Theo, confused, asked, "What do you mean?"

"I think they want to run a scan on him, like they did with Tejas," Godric suggested.

Zoraver nodded. "Yup! You got it!"

Godric then asked, "Then how would we tackle them?"

Zoraver replied cryptically, "The art can't be done; it happens! There's a difference between using a Siddhi and the occurrence of a miracle."

Harold, feeling frustrated, said, "Can't you use simpler words?"

Suddenly, Aldous shouted loudly, "Be alert! A drop ship is coming down!" He pointed towards the sky over the alien army.

A drop ship descended between the two sides. Pranja and his fellow scientist emerged from it with a few alien soldiers.

Pranja called out in pride, "Harold! Aldous! I won't hurt you or anyone else if you hand over this enlightened human to me. Otherwise, you know very well what I am capable of."

Zoraver greeted him with disdain, "Hello, Dog! Do you really think all these humans trust you just because I call you a dog?"

Pranja sneered, "Maybe you can kill a couple of thousand of my soldiers and even me! But your big mouth will be the doom of every human on this planet! You can't save all of them. Millions of my soldiers are hunting humans like pigs right now. I can make it stop, but you must surrender for that. Now, surrender yourself!"

Zoraver asked calmly, "Why?"

Pranja raised his voice, "Because we will kill all of them!"

Zoraver shrugged, "What's that to me?"

Pranja, growing impatient, demanded, "Don't you want to save them?"

Zoraver replied coolly, "A soul never dies. They'll be born again."

Pranja shouted, "Humans! Look at this arrogant bastard you think is here to save you all! Look at your coward saviour! He can't even surrender himself to save your world! Look at the fear of death in his eyes!"

Pranja's fellow scientist commanded his soldiers, "Bring them out!"

Two soldiers went inside the ship and emerged with a Sikh man and a child, both bound in chains and looking terrified.

Pranja taunted Zoraver, "Do you know who they are?"

"Oh God!" Godric gasped.

"Who are they?" Isla asked, turning to Godric.

"Yes! They are my family like the all creature from every corner of the whole existence!," Zoraver said solemnly.

Pranja sneered, "That means it won't hurt you if I kill them right here right now in front of you!"

Zoraver replied calmly, "That's a human thing to say."

Pranja grabbed Zoraver's son, making him stand before him, his face towards Zoraver. With one brutal pull, Pranja tore both the boy's arms from his shoulders.

"AAAAHHHHH!!" Zoraver's son groaned in unbearable pain.

Seeing his father crumble on the ground, the child is also suffering but Pranja and his companions are feeling very proud after seeing all this.

Witnessing the scene unfold, Harold and everyone else shot to their feet. Anger simmered in the air as those surrounding Zoraver wore furious expressions. Even the Angel joined them, standing beside Zoraver with a fierce look of aggression on her face. Yet, Zoraver remained still, his gaze fixed on Pranja, his expression unreadable.

Now, Pranja placed his right foot on the back of Zoraver's son and, with his right hand, grabbed him by the neck and separated the head from the torso. After that, he crossed his right leg over his left, grabbed his right leg with both hands, and tore the body into two parts.

Harold shouted, "What is honour in hurting the weak and an innocent man!"

Pranja sneered, "You have no idea how far I can go to hurt you! Now tell me if he's ready for the surrender!"

Zoraver defiantly replied, "No!"

Pranja picked up the crying child by the head. The child struggled desperately to free himself, but there was no way for the bird-like kid to escape the claws of Pranja.

Godric cried out, "Save him! He's your grandson!"

Zoraver declared, "Not only him, you all are mine!"

Pranja growled, "Surrender!"

Zoraver spat, "Nah!"

With a heartless grip, Pranja crushed the child's head in his hand. The body fell to the ground, wriggling in its final moments.

The brutality of the act caused Isla to faint, her legs giving way beneath her. She collapsed to the ground, sobbing uncontrollably. Godric rushed to her side, gathering her quickly into his arms. Pranja's merciless deed sent shockwaves through the hearts of people across the world, leaving them shaken by the cruelty they witnessed.

Bella screamed, tears streaming down her face, "What are you waiting for?"

Zoraver said, "There was zero percent chance he could let them live. But by killing a child, he just lost a lot of spiritual power."

Michael asked, "But you didn't even try to save them. Why didn't you stop the time?"

Zoraver replied, "I can't use any Siddhi for the sake of my earthly feelings."

Michael questioned, "What's wrong with using your powers to save your own family?"

Zoraver responded, "Even in this very moment, I can't let Maya play with me. Only one selfish action can put me in the birth cycle again."

Isla cried, "How can you be part of the birth cycle again by helping your own child?"

Zoraver said, "You all are mine and I am yours."

"Excuse me! Excuse me! Excuse me please!" A vampire moved Harold, Aldous, Theo, and Bella aside and approached Zoraver from behind.

Bella and Isla screamed in terror, clutching their husbands tightly. Including Harold and Aldous, even all the soldiers flinched in fear as they caught sight of the ugly creature, five feet tall with two long, jagged teeth protruding from its mouth. Pranja and the rest of the aliens, including their king, stared at the vampire in astonishment, never having encountered such a being before.

Zoraver glanced over without even looking at the speaker. "What do you want?" he asked.

"My lord!" the vampire exclaimed, "I came all the way from England to ask you just one question."

"Ask!" Zoraver replied.

The Angel smiled upon seeing the vampire and looked at Zoraver.

"Why should my people fight this war for humans?" the vampire questioned. "It's their problem. I think human problems need human solutions."

"You idiot!" Zoraver snapped. "Whose blood are you going to suck if there are no humans left on this planet?"

"Do they gonna kill them all?" the vampire asked in a disappointed tone.

"Now go back to your place and attack with full force," Zoraver commanded. "But... Don't you dare to take advantage of this moment. Only take what you need."

"As you wish, my lord!" the vampire replied, vanishing into the air.

Everyone around looked at Zoraver in surprise.

"Did you just make a deal with a vampire?" a soldier asked.

"Deal? Nah," Zoraver said dismissively. "I gave an order to a vampire."

"You coward!" Pranja shouted. "This is your last chance. Surrender right now or get ready for the war."

"Dog! Let's play the war!" Zoraver retorted.

"Soldiers! Attack!" Pranja ordered.

All the aliens immediately drew their swords and axes from their sheaths and surged forward, waving their weapons in the air.

"My lord!" an advisor said to the alien king, "I am suggesting again that we must kill him on the spot with the full force of all our cannons."

"Don't you understand?" the king replied. "I need Harold's grandson and that enlightened man both active and alive on this battlefield."

The aliens advanced towards Zoraver, pushing each other aside to reach him as quickly as possible.

Everyone around Zoraver quickly reformed the circle and opened fire. Some of the aliens fell as bullets pierced their chests, yet they seemed utterly unafraid of death. Their relentless pursuit resembled that of hungry wolves closing in on their prey.

Zoraver is in the middle of the circle, a mysterious smile on his face, creating millions of questions in the mind of the alien king.

The king said, "Come on, you filthy human! Fight!"

Aliens are coming closer and closer. The whole ground is shaking from their heavy and fast footsteps. Everyone around the world is watching the live telecast without blinking.

Zoraver closed his eyes, diving deep into the recesses of his mind. A radiant white aura began to spread around his body, growing brighter with each passing moment. The angel, sensing the change, knelt in front of him before launching into the sky like a rocket, disappearing swiftly into the clouds above.

Every alien and human around the world held their breath at this terrifying moment. Even the enslaved humans confined in chains watched among alien soldiers on the big screens inside the hundreds of alien army camps scattered globally.

Everyone in the circle tried to kill as many aliens as possible, but the mountain-like alien warriors did not retreat. Godric and the others, firing bullets at the aliens without fear, were driven by a spiritual zeal for sacrifice that gave them an almost supernatural strength. Godric, remembering his tormented masters, roared like a lion, opening skulls with bullets and hitting every target with precision. Isla and Bella, their courage as fierce as lionesses, also fired into the eyes of their enemies.

Seeing this, Pranja picked up an eight-foot-long heavy metal spear from the wall of his dropship and aimed the one-foot pointed crystal at its end towards Zoraver. His steps quickened as he approached, and with a powerful thrust, he hurled the spear at Zoraver. The aliens, gnashing their teeth and waving their swords and axes, stirred up a frenzy in the shadow of the spear as it tore through the air. When the spear was within 50 metres of Zoraver, he opened his eyes, caught the spear with his right hand just inches from his forehead, and drove it into the ground beside him.

As the aliens drew dangerously close to Zoraver, several of them leapt into the air, poised to strike down everyone standing around him. But suddenly, with blinding speed, twelve giants, each towering three metres tall, erupted from the ground. In a terrifying display of power, they snatched the airborne aliens mid-leap and tore them apart, ripping legs and arms from their torsos with their bare hands. The sight of these monstrous beings, sporting massive horns on their heads, wide jaws lined with pointed teeth, thick skin like rhinoceros hide, and bony knees resembling steel beams—instantly halted the charge of the alien horde. The aliens, who moments earlier had charged like furious bulls, now hesitated, fear evident in their eyes. Even Zoraver's companions recoiled, taking a few cautious steps back, stunned by the giants' aggressive and battle-hungry presence. A tense silence fell over the battlefield. The alien king, visibly unsettled, gestured towards a scientist alien nearby and asked him something in a low voice. The scientist, after scanning the battlefield on a tablet, shook his head and indicated to the king that no detectable patterns were found.

King commanded, "Commanders! Move your soldiers." He spoke into the mic of the radio device on his wrist.

All the comrades standing around Zoraver looked at each other and stared at the giants, who had their backs to them and were gazing at the aliens and roaring in awe. Amid all this, Zoraver glared aggressively at Pranja, who stood in the middle of the aliens.

Zeh REE dee ah!!

Zeh REE dee ah!!

The battle cry thundered across the field, and the aliens, reinvigorated, charged forward with renewed courage. But their advance was short-lived, as the earth burst forth with thousands of demon warriors, who rose up from the ground. Simultaneously, a deluge of angels descended from the sky, plummeting down like a hailstorm, tearing through the clouds with incredible force. With lightning-fast speed, these spiritual warriors sliced through the alien ranks, sending limbs and torsos flying across the battlefield in a grisly display of divine fury. The angels also unleashed devastation on the alien fleet, breaking the cannons of the warships, tearing apart the bodies and engines of the ships, extracting the aliens from their vessels, and hurling them to the ground.

Across the entire globe, millions of supernatural beings – ghosts, vampires, demons, and angels – burst forth from every surface, converging on the aliens wherever they were found. United in their quest for victory, they fight as one, exchanging weapons and tactics as needed. Ghosts possess aliens, blasting them from within, and in a gruesome display, groups of ghosts tear aliens limb from limb, ravaging them like a horde of ravenous dogs devouring a helpless rabbit. Vampires flay the aliens' skin, exposing their internal organs, and rip out their entrails with razor-sharp spears and axes, feasting on their very essence. Demons wield burning swords and spears, igniting the aliens' flesh, and devour their bodies with frenzied relish, tearing into them like a school of piranhas consuming their prey with insane hunger. Angels strike down aliens with explosive arrows, bursting into flames upon impact, and chop off their heads with their wings, the feathers slicing through the air like a hail of bullets, piercing the aliens' bodies from one side to the other, leaving a sea of smouldering, lifeless husks. The spider machines, once thought invincible, are also facing the wrath of the supernatural beings. They tried to hide, but creatures like scorpions, similar in size to the spiders, are hunting them down in every single place around the world, breaking them apart with ease, like hounds chasing down their prey. The legs of these spiders, along with other mechanisms, lie shattered everywhere, a testament to the supernatural creatures' unrelenting fury. The supernatural army moves in perfect sync, orchestrating a macabre waltz of annihilation, leaving a trail of shattered alien bodies in their wake. The tide has turned. Just hours ago, humans were fleeing for their lives, but now the aliens are the ones desperate to escape. The screams of the vanquished aliens echo through every road, street, and building, a chilling symphony of terror.

Seeing the tyrants who oppress the weaker human beings wailing in agony, shrieking in terror in front of the ordeal of death, a wave of enthusiasm spread among human beings all over the world. The supernatural creatures bathe the earth in the blood of their foes, purging the planet of the alien scourge. And as the carnage unfolds, humans emerge from their hiding places, jubilant and triumphant, reveling in the spectacle of their tormentors' demise.

The eye-opening and ego-bursting unexpected situation, totally out of the math of war, as beings from other realms slaughtered the entire alien army, left Pranja and his fellow scientist both struck with goose bumps. They ran and entered the drop ship. When Zoraver saw the drop ship rising 50 metres into the air, he took the spear and delivered a blow like thunder. The spear ripped through the nose of the ship, burst through the alien scientist's chest, and exited the ship through the engine at the back.

Pranja's ship crashed to the ground as Zoraver, removing his gun from his shoulder, joined his companions in attacking the aliens. The alien army began to retreat, but their escape was thwarted when more demons emerged from the ground and angels descended from the sky. They surrounded the battlefield from all directions, tightening their encirclement towards the centre. The aliens in the middle, desperate to escape, pushed outward, but the ones on the periphery were forced back by the advancing demons and angels. The chaos ensued as the aliens crushed each other in their frantic bid for survival. Even the Alien King, who had stood proudly for so long, began to tremble with fear at the sight.

About 500 angels attacked the Alien King's ship, but none of them could touch it. Some kind of dark energy mixed with golden sparks threw the angels away as they tried to attack the ship.

"My King!" an alien commander said, his voice shaking and embarrassed. "An unknown virus has hacked our whole system, and our warships are failing all over the world. If we don't leave now, we may get stuck on this planet."

"Take my ship away from these creatures. Hurry!" the Alien King shouted loudly in panic.

Godric and all his fellows, moving forward along with the giants, demons and the angels, were shooting the aliens and piling up their corpses. Their speed was 50 times faster than a normal soldier's.

Zoraver was chopping off every alien in his path and reached closer to Pranja. With a bazooka on his right shoulder, Pranja waited for him with an angry expression.

"Bruuummm!" Pranja attacked Zoraver with the bazooka, and Zoraver fired his gun simultaneously. The bullet from Zoraver's rifle tore through the wave of the bazooka in the middle, scattering the bazooka into pieces.

Pranja grabbed his gun and fired quickly, but the laser beam disintegrated upon hitting Zoraver's chest. Realising Zoraver's formidable power, Pranja attempted to flee, only to be seized by a giant. The giant hurled him against the wall of the dropship from ten metres away. Dazed, Pranja rose and gazed up at his king's ship in the distant sky. Meanwhile, a circle of demons and angels formed around Zoraver and Pranja, their presence imposing within a 50-metre radius.

Zoraver said, "He won't save you! Even if he tries, you still won't be able to escape! Your karma is moaning and death is dancing over your head." He took his Kirpan out of its sheath and moved forward with a loud roar.

Godric, Harold, Isla, Bella, and Theo stepped into the circle and positioned themselves alongside the spiritual warriors. Angel, standing between Godric and Isla, held a sword in her right hand and an alien commander's head by its golden hair in her left. With a deliberate motion, she tossed the severed head at Isla's feet.

Pranja looked at the surrounding area. All the giants, demons and angels were staring at him with very aggressive expressions. He glanced at the sky, where the angels flying above the circle gazed at him in anger. The surveillance cameras fixed around the dropship were broadcasting the scene to the entire world. Seeing no other choice, Pranja drew his sword from its sheath and rushed towards Zoraver with a roaring attack. Zoraver, closing in swiftly, slapped him with lightning speed, and Pranja fell several yards away.

Meanwhile, in the control room of the warship, the alien king watched intently as the battlefield's perimeter was displayed on a large screen. Multiple monitors showed footage of warships that had crashed around the world. The alien commander and the entire crew looked visibly terrified, their fear palpable as they observed the chaos unfolding outside.

King frowned. "Why is it not working?"

The scientist replied, trembling with fear, "I think he is not using any of his superpowers! It seems like all his powers are happening without any single thought of his mind!"

One of the commanders said, "I think we must leave, my lord."

The King shouted, "No! I won't give up. Use all the cannons with full force."

The commander standing by added, "Sorry, my lord, all our cannons have been jammed!"

The advisor urged, "My lord! We all need to leave right now!"

The battlefield had fallen silent. The legs, arms, and heads of aliens were scattered around, along with their organs. The entire field was soaked in blood, and the people who had escaped from the aliens in the surrounding villages had also walked towards the battlefield.

Pranja regained his consciousness and saw that Zoraver was standing with his foot on his chest.

Zoraver said, "Even a witch spares the children within her seven-house radius, yet you slaughtered your own kids to fuel your dark ambitions?"

Pranja asked with a shaking voice full of fear, "Who are you? How do you know about my children?"

Zoraver seized Pranja by his hair and hurled him into the middle of the field. Groaning and struggling to rise, Pranja barely had a chance before Zoraver, moving with lightning speed, grabbed his leg by the shin. He slammed Pranja into the ground repeatedly, each impact resonating with a bone-jarring force. Pranja's anguished cries echoed across the field.

Zoraver said, "Have you ever thought how much pain your daughter suffered? Ever thought about the thousands of women whose wombs you kept using as a test tube?"

Pranja, lying on the ground below and groaning in pain, cunningly drew a dagger from his belt.

Thak!

Godric fired at Pranja's hand, tearing it apart from the wrist.

"AAAHHHHH!" Pranja groaned in pain and started rolling on the ground.

Zoraver placed his left foot on Pranja's right knee, grabbed his leg by the ankle, and tore it apart with a jerk.

"AAAGGGHHH!" Pranja writhed on the ground in pain.

Zoraver placed Pranja's leg on his shoulder and started walking around him in a circle.

"It was you who made those aliens brutally kill your wife and two children!" Zoraver said. "It was you because of whom the child of a saintly man like Kashyapa was killed by his own hands! It was you because of which I got cursed and yearned for salvation by taking birth again and again!"

"Who are you?" Pranja asked, his voice trembling with pain.

Zoraver hit Pranja's leg ten times on his face like a baseball bat, tearing all the flesh from his mouth and disfiguring his jaw.

"Monster! Do you really dare to escape your karma?" Zoraver said. "Look where your actions have brought you." He put his foot on Pranja's cheek, making him face Isla and Bella.

Pranja saw Arambha's reflection in Isla.

"How can it be possible?" Pranja said in a gibberish tone.

He turned his gaze towards Bella and saw the reflections of Prisha and Kashyapa in her. Seeing all this, his whole body trembled.

As soon as Pranja turned his face back towards Zoraver, he saw Arva instead of Zoraver.

"Father! Why did you kill me?" Arva asked in a very sad and innocent way.

"No, no, no! Don't do that. It can't be true. It's your maya," Pranja said.

Seeing Arva and listening to him wrenched Pranja's heart. He turned his face to the other side and began to slide away from his son.

"Father!" Arva called.

Pranja stopped sliding and turned his face back to his son, who looked at him with a very innocent face.

"Please forgive me, my child!" Pranja said.

Arva suddenly disintegrated into dust. With tears welling in his eyes, Pranja rushed toward the scattered remains, desperate to find his son. But as he drew closer, he was met by Zoraver's furious gaze. Panicked, Pranja scrambled in the opposite direction, using his elbows to push himself away. Zoraver swiftly closed the distance, placing his left foot on the back of Pranja's left knee and seizing his ankle with his right hand. With a powerful jerk, Zoraver wrenched Pranja's leg from its joint.

"AAAAAGGGGGG!" Pranja snarled with pain.

Zoraver started beating him with his leg. Pranja screamed in agony as Zoraver beat him blindly, breaking the armor. After that, Zoraver threw the leg away and sat on Pranja's stomach. With sadistic ferocity, Zoraver savagely ripped apart the skin around Pranja's collars, chest, with his bare hands, and then grasped both collarbones, yanking them out with a gruesome crunch, leaving Pranja convulsing in torment, his body shuddering like a fish in death throes. Zoraver then got up and started skinning Pranja from the belly and the back. As Pranja screamed, people all around the world watched live, their horror and revulsion growing with each passing moment.

Zoraver grasped Pranja's left wrist and, with a single, brutal tug, ripped the entire arm from its shoulder socket, Pranja's anguished shriek pierced the air as his body contorted in torment.

"You ugly Asura!" Zoraver declared. "Today, your last breath will be taken with the same pain you inflicted on every woman who worshipped you like a god."

"Maayavi manav!" Pranja cried out. "Tvam pishaachat nyunah nasi!"

"Nah!" Zoraver retorted. "I am more than that!"

Zoraver seized Pranja by the back of the neck with his right hand and threw him twenty metres up into the air. As Pranja descended, Zoraver pushed Pranja's entire arm between his buttocks.

"AAAAHHHHHHHHH!" Pranja's blood-curdling scream resonated throughout the battlefield. He writhed on the ground, his body twisting in tortured spasms, his torso flailing wildly.

All the supernatural beings, including the humans standing nearby, trembled at the sight.

In a fit of agony, Zoraver seized Pranja by the head with both hands and lifted him effortlessly. Locking eyes with him, Pranja's eyes widened in terror as a faint whimper escaped his lips, and Zoraver let out a deafening roar and crushed Pranja's head like a shattered porcelain vase. A crimson geyser burst forth from the shattered skull, bathing Zoraver's arms in warm, viscous blood. The headless corpse of Pranja collapsed to the ground, convulsing briefly before going still. With a triumphant gesture and a mighty roar, Zoraver raised the shattered remains of Pranja's golden-haired head aloft in his right hand, like a trophy, to the sky. The giants, demons, and angels surrounding them knelt in reverent respect, followed by Godric and the others.

Zoraver said, "Oh come on! You have no need to do that! I know you all love me!"

After hearing this, everyone started dancing in joy. Harold and all the other companions came to Zoraver and lifted him in their arms. Seeing all this, the whole world was filled with a festive atmosphere. People danced on the dead bodies of aliens in the streets all around the world.

Amidst the jubilant atmosphere, nuclear bombs around the globe were suddenly activated. Within minutes, thousands of missiles began to encircle the Earth, their ominous presence plunging the world into an eerie twilight.

Aldous pointed to the horizon and called out, "Zoraver! Zoraver! Look!"

Around fifty missiles flew in different directions, casting a pall of dread over the battlefield. The songs of victory were abruptly silenced, replaced by an unsettling stillness. The warmth of triumph's first light, kindled after the darkness of alien domination, was now overshadowed by the specter of extinction, as if the Queen of Death herself had arrived to claim her due.

Harold asked Zoraver, "So now they are going to bombard our entire planet?"

Zoraver merely smiled, his eyes gleaming with confidence, as his voice rang out clear and commanding: "Three, two, one! Blast!"

All the missiles exploded in the sky simultaneously.

Michael remarked, "That won't work, mate! The fallout's still gonna kill us all."

Everyone's faces were sad.

Bella said to Theo, "You've always been a caring husband. I am not mad at you for hiding those secrets. I know that was part of your job. I just want to say, I love you more than anyone and anything."

Theo replied, "You are every colour of my life. A godly wife who looked after me beyond my expectations. I love you too, my angel."

Godric said, "I never gave you priority over my work, but you were the only one whom I trusted and loved the most. It's strange; now all my work is finished, but I have no time to grow old with you. My doll, forgive me please."

Isla responded tearfully, "You are my first, last, and only one. I never had any conditions to love you. My lord, we may not grow old in this life, but we will surely be together in the next one."

Aldous said, "It was nice to see you again, my son. But who can change fate? Just keep in mind that I am proud of you, my lion."

Michael expressed, "I love you, Dad. You are my hero."

Harold said to Zoraver, "What can I say? I am already dead. And yes, I want to apologise for that shot. I thought you were running from the battlefield."

Zoraver replied, "Oh, I remember you called me a fucking slave!"

Harold exclaimed, "Fuck! Did you hear that too? Look... I am... really, I am very sorry for that too. Please don't send me to hell for that."

Zoraver did not reply and looked into the sky.

All the people standing around had wet eyes. The angels and giants nearby looked at them with love and mystical smiles.

All the WWII soldiers embraced each other, forming a tight circle and holding hands. Harold's entire family, along with Aldous, Michael, scientist and all the soldiers, gazed at one another with tear-filled eyes. After a few moments, everyone closed their eyes, and a profound silence enveloped the group. The air was thick with the sense of impending doom, as if death itself was looming on their doorstep.

Suddenly, flowers started raining from the sky, demons and giants, including angels, began dancing in happiness.

"Ha ha ha ha! I got you... ha ha ha," Zoraver said to Harold with loud laughter.

Seeing death near, all the people standing with wet eyes began shedding tears of happiness upon breathing the fragrance of life from the shower of flowers instead of fallout. Everyone hugged their beloved partners. Everywhere in the world, flowers were showering and people were celebrating.

"What was that!" Isla asked Zoraver, tears streaming down her face as she walked alongside Godric.

"Prank!" Zoraver replied.

"You know, you are just too much!" Isla said.

Isla and Godric both hugged Zoraver.

Bella said, "What if I had a heart attack before this rain of flowers?" She pulled Zoraver's ear playfully.

"Oh, come on," Zoraver said, "It was the main part of this celebration. I even gave you all a hint about it."

"You and your words!" Harold exclaimed. "I'm never going to understand any of this. Come! Give me a hug!"

Zoraver embraced Harold and closed his eyes, as the angel approached and wrapped him in a tight hug. Around them, Godric, Isla, Aldous, Michael, Bella, Theo, the scientists, and all the soldiers formed a close-knit group, creating a comforting pile of embraces around Zoraver. Seeing this, the thousands of giants and angels encircling them moved closer, creating a collective cuddle. Across the globe, every being, humans, vampires, ghosts, giants, and angels, joined in, forming a vast chain of love through their embraces. Zoraver's body radiated waves of pure white light, emanating love and joy that spread across the land, mountains, and seas. A divine melody, intoxicating and celestial, resonated in the ears of every living being. In this extraordinary moment of heavenly bliss, no one dared to open their eyes, overwhelmed by a sensation that defied earthly explanation and stirred deep agitation.

After a few minutes, Harold opened his eyes and saw Godric and Isla hugging him tightly.

"Zoraver? Zoraver?" Harold called out.

Everyone opened their eyes and looked around. Zoraver had vanished, along with the giants, demons, and angels. The entire battlefield was littered with piles of dead alien bodies.

"Zoraver! Where are you?" Bella cried out loudly, tears streaming down her face.

NEXT DAY

Godric, Isla, Aldous, Michael, Harold, Theo, Bella, and the scientist were sitting around a table inside Archer's broken house. Archer was lying on a sofa, and Isla's mother was sitting in a chair next to him.

"Listen!" Isla whispered to Godric.

"Yes?" Godric replied.

"I saw that angel of yours. Does she always look that beautiful?" Isla asked.

"Oh God! Really?" Godric responded, surprised.

"Please tell me! Does she look more beautiful than me?" Isla continued.

"Isla? Is there anything wrong?" Bella asked.

"Sorry, Mother! It's nothing," Isla said.

"Before we start our discussion on political matters, I need your permission to bring my five masters back into my life," Godric said.

"That's totally fine," Theo replied. "But first, we need to get our hands on the time machine, which is inside the alien base on top of Mount Everest."

"That can be arranged, but I don't need the time machine to bring them back," Godric said.

"Then how would you do that? Do you also know some voodoo stuff?" Aldous asked.

"His plan is to create clones of his masters. We already have their consciousness in our data storage, which we got from each of them to teach the subjects of the World Religion," the scientist explained.

"Son, I have objections to this plan of yours! This is totally against nature! Your masters died an honourable death. They are our martyrs," Bella said.

"Mother..." Godric started.

"No! I won't listen to any nonsense from any of you," Bella insisted.

"Bella! I know you are really good at spiritualism, but Godric just needs their clones in his life, and clones won't have the same souls as his masters. They can rest in peace, and Godric can have their wisdom. It doesn't seem to go against nature to me," Harold said.

"Harold! I think we must listen to her. It was only her who brought a superhuman into this world and made us win this war," Aldous said.

"I agree with you, Chief! We all would have died by now if she hadn't taken charge when we had lost hope of saving ourselves from those monsters," Isla added.

"Theo! What do you say?" Harold asked.

"I think she is right. We shouldn't play with nature. Now, our focus should be on building a government body for the whole world again," Theo replied.

"Alright, I won't do that, but I need your permission to transfer the consciousness of my masters into my mind," Godric said.

"That should be fine. I can agree with that," the scientist said.

"Bella! Should we agree to this?" Theo asked.

"Yes, but only if he won't forget me after that," Bella said, a hint of vulnerability in her voice.

"Is there any chance of that?" Isla asked, her eyes narrowing slightly.

"Nope! That would be totally fine," Godric replied with a reassuring smile. "I will be the same. Does anyone have any objections?"

No one said anything, and they looked at each other's faces.

"Alright! I think you have permission to do that! Congratulations, Grandson!" Harold exclaimed.

The room erupted into applause, with everyone clapping. Amidst the commotion, Michael's voice cut through.

"Wait, hold on... I think the most important thing we must focus on is how we build a strong government for the whole world again," Michael said, his words quieting the room. "We have no army, no leaders. Where should we start?"

"Zoraver! Zoraver should be declared a Masiha who saved the whole world. Everyone saw you all along with him. Whatever you say, the whole world will listen and follow you blindly!" Archer suggested.

Archer's words shocked everyone.

"But he never said that he is a Masiha," Bella said.

"Do you have any better idea, my love?" Theo asked.

"Why can't we just live a simple life? Let the world be like it has been for thousands of years. I want my family together without worrying about any kind of political conflicts. Why do you all want to put the burden of whole world's problems on your shoulders?" Bella asked.

Harold said with a teasing smile, "Theo, can't you handle your wife for a minute?"

Everyone laughed, except Bella, whose lips pursed slightly in annoyance and her eyes flashed a warning glance at Theo.

Theo quickly intervened, noticing her expression. "Oh, come on, Dad! You know her nature well. She's just—"

Harold interrupted, chuckling. "Archer, I love your idea!"

"I completely agree!" Michael added.

"Count me in," Aldous said.

"This is a brilliant idea! It's exactly what we need!" the scientist exclaimed.

"Father! I never knew you would be such a bold politician," Isla said with a smile.

"I'm not sharing any political strategy; this is genuinely how I feel. It's an absolute truth that Zoraver saved the world with an army of supernatural beings. An ugly alien was about to kill us both when an angel appeared out of nowhere. With a flash of lightning speed, she sliced the alien with her wings, shimmering silver blades, crystal-sharp, and took its head with her. The world witnessed Zoraver's power. He's a Messiah, and there's nothing wrong with forming a government in his name. Wherever that mighty warrior is now, may God bless him," Archer said.

Isla sprang up and wrapped her arms around her father, holding him tight.

"Oh, you stubborn atheist!" Harold teased, a sly grin spreading across his face. "It took an enlightened man oppressing millions of innocent devils to make you believe in God."

Archer chuckled, his eyes crinkling at the corners, as the others joined in, their laughter filling the room.

FEW HOURS LATER

As people laboured to clear the battlefield, loading alien bodies onto bullock carts, trucks, and tractor-towed trolleys, the spider machine suddenly emerged from the dropship in the ravaged sugarcane field. It soared into the sky at incredible speed, leaving the dropship behind. Workers exchanged fearful glances and fled the area. Reaching an altitude of 5000 metres, the machine unleashed a deafening sound wave in all directions, akin to a nuclear blast, before self-destructing in a catastrophic explosion.

A kilometre away from the battlefield, Zoraver's face twisted into a cryptic smile as he gazed at the explosion in the sky, his eyes glinting with an unnerving intensity. Meanwhile, sitting by a crackling fire beside a tube well, he wrapped himself in a brown blanket, his features shrouded in shadows. As the flames danced, a golden-coloured Cobra crawled around his left leg, its sleek body winding effortlessly around the calf, like it entwined the sacred wood of Chandan. Nearby, a dog lay faithfully, while a curious cat groomed itself by his right leg. Amidst this tranquil scene, a gentle rabbit nibbled on a nearby leaf, and a flock of sparrows perched on the tube well's rim, their soft chirping a stark contrast to the chaos raging in the distance.

CREDITS

Images generated by Meta AI
Translated with Google Translate
Editing and proof reading done by British Proofreading
Illustrations by L Bareta